praise for michael guillebeau and
MAD Librarian

"Guillebeau (*Josh Whatever*) blends humor and mystery
perfectly in this comic thriller set in the small city of
Maddington, Ala. ...Guillebeau keeps things light with
frequent laugh-out-loud lines."

-Publisher's Weekly

praise for michael guillebeau and
Don of the Q

"The tongue-in-cheek humor, social insights, and action-
packed encounters will both entertain and enlighten readers
interested in a lively blend of honor, world destruction,
warped family relationships, and comedy.

Don of the Q is highly recommended as an original, involving
read that pushes the boundaries of comedy, stormy
relationships, and social commentary alike."

-D. Donovan, Senior Reviewer, Midwest Books Review

Things to Do When

You'd Rather be Dead

Michael Guillebeau

Madison Press
Madison, Alabama

Copyright © 2020 by Michael Guillebeau

Published by Madison Press
Madison, Alabama
madisonpresspublishing@gmail.com

Book Layout © 2017 BookDesignTemplates.com
Cover Design by
PRE09302020

Things to Do When You'd Rather be Dead
Michael Guillebeau. – 1st ed.
Paperback ISBN: 978-0-9972055-9-6

acknowledgements

As always, many people helped on this book. Victoria Skurnick believed in it when the rest of the world kept giving that deadliest of all compliments, "Almost." Bob Spears and Randy Bachmeyer gave their usual thorough comments, joined this time by Mic and Steven Butler.

But since 1980, one woman has given me an amazing life. Let there be no doubt: every book, every smile, every prayer and every exaltation came from Pat Leary Guillebeau.

Sometimes it feels like you're drawn by a Looney Tunes cartoonist on a bad day.

Picture this: a second-grade classroom full of tiny human beings, each with ten times the frenetic energy of the full-grown models. Running and bouncing for no reason other than that they can.

I sat at the front of the class, three-hundred-and-fifty pounds of obsolete cop teetering on a second-grader's chair, the wood creaking and moaning, threatening to go at any moment. The buttons on my too-small blue uniform are threatening to pop free and join the kids in bouncing around the room, possibly with sound effects like ricocheting bullets.

But I sat here, again, today, in front of a class of rug rats not much bigger than my hands, praying my chair won't break, or my buttons won't fly off like cartoon bullets, and the kids won't all run screaming for the door.

It didn't seem to bother the spiky-haired little girl hugging my leg as far as her arms could reach around it.

"He's my huggy bear," she said.

The teacher was a mournful-faced middle-aged woman. Probably sad-faced because of the way the years had pulled her body down until she looked like a pyramid on top of tiny scurrying feet. Or maybe because someone had shoved it all into a purple mu-mu like some kind of bad cosmic joke.

I reached down to pat the girl on the head and the teacher pulled the girl away, "Jessi, today your huggy bear is a cop—police officer." The girl gave me a finger wave and a farewell smile.

I tried to return the smile. My smiles never come out right.

"Please don't make that face around the children," said Ms. Purple Tent.

Off on a bad foot, again. Even the last woman who loved me had described my face as looking like an old-school prize fighter who had just lost a bad fight and was sad about it. And that was a hundred pounds and several chins ago.

I did my best to look serious and presentable. I put on a blank face and sat completely still and completely expressionless, my eyes flitting back and forth as I searched the little faces.

Purple Tent rapped a ruler on her desk and the faces all got quiet. Her mouth had the tight lines of someone who fought a losing battle every day to impose authority amid the rampant anarchy of the world. "OK, everybody, let's get quiet for—I'm sorry, what was your name?"

"Officer Joe. What's yours?"

I was trying to be friendly, but the class giggled anyway.

The teacher had those angry lines again. "My name is Ms. Capulet. You need to give the class your proper rank and—"

"Just Officer Joe."

A huff and an eye roll, and I thought the ruler was coming my way. "Very well. Officer Joe." She turned back to the mob-in-training. "Class!"

There was silence again.

"Officer Joe has been sent here to tell you why you shouldn't do drugs."

She hissed at me. "As if we need this kind of fascist government crap in the second grade."

Out loud, she said. "They're all yours. I assume you have a presentation."

"I do." I started to stand. Decided there was too much risk of winding up with a chair leg up my ass, so I carefully and slowly reached over and picked up the spiral-bound poster boards our community outreach people had given me.

Jessi giggled. "You're funny." The class laughed with her.

"I try to please." More giggles.

I flipped to the first page. "This is Henry. He ate some drugs that the bad man there, named Alphonse, gave him, and now Henry doesn't feel good."

Ms. Capulet said, "Alphonse looks very dark-skinned. It's important to tell the children that the bad man could be any color."

"He certainly could. In fact, he could be a man or a woman, young or old, even a neighbor or a teacher."

The tent had sat down, but now it stood up. "What's that supposed to mean?"

"Nothing. Look — I'm trying to agree with you. And I try to be honest with kids."

She snorted. "Go on."

I tried. Jessi waved her hand furiously. I felt like thanking her for the interruption, but I only nodded.

"Henry looks sick, like I look after my mom gives me medicine. Are drugs like medicine?"

"No. Well, yes, but not good medicine."

A boy slouching in the front jerked his chin at me, a seven-year-old with a teenager's attitude. "Medicine tastes bad. I won't take drugs if they taste bad."

I didn't want to lie.

"Well, sometimes people make them taste like candy."

"I like candy." He hesitated. "But they make you feel bad like Henry?"

I paused. "Well, yeah, eventually." I sighed. "But sometimes they make you feel good at first."

This wasn't going the way community affairs planned. It rarely did.

"Maybe," I said, "we should put off talking about drugs for right now. Let's talk about Henry being safe. If Alphonse tries to talk to you, what should you do?"

Tough Kid tilted his head to one side. "I'm going to ask him for drugs, if they taste like candy."

Ms. Capulet gave a harsh laugh, "Good work, Officer Joe." She turned to the boy. "Juwan, you should tell your teacher if a strange man tries to talk to you."

I looked at Juwan and tried to hold his eyes. "No. You should tell a police officer. Like me."

She looked shocked, then her mouth got that tight look again. "Teacher."

I knew she expected support, but I couldn't give it. "Cop."

She opened her mouth, but Jessi got the last word in. "What if Alphonse tries to grab me?"

I thought about what I would have told my own daughter. "Kick him in the balls as hard as you can and run away."

The class all giggled and Ms. Capulet rapped the table with her ruler. "Enough. I think we're going to lunch now."

Jessi said, "The bell hasn't rung. I want to talk to Huggy Bear."

"We're going to lunch early. Line up out in the hall and wait for me."

While the kids were filing out, I stood up, towering over Ms. Capulet. She seemed to take affront at my size and stepped into my space.

"Some job."

"Believe it or not, I'm trying."

She softened, a little. "Sorry. I get tired of all the crap that the Birmingham School Board and the State of Alabama wants to cram down my children's throats, while ignoring the things they really need." She paused. "The kids seem to love you, though."

"Younger ones, anyway," I said. "Older ones get suspicious of the uniform. I try to catch them before they reach that point. While I'm still a big huggy bear."

"Yeah. Kids are naïve and will trust anyone, including cops." She waited for an argument and didn't get one. "You really think kids should go to the police first, tell on their parents and teachers? Beat people up if they need to?"

"Yes."

"You really think the police can always help?"

"No."

She put her hands on her hips. "You can't teach them self-defense yet. I don't think giving every second grader karate lessons or teaching them to kick people in the balls will help."

"Kids are getting hurt every day. So-called grownups aren't taking it seriously enough. Karate lessons might not be a bad idea."

She said, "You're not the one who has to supervise recess."

I laughed and looked at her to see if she thought it was funny. Hard to tell.

She reached up and poked her finger into my shoulder. "That's a detective rank, pretty high to be doing community relations. Is this just a day of volunteer work for you? Acting like you know something about kids?"

"No."

"This is your full-time assignment? Basically, a clown in a cop suit?"

I thought about it. "Yes."

"Quite a comedown, wouldn't you say?"

"Probably."

"You weren't always called 'Officer Joe.' "

"No." She was waiting for more. "Detective Third Brosette. Hard for kids to remember."

"Hard for adults to believe you're a detective."

"Yeah, I know I don't look like a detective. Anymore." I wanted to change the subject entirely. "You know your police ranks."

"My dad was on the job. Brothers, too. We don't get many detectives in here for school officers."

"No." I didn't elaborate even when she waited. Finally, she won and I spoke first. "You seem to be older than the suspicious teenagers I talk to in the high schools. Not sure why you're so suspicious."

"Like I said, my father and brothers were and are cops. I know how you guys think. And I spend enough time battling school boards and the city that I assume anything they send down must be crap."

"I'm not sure you're wrong about that."

She studied me for a minute.

"Not trying to be confrontational, but when I said the young kids love you, I'm not sure that's all good. I may be overly suspicious—some say paranoid—about threats to my kids, but you do seem to take an unusual amount of interest in kids."

I thought about it a long time.

"Yes."

I picked up my props and walked out the door.

There's a traditional Birmingham cop bar in the Five Points area that's always packed with shiny cops in starched blue uniforms, proud to show off.

I've never been there.

The joke about Johnson's Bar, where I was going, was that it was called that because only a real dick would go there. A shabby bar next to a shabby payday loan store, it was so dark that you were tempted to light a match when you went in. Probably get shot if you did. The protocol was that you came in and closed the door tight behind you to seal out the unwelcome Alabama summer sun, or even the equally unwelcome light of the one working street light outside. You stand very still for a few seconds while your eyes adjust, and the unseen eyes inside check you out. When the steady low growl of the place returns, it's safe to go deeper.

"Joe," I heard a whisper in the darkness and went toward it. As I got closer and my eyes adjusted, another wrinkled blue uniform emerged from the darkness, then I could see the dark bar he was hunched over, and then another figure across the bar.

I hauled myself up onto a stool, feeling like a big blue popsicle on a stick.

"What you hear, Ron?" I said.

"Nothing."

A woman with white cropped hair and a body that wouldn't be out of place on an NFL line leaned across the bar. "You're almost too late for dinner, Joe."

"It's always time for Myers's rum, Wendy."

"Only cop I know who gets fat on rum, and the expensive one at that."

"What else am I going to spend my money on?"

"I don't know. Peace, love and understanding, maybe. I'm going to get Joyce to make you a sandwich before she goes home."

"Make it three. Never turn down free food."

She laughed a harsh laugh. "Who said free?" She turned away but said, "You know, you're eating and drinking yourself to death."

"You got a better way?"

She thought about it. "Not as long as you're paying."

I turned to Ron as she walked away. Too dark to read expressions, but Ron could feel the focus and shrugged.

"Really, I haven't heard anything." He shifted. "Hey, you hear more in schools than I do on the street."

"Yeah. What I heard today was guff from teen-agers at two high schools. Can't blame them, with the crap I'm supposed to hand out. The young kids love me."

"Yeah, that's you. Mr. Lovable."

"One called me Huggy Bear today."

"You want me to make an announcement in here, tell people to call you that?"

"Probably not. Look, though, you got anything at all? You never know when you might hear some little something that matters."

"Nothing. Joe, it's been two years. Maybe it's over."

"No."

For a few minutes, we engaged in our favorite conversation, which was no conversation. A white face emerged from the murmuring darkness. From the corner of my eye I saw someone dressed in a suit that might as well have said Detective on the back, except that it also said money and taste.

He stopped five feet away from me and said, "So, this is where Birmingham's kiddie cop comes when he's not bouncing little boys and girls on his knee, asking them if they've been good enough for him?"

Ron and I didn't say anything, but the murmurs around us started dying in an expanding circle, a ripple of silence as the room stopped to listen.

He stepped in closer. "TV hosts and grade school teachers might be fooled by a burned-out cop who can't hack it anymore. But tell me this, what kind of a man—an old man at that—wants to do nothing but stay drunk and play with kiddies?"

Wendy put a plate and a glass down in front of me.

"What the hell are you doing in here, Vinzini?"

He tried to give her a cop-stare but couldn't match her look.

"Had to talk to one of your bottom-feeders. Done with this dump now."

"You've had enough slumming. Go somewhere else."

Vinzini opened his mouth but something bumped him from behind. He half-turned, blocked by a crowd of men dressed in faded blue uniforms and cheap suits.

"Go back to McGinty's, Vinzini," a voice said from the back. It was slurred but clear. "Go back to the pretty boy cops. We don't like showoffs and pretend heroes in here."

Vinzini moved away and put two steps toward the door and away from the crowd.

"Real cops toe the line and that's what makes us heroes. And we don't like being associated with burnouts like this guy. Or the rest of you in here. You keep it so dark that I can't recognize half of you, but the ones I know are all disgraces to the force and don't even know how to be modern cops."

"We know how to protect people," said a voice in the front.

When Vinzini hesitated, a voice in the back said, "And we know how to hurt people."

He put his hand on the doorknob. "Sorry I fell into this shithole in the first place." Then he was gone and the figures faded away.

I downed my first double of the night. "I don't need any of you to stand up for me. Been coming in here for two years to be left alone." I said it to the wall, but I said it loud enough to be heard.

Ron's voice at my back. "That's the Mr. Lovable I know."

"Blow it out your ass. All of you."

But the room was back to a murmuring darkness and gave no notice.

When I felt like I had drunk all the rum in Johnson's and could hold no more, I signed the credit slip and hoped Wendy hadn't cheated me. From habit, I scanned the dark room carefully before standing up. Most of the figures were gone now, the bar-back stacking chairs on tables. Ron was gone and I didn't even know when he had left.

My stomach bumped the next stool as I stood up and I looked down at the belly that sloshed with every step. Walking out, it felt like I was wading in a small rolling sea of my own sins.

I blinked at the streetlight, belched, and turned toward home.

three

Before I started my journey, I stood outside in the two a.m. darkness and looked up at the rusted sign. Underneath the neon "Johnson's" there were still the painted letters, "Groceries," in script that had once been bright white. I stood here remembering the neighborhood the way it had been when Luz would send me here and I'd stand outside, kind of like this, trying to think of what I had forgotten from the list of things she had sent me to the store for—a list I always refused to write down, a list from which I always forgot at least one thing.

Now that it was a bar, it was easier to remember what I came for.

Everything around Johnson's was different now, too. When Luz and I moved in, the Pinewood neighborhood was urban middle class. But, like a lot of urban Birmingham neighborhoods, Pinewood had slid downhill fast, the neighborhood shops and day care centers turned into tattoo parlors and head shops and empty windows with "For Rent" signs on them. Now, in the last year, it was starting to become yuppified, with drug stores that had turned into tattoo parlors now becoming coffee shops that charged five bucks for coffee. Progress, I guess. It was like an old building with so many coats of paint that you had to know where to look to see what it had once been.

I stood looking at the sign, trying to remember if I were going in or coming out. The "Johnson's" neon winked out and reminded me.

I walked a tired walk down the empty business street and turned into a row of small homes. My plain little house looked to be neutral in the war between decay and gentrification—still square and solid and maintained, but with no cutesy upscale modern flourishes.

It took two tries, but I got the key in the door. When I hit the light switch, the same old sadness washed over me. Everything looked exactly like it had for two years.

A small crucifix on the wall, doilies on the easy chair in front of an old CRT TV. A dining room table unused for years, but still dust-free and ready. I went into the kitchen and put on a pot of coffee. Stood looking out the window over the sink while I waited, scanning and drinking a glass of water from the tap. I picked up the pot and was holding it over my cup, about to pour, when the thought came to me like a vision: not tonight. Maybe tonight I would sleep. I poured the hot coffee down the sink, washed the coffeemaker and loaded it for the morning.

The oak floors creaked as I walked back to the bathroom. I spent five minutes unpinning the service medals and insignias from my uniform shirt and folded the shirt before putting it in the laundry hamper on top of the uniform from yesterday. After I added the pants, I caught a glimpse of myself in the mirror, standing in my underwear.

I'd never seen anything so goddamned broke-down.

I shook my head and went into the bedroom. I took the throw pillows off the bed and stacked them on the reading chair to the left. Walked around to my side of the bed and slid under the covers without pulling them all the way back. My eyes closed as soon as I snapped the switch on the lamp.

They stayed that way for maybe an hour before I woke with a start. I'd forgotten something, gotten something wrong, missed something and I didn't know what. I picked up my gun from the nightstand and stumbled out into the darkness to the bedroom across the hall and flipped the switch, scared of what I would find there.

But the room was perfect. A pink canopied girl's bed, a neat desk with three-year-old school books on it. My Little Pony painted on the wall.

In the middle of the bed was a pile of pillows. I realized I was afraid I'd forgotten to put the pillow shams on yesterday when I had washed the linens. Looked down and wondered why I thought I needed a gun to make pillows right.

I hadn't forgotten the shams. The bed was perfect. And the room was a perfect room for a little girl. Still, I stood staring out the window, standing guard against something dreaded and unseen, sweeping the horizon over and over without moving, until the light came up and I could leave safely.

four

There is something elemental about the sound of a
rattlesnake clattering that connects instantly to the terror
sensors in human beings.

So, what asshole set my ringtone to a rattlesnake?

I almost ran my black city Impala into a dump truck
when I heard the rattle. At the stop light, after my heart
slowed down, I looked at the caller ID and threw the
phone, unanswered, onto the pile of fast food wrappers on
the passenger seat. I pulled the large Styrofoam coffee cup
out of the center console and swallowed as much hot coffee
as I could.

The light turned and a kid in a buzzing, tricked-out Scion
cut around me and flipped me the bird as he screamed
away. Pissed at him and rattlesnakes in general, I stomped
the gas to go after him. Two seconds later, my better
judgment returned and told me to ease off. A waste of time
to try to kick every ass I saw.

Maybe I needed a way to mix Valium with my morning
caffeine, keep me awake but calm. Now that would be a
drug that Alphonse could sell.

I pulled into the grade school parking lot and the
rattlesnake buzzed again in its nest of dirty waxed papers

and plastic boxes. I snatched the noise box up with a hamburger wrapper sticking to it.

"You're not going to go away, are you Shirley?"

The rattlesnake spoke. "Where the hell are you? I just got a call from the counselor at Westlawn Middle. You were supposed to be there half an hour ago."

"Shirley. How nice to hear from you." She snorted, but I ignored her. "I've got a priority call first. They'll have to stay drug-free-and-all-they-can-be on their own for a little while."

"You're not a detective anymore. You don't have priority calls, except at donut shops. Do you not know that you have a job and people are counting on you?"

"You mean my bartender?"

"Very funny. Do you use these lines on second graders?"

"Sometimes. They have a more mature sense of humor than you. Listen to this one. Knock knock."

Another snort. "Knock it off yourself. I don't know why we put up with you. We need to replace you with a telegenic twenty-five-year old."

"Do it."

"You know they won't let me. I don't know why the captain sent us a burned-out old fart detective rather than somebody useful and made us put up with you for almost a year now. A year of complaints. What have you got on him anyway?"

"Every time he threatens me, I tell him." I paused for effect. "I tell him that I'm going to tell the world that he's having an affair with that nasty, dried-up skank in the community affairs office. The mere image of that scares the hell out of him."

"Screw you, Joe. Get to Westlawn today."

"Later."

I was proud of myself. Calls like this were more fun back in the days of real phones, when the person I pissed off would slam the receiver down. Imagining Shirley angrily punching a button on a cell phone didn't give the same satisfaction. But it gave some.

The office volunteer at the elementary school I'd been to yesterday yelled at me to check in as I went by, but I waved and kept going. I opened the door to Ms. Capulet's room and walked in.

She stopped mid-sentence, hand in the air, and turned her head to the door. Then she rotated her whole body like a battleship gun turret coming around and pointed her finger.

"Did you forget something?" she said. "Like how to knock?"

"No." I searched the classroom and found what I was looking for. "Yesterday, you had everybody sitting in precise rows, everybody with an assigned seat."

She marched over and hissed in my face so the class wouldn't hear. "Discipline's important, Detective. Sitting in the right place. Using class time for—you know—class rather than getting organized. Or random police intimidation."

"And that seat," I nodded past her, "was empty."

"Maria was sick yesterday. As if that's any of your—"

"Let me guess. You told your class a few days ago that you'd have a police officer coming yesterday. And yesterday, Maria was sick."

"Oh, for crying out loud, Detective. This is a new low for police paranoia. Yesterday I saw you give Sheila a suspicious look when she gave you some back talk. Now you've added a girl who wasn't even here to your suspect list. What set our heroic police force off? Was a bank robbed by a daring team of seven-year-olds—"

"No. Probably is just paranoia." I pushed her aside to keep eyes on the child. "That mouthy girl yesterday? Sheila? Yeah, I looked at her but decided she was an angry girl with a problem with authority. Nothing wrong with that." I turned to the girl who hadn't been there.

"What's your name?"

"Maria."

"Maria what?"

"Maria Trap."

"Trap. One p or two?"

The girl hesitated and my police paranoia screamed louder.

Capulet stepped between us.

"Enough. Get out of my class. Now."

I started to open my mouth.

"Now!" She shoved her face into mine. Or my chest rather, with the height difference. "Get out now or this gets ugly fast."

I decided not to make the obvious comment and stepped outside. The door slammed at my back. I smiled.

Sheila wasn't the only one in that class who had a problem with authority.

The captain didn't want me back in his office, but there I was. He sat at his desk with his head in his hands. His voice was muffled, coming out of his hands. "You never heard the story about the boy who cried wolf, back in school or church maybe?"

I said, "The boy was right, the last time. Whole village would have been better off if they'd listened. He did his job."

"Yeah." The captain pulled his head up and looked at me. His eyes were brown with a red tinge that made him always look angry, his face younger than mine, but more creased under his chocolate-brown shaved head. "We'd like you to do your job now. Go out and show the flag and preach the gospel of clean living. That's all. I left you with your detective rank out of respect for things you'd done, but took away any real police assignments because..."

I thought of a scene from an old movie. I looked up at him with fake sad eyes. "Mungo Joe just a clown in a cop suit." The captain didn't laugh. I said, "But you still need to listen to this."

He stared at me for a long time. I said, "Look, I really am sorry for all the trouble I bring you. And I'm sorry about what you're thinking but too polite to say."

He waved his hand like he was batting a fly away. "Joe, I know you think you're some kind of guardian of the universe, but you're not. Stop coming in here with your false alarms. We've wasted enough time chasing your paranoia. Stay out of trouble and keep people from calling my office with complaints."

I was supposed to leave now but I didn't. I didn't mean to smile as much as I did. "Shirley from Community Affairs called?"

The captain fished a pink message slip from the pile on his desk. "I haven't even gotten to hers yet. Joe, I was your Lieutenant the last time you were a working detective."

"Yes, sir. And, once again, I thank you. If you hadn't stood up for me and pushed for me to take this job, I'd have been forced into early retirement and off the force."

"Medical. It would have been medical retirement. We gave you a year as a community affairs officer. Frankly, your year is almost up and I've got nothing but complaints, so I don't know what we're going to do with you. But you're also not a real detective any more, even if we let you keep a desk." Something occurred to him and he brightened. "And a chain of command. Next time you get a wild idea, take it to your Lieutenant. Not me."

"Captain, there are still bad guys out there. Remember? All those little people who try to make themselves feel big by hurting kids?"

The captain's jaw locked and I couldn't tell if that was from irritation with me or agreement. He gave a terse nod.

"Tell me what you got. Anything to it, I'll kick it down the chain. But make it fast."

"I think I've got a kid who was abducted and is now in school under an assumed name, maybe living with the guy who abducted her."

The captain waited.

"I went to Morningside Elementary yesterday. There was one girl missing. Teacher told the class a cop was coming, and her parents kept her out of school to avoid me."

The captain shuffled some papers on his desk. "Or she was sick."

"Yeah, but when I asked her today, she wasn't sure how to spell her last name."

"So, you want me to send out a SWAT team because a second-grader can't spell? Go do your job and let me do mine."

"One more thing: she's got dark skin, dark eyes, dark brows. And blond hair."

"It happens." He looked at the wall. "Could be a hundred reasons," he said. "Probably completely innocent."

"Probably."

"It's certainly not the guy you think it is."

I said nothing, but didn't move.

The captain finally said, "OK. No investigation. No report. No ruffled feathers. Go back and talk to her teacher. See what she says."

I smiled. "She'll be glad to see me."

I found her in the teachers' lounge, eating lunch by herself with her head in a book. I stood by the door and watched as she took a bite of a Macintosh apple without interrupting her reading. She sensed something, looked up at me and made a face.

Glad to see me. "Must be a bad apple," I said, "judging from the look on your face."

"Yeah. Must be the apple. So, if you're back to harass my students, I'm afraid they're in the cafeteria with the aide. Probably hatching plots to rob the First National Piggy Bank, or maybe get the first graders hooked on Fruit Loops. You know how the Morningside Mob operates, at least in your mind."

I tried to twist my face into an ingratiating smile.

"Where do you get off?" She closed the book and warmed up to the current ass-whipping task at hand. "Let me guess, Detective Stripes, you used to be a real cop, saw yourself as a hero. Now you're a washed-up cardboard pretender, and not a very good one at that. So, you see dragons and monsters that the world needs you to battle everywhere: in politics, in neighbors, and—heaven help you—now even in little girls. And maybe that's not even all you see in them. And maybe that's why you eat way too much and probably drink too much, too."

She waited, but I didn't give her an argument.

"Sorry." She stared at me for a long few seconds. "Old age is a bitch, isn't it?"

I thought about it. "It's not what I expected."

She laughed. "Let me guess. You grew up wanting to be Wyatt Earp and Matt Dillon. Went far enough to make detective, but fell over the line some place when somebody insisted on doing things according to the constitution instead of the Wild West?"

"No." I started to leave it at that, but couldn't. "I always followed the Constitution, and the hundred picky rules to protect the accused. Figured we were out there to protect the accused as much as anybody else. No. You know that song, the one with the line about "bad guy wins every once in a while"? Well, in my case, the bad guy won, big. The department decided I needed to be someplace where they didn't have to look at me. They were going to send me home, but I begged my Lieutenant that home was the last place I wanted to be, so he got me the community affairs job. Still a cop. Sort of. Long as I don't mess up too much here."

"For my money, you don't have long in this job."

"Maybe not. But they're going to have to kick me out. Do my job until they do."

She studied me for a long couple of seconds. "My fall from grace was from a different mountain, the one next door to cop mountain. Everything in my family background said to be a cop, but I was a rebel. Thought of becoming a bank robber, but became a prosecutor instead because they get to fight with cops more. Worked out well until one of my brothers assumed his baby sister would lie for him in court to put a bad guy away. I didn't, the bad guy walked, the police looked bad."

"So, they fired you?"

"At first, they wanted me to bend. I don't bend. So, they broke me. Fired, run out of town."

"Not from Birmingham?"

"Oh, hell no. Not 'we dare defend our rights, the South will rise again' Alabama. Madison, Wisconsin."

"Not so bad here. We don't have snow."

"Yeah, instead you've got tornadoes, heat, humidity, judges who defy the law if they don't like it..."

"There's all that. So, teaching second grade seems as far from the law as Alabama does from Wisconsin."

"That's the idea. Catch them when they're young. Instill the importance of disciplined thinking and rules while you still can."

"And you follow the rules?"

Her mouth got tight. "Yeah. The one rule I follow is that I protect my kids from anyone and anything that can hurt them. Including the police."

"Nothing wrong with that."

"Damn." She put down the apple. "I was hoping to replay one of my favorite fights with my father. All right, if we're not going to fight, what can I help you with so that you and I can go back to growling at other people?"

Good. I was tired of trying to make nice so she'd help me. Ready to get down to business.

"The Trap girl."

"Pretty sure she hasn't killed anybody in weeks."

"What's her mother like?"

"Never met her. Her father registered her a couple of weeks ago."

I nodded.

She looked at her watch and rolled up the paper bag on the table. "I can see you expected that. Doesn't prove anything."

"No. It doesn't. What's he like?"

She took a last bite of the apple and, from her expression, it was sweeter this time. She took her time chewing before answering.

"Never met him either." She paused. "It happens, sometimes. Most parents want to meet their child's teacher. Some don't." She laughed. "Most don't want to meet their teacher a second time after they've met me." She looked at the door for a minute. "But I do wish I'd met him."

"I do, too."

"So, if I don't do something, you're going to take a SWAT team and bust his door down and demand answers?"

"Not today. SWAT team's busy torturing ACLU members."

"But you won't give this up?"

"Probably not. May go see him myself."

"Have you looked in the mirror? I'd rather have that SWAT team show up at my door than you."

"I could wear a disguise. Fake mustache and glasses. Blonde glamour wig."

She laughed. "Oh yeah, that'd do it." We locked eyes. "Tell you what. You've got me curious, too. Maybe I could drop by their house after school, just a teacher returning something Maria left at school. A friendly teacher-parent visit. Then, tomorrow, I could tell you that he's a nice guy and your fears are groundless, and you can go back to drowning your frustrations rather than taking them out on little girls."

I nodded.

I thought my desk was still in the old precinct house, but I wasn't sure. I stood in the doorway of the detectives' squad room and felt like I was seeing ghosts. Ghosts from a year of terror and frustration, then more ghosts from a year of collapse and burning bridges. All followed by a year exiled to sitting in second-grade classrooms.

It had only been one year since I'd been back here. Seemed longer now. I realized that I was the ghost, not them, that I was fading away from here as fast as my body was growing larger.

The real people occupying the room now had their own rhythm and walked by the steel desks without seeming to even see me. I picked my gaps in the traffic and made my way to my old corner. My desk was shoved out of the way, empty except for a couple of dirty cardboard coffee cups. But it was still there, with my nameplate on it. I stood there wondering what to do next. Something bumped me from behind.

"Get out of the way, rummy. Go back to your shit hole."

I turned around and saw Vinzini. Everyone pretended not to hear, but they all got quiet.

A tall, skinny kid with coffee skin stood up from the closest desk. "C'mon, man. Let it go."

Vinzini let himself be directed elsewhere, but sneered as he walked away.

The kid smiled at me. "Don't pay him no mind. I heard the story why your desk is still there. I respect it."

"Yeah."

The kid laughed. "Heard you didn't like to talk about it. Or about anything." He put out a hand. "I'm Detective First Coltrane, like the sax player. Let me know if there's anything I can do to help. Youngest one here, I got lots of time on my hands. Mostly they let me run errands."

I took his hand. "Thanks." I thought I needed to say something more. Didn't know what, so we stood there.

Coltrane laughed again, like laughing was what he did to fill the spaces. "I'll get you a chair."

"Thanks. Yeah, I guess that'd be nice." I tried to figure what to do with my hands. Or anything else. "Yeah, that and a computer. I don't have a computer."

Coltrane scooted a chair. "I guess they figured that was too much. Here." He unplugged the laptop from his desk and set it on my desk. "Take mine." He laughed again. "No surfing for porn."

I stared at it for a long moment.

Coltrane said, "You know how to use it?"

"Of course. Well, last time I was here they had older ones. Bigger. I knew how to use those. Well, a little."

Coltrane laughed again, collapsed into his chair and pulled his computer back to his desk. "Tell me what you need."

"I really don't know what I'm looking for."

There was harsh laughter somewhere behind my back.

Coltrane said, "That's kind of where I always imagined the heart of a real detective's work to be. You don't have a specific crime, or even a specific question, but just kind of an itch. So where are we looking?"

I suddenly felt like this was a mistake. "Little girl. I've got her full name, and her father's name, nothing more. Probably nothing more to find, either."

"Probably. Why don't you pull your chair around here where you can see what I'm doing? If nothing else, it'll give you a chance to see

I pulled my chair around. There were a couple of sidelong glances from around us, but mostly the other detectives had their own cases and their own lives.

"OK. School records," said Coltrane. He pulled up a summary page while I gave him the background.

"Looks clean," I said. "It's probably nothing but a girl with a bad haircut." Maybe the captain was right. This was a waste of time, one more old fat man crying wolf. I looked at my watch. "I'm supposed to show up at a middle school basketball game in a little while. Show them what they can become if they choose law enforcement as a career. Take the mic at half-time and tell them this American Dream can be theirs if they don't do drugs. I better get going."

"Sounds exciting," said Coltrane. He paused. "If you don't mind, before you go, let's look at Dad, see if we can find anything on him." He pulled up another screen and typed the name in. While the computer was working, he turned to me. "What I was going to say was, you're part of the reason I'm here. In high school, my dad was really pushing me to music. John Coltrane's like a third-cousin twice-removed or something, and my dad always had the same dreams for me.

"So, I was good enough on the sax, even in high school, to play with a lot of local bands. Probably not good enough to go much farther, but enough to make a living. What kept me hooked on music was the look you saw on the faces of the greats: Monk, Bird, Robert Johnson. Haunted looks, men with stories, not only songs to play, but stories to be a part of."

I shifted. The chair was set up for a smaller man. "I never was a musician. Don't know where you're going with this."

"I'm getting to it, sir. See, I never saw that look in the faces of the local guys I played with. They were just guys with a job. And that's all I was ever going to be.

"Then, one day when I was in high school, your picture was in the paper from a case you were on. You had that same look the greats had. Like you were haunted by the stories around you, driven to close some of those stories yourself. I looked you up, after. Saw what you were doing as a detective. Knew that's what I wanted."

I made a rude noise. "Sorry for the false advertising, kid."

"You took a beating, sir. Yet here you are. You're no failure." Coltrane turned back to the screen. "Let's see what we got. Dad looks pretty boring. Moved around a lot. Only got to Birmingham about ten months ago."

"Record?"

"Nothing. Well, speeding tickets and such. Not even many of them. Keeps a low profile."

"Like I said, probably nothing. Sorry I wasted your time."

"Keeping our eyes open isn't a waste to me, sir. And it was an honor meeting you."

He closed his computer, but I didn't get up. Coltrane turned back and waited in silence.

I said, "Still..."

Coltrane studied me and opened his computer back up. "Let me do a little more playing. We've got fifty different states and about a million towns and counties. Big things like convictions and fingerprints are centralized, but there's still a lot of things that aren't. I'm going to build a search that will go across the lines and see what we get."

We sat and waited in silence as seemingly random screens popped up.

"This is mostly worthless," said Coltrane. "In fact, I'm surprised at how little we see about Maria and Dad. Usually, you see a lot of crap: pictures from local newspapers of kids in school plays, that sort of thing. We don't have much of that here... huh."

"What's that?"

"Funny. Same name, in a school in Indiana four years ago. Also in the second grade."

I said, "Still, Maria Von Trapp was a famous name from *The Sound of Music*. Could be more than one of them sort-of named after the movie."

"Maybe." Coltrane looked. "Here's another one. California, seven years ago." He glanced at me and pulled two windows forward. "Look at the pictures. Looks like the same guy was in both places at those times. Had a daughter in the second grade with the same name both times."

I said, "May be a coincidence."

Coltrane said, "Maybe not. "

We agreed it would be best for Coltrane to take what we'd found to his Lieutenant—our Lieutenant—without my being there to muddy the waters. Coltrane promised to call me when he had something. We both knew that might be an hour or a week, or never.

I went and played clown at the middle school, then found myself standing outside of Johnson's as the sun was going down. Checked my cell phone for the hundredth time; the rattlesnake was quiet.

I decided not to go in. Be sober if Coltrane called.

I walked home, and stood with a big cup of coffee in the back bedroom, the one stripped of furniture except for one desk in the middle of the room, the walls paneled with corkboard covered with yellowing newspaper stories and pictures and police logs and notes and diagrams.

One wall had only one thing: a framed picture of a heartbreakingly beautiful brown-skinned woman and a young girl who—if you squinted just right—looked like me.

I stared at the wall to the right of the picture, the wall with the earliest stuff, and walked a familiar path around the room. The first case was a young girl kidnapped and killed. Hot senior detective assigned to the case. I went to the next case. Then the next. The killer called himself the Angel of

Mercy and he kept killing Birmingham's children, and the detective could do nothing, at least as far as the papers were concerned. Finally, the detective started taunting the Angel in the press, hoping to push him into a mistake.

Then the last set of articles. The Angel killed the detective's wife and daughter. And was himself killed by the detective.

Or so the papers said.

The papers were too kind to print the stories of the detective's slide into obsession after the case was closed. No story about how his lieutenant at the time refused to fire him even after a year of the detective fucking up; instead he made him a community affairs cop, where he couldn't do any harm.

I circled the walls, chanting every word out loud like a long familiar rosary. Looking for any connection between the Angel and Maria Trap. This had to be him. He was back and I would get him this time.

I came to the end, to the picture again. I stood in front of my girls and prayed the only prayer I ever prayed

Prayed that none of this was real.

But it was.

I circled round and round the room, coming back to the same prayer, until the next morning. No rattlesnake clatter of my cellphone interrupted me.

The next morning, showered but sleepless, I found myself sitting, irritated and exhausted, in front of a class of seventh graders and trying to focus.

"Officer," said the teacher. "Officer, could you please at least stay awake?"

"I'm not...sorry. I'm not asleep, I'm...distracted, I guess. Sorry."

The door burst open and Capulet burst in. The teacher turned on her. "Please check in with the office, ma'am. And don't interrupt my—"

"Oh, blow it out your chalkboard. Joe, you're right. There's something wrong there. I went to Maria's house. Her father wouldn't even let me in the house, just talked through the door. When I went around to the back, he waved a gun at me through the window. And Maria's not in school today. I called your community affairs office and a very rude woman finally told me you were here."

"C'mon." I stood up. "Let's go see the captain."

We moved fast for our size.

A few hours later, I was in the front seat of Captain Jordan's Explorer, Capulet in the back fidgeting.

She leaned over the seat. "Why don't we—"

"Shush." I turned to the captain. "Told you not to bring this one along."

"And she made a phone call to her brother who's a cop somewhere and a buddy of the commissioner's, and he told me to move on this and bring her along as a witness." He turned to Capulet. "Which is why we're here today, violating everything in professional police methods, which say investigate thoroughly, take your time, and don't fuck up. Don't make me regret this." He turned back, said something into his radio and heard some crackling noises that meant something to him.

"Five minutes out," he said. He swiveled around and faced her. "You're doing this as an observer. Who stays in this car." He swiveled back. "In five minutes, we've got an undercover guy posing as a DHR worker who'll politely knock on the door of the Trap house, with a uniform beside him in case Trap gets any ideas. They will get into the house and have eyes on him and make the call when the rest can move in safely." He turned to me. "Nice and quiet. If this turns out to be another wild goose chase, we'll smile, thank him for his time, and disappear without having this on the six o'clock news."

She said, "But what about the other girls?"

The captain turned and gave me a look. "What did you tell this civilian?"

I squirmed. "I told her a couple of things, to shut her up."

"Yeah, that worked. She hasn't stopped telling me how to do my job since we met." He turned around in his seat. "Ms. Capulet, I can let you stay here with us and observe, if you can remain silent."

"I can if your detective can."

"He can. He will."

The radio crackled and a minivan pulled up in front of the house.

The captain keyed his radio. "Everyone, positions."

Doors opened on the houses adjoining the Trap house and men came out trying to look bored. A guy across the street cutting the grass stopped his mower and bent down to check it; I could see the gun and badge in the back of his jeans. A man in a sport coat carrying a notebook and a uniformed officer got out of the minivan. They walked up to the front door, pretending to laugh at some joke as they went.

Still laughing, they rang the doorbell until Trap came to the door. After a minute, he let them in.

The captain keyed his mic. "Everyone, stay off the air. When Remnick is satisfied we've got cause, he'll key his mic twice and I'll give the word to move in. Until then, nothing."

For a minute they were silent.

"This is exciting," whispered Capulet.

"Quiet," I said.

The captain gave us both a glare.

There were two clicks on the radio, and the captain said, "Go." The men sprinted for the door and a Birmingham PD van came up the street, followed by an ambulance. Capulet saw the ambulance and jumped. "She's hurt?"

I said, "Precautionary."

"What do we do now?"

"Wait."

The radio crackled with one clear word: "Secure."

The van opened and a real DHR worker came out and ran toward the house, followed by an EMT from the ambulance.

"OK." The captain opened his door and got out with the window down.

"Can we go in now?" Capulet said.

"No. You two will stay here and keep quiet. Remnick's got control of everything in there." He spoke into the radio.

The grass cutter came out with Trap in handcuffs.

"Where's Maria?" said Capulet.

"Actually," the captain said, "we think her name's Carmen, Carmen Del Sol. She's safe. DHR workers are inside now, looking out for her until her family is called and can get here."

Capulet said, "I hope she's not scared."

Another time I should have kept quiet. "Of course, she's scared. What the fuck you think? Little girl surrounded by strangers with guns."

Capulet pushed her door open. "I've got to get in there. I'm not going to be so passive about these things anymore."

"Heaven help us all." I hit my door and went after her.

Maria/Carmen appeared at the window. She recognized her teacher, screamed and ran for the door. A patrolman caught her on her way out.

"Ms. Capulet!" the girl screamed, reaching out to Capulet. The patrolman dragged the girl back inside.

Capulet picked up speed. I caught up and grabbed her arm. She shook me away. "That child needs somebody on her side."

I said, "They won't let you in."

She flashed me a manic grin. "Heaven help them."

She was fighting with officers at the door when the captain came up to me.

"You're not going to stop her," I said. "And she'll probably be good for the girl."

The captain waved and they let her in.

He looked at me. "You earned your stripes today."

I paused. "When I first saw that something was hinky with the girl, I thought it might be a shot at the Angel."

We stood in silence for a moment.

"This might be more important than even that, Joe. A few minutes before we left, we got word from one of the cities where Coltrane found other girls. Police there have found a body—young girl's body—in the backyard of the house where this guy lived. Starting to look like maybe this guy keeps them for about a year, grows bored and gets rid of them and looks for another one in another town."

"How long has he had Maria/Carmen?"

He bit his lip. "Been in school here for nine months."

"So…"

"Yes." He pointed over at Capulet hugging Carmen. "Could have been anytime now. Don't tell your friend, but if we had followed correct police procedure this time, that little girl might be dead."

The captain said, "Jesus Christ."

I followed his eyes up the street and saw a big white van with a mural on the side and satellite dishes on top rolling up the street.

"WBHA." The captain read the letters off the side. Not easy to do with all the happy reporters' faces smiling around the letters. Birmingham must be the happiest place on earth.

"Stay out of sight." he said to me.

"Want me to hide behind a light pole?"

"Yeah. A really big one. WBHA is the happy news station. Everything has to have a happy spin. Preferably young and good-looking, which is why we've got a new assistant commissioner for media affairs. I got a royal ass-chewing from the brass for frowning on camera while I was talking to a reporter about a little old lady who got pistol-whipped during a robbery."

The captain shoved his hands in his pockets and rocked back and forth, slapping on a smile. Casual. Two happy guys enjoying the happy Birmingham sun while cheerfully serving and protecting. He kept his face frozen and happy, and cut his eyes at me. "If you have to be on-camera, smile."

I gave him my social smile.

"Jesus Christ. We can't put that on TV." He risked looking away from the truck for a moment. "Coltrane! Get over here."

Coltrane walked up, a genuine smile on his face. He placed a hand on my shoulder. "Captain, I want to take this opportunity to compliment Detective Brosette on some fine police work, and thank him for showing me a great example—"

"Yeah, fine," the smiling stone face of the captain said. "It's your police work now. Keep that smile on your face, and stand here beside me. Brosette, get behind my car, completely out of sight."

The reporter was striding toward us, a tall smiling blonde with a microphone in her hand and a cameraman trying to keep up.

I said, "Gladly," and faded behind the car. Realized that, for me, hiding behind a car was about as good as hiding behind a light pole. I bent down. Maybe they'd think I was fixing a flat tire.

As the blonde reached the captain and Coltrane, she turned so the camera caught her intro as she was moving to heighten the image that Big 11 News was, yet again, running to find news you could use

"Paula Light for Big 11 News."

The captain put his hand out, but she turned back to her cameraman. He gave her a hand signal.

"We're in Legion Park where the Birmingham police force has just rescued a child at great risk to their own personal safety. I've been getting the full story from a

Birmingham police spokesman. What can you tell us about this rescue, Chief?"

The captain's smile turned to a snarl before he pasted it back on. "I'm not a chief, I'm—never mind. No, there was no real danger to the officers here. Acting on a tip, we sent a team to the door. The suspect recognized the situation and gave himself up without a fight. The young lady was recovered safely, and we're now in the process of reuniting her with her parents."

"Can we see the child, let our viewers see that she's OK now?"

"No, she's inside, and safe. I would like to introduce your viewers to Detective Coltrane here, whose fine police work resulted in this rescue."

He stepped away, and the reporter pointed her smile and microphone at Coltrane.

Coltrane said, "Well, actually, it was another officer—"

The captain stepped back. "A team effort. But Officer Coltrane will be the face of BPD for this. He'll be making a full statement, once we've gathered all the facts."

Coltrane's smile became bigger. "Yes, sir, but—"

There was a commotion at the front door and a blue-uniformed back appeared, the officer saying something about not going out there. As we all watched, the officer flew backwards off the little porch and landed in the weeds. Capulet and Maria stood in the door.

The camera swiveled to them.

Capulet stepped outside and looked down at the officer. "Sorry, didn't know you were that easy to push around."

Lying in the weeds and looking up at her, the officer said, "Ma'am, you can't—"

"Oh, blow it out your holster. Where's Joe?" She scanned the crowd. Maria spotted me first. She ripped her hand away from Capulet and ran to me, crying, "The Huggy Bear saved me."

The cameraman got all of it, including Capulet catching up and putting her finger in Light's face. Now they were all in the picture.

"This is the story for you." She pointed at me.

Meanwhile, I was still trying to hide behind the car with Maria wrapped around my arm.

"Here's your hero," Capulet continued. "That's Officer Joe, the only name this hero goes by as he travels to our schools, showing our children what a Birmingham policeman can be. And saving their lives, when they need him. Using his skills as a trained detective, Officer Joe ... "

The captain looked at Light, who was shaking her head in a furious "Yes, yes," as Capulet unfolded the heroic legend of Officer Joe.

"Jesus Christ." The captain waved me over to the reporter. Off-camera, his smile was gone.

Capulet gave the captain her teacher look, and he shut up and walked away. But he stayed close enough to hear. Which wasn't hard with Capulet.

"This man is an American hero," she shouted.

"Yes, ma'am," Light said. "You were saying this man— Officer Joe? Did what exactly? Is he a patrolman? I see he's got a blue uniform, not plainclothes like a real detective."

"No, he's real. He's a detective, but he goes around to schools and talks to kids."

Maria said, "Jessi says he's our Huggy Bear."

"And he's a hero. I'm Juliet Capulet. Yeah, I know, what a joke, name a woman built like me after Shakespeare's Juliet. Talk to my parents about that. Hey! Who cares who I am. Officer Joe's the story here. Keep up."

"Yes, ma'am," Light said.

"Detective Boy—no, he prefers Officer Joe, so I'm going to respect that. While presenting standard police propaganda to children, Officer Joe picked up on clues that Maria was being tortured—"

I opened my mouth, but the captain jumped in first. "We don't know that. And it was a team effort on the part of the Birmingham PD."

"We don't know that she's been tortured?" Capulet's volume made the captain take another step back. "Look at this poor child, torn from her family. Even if that monster did nothing but force her to watch reruns of *Saved by the Bell*, it was torture."

She was not finished. "And, as for the all-powerful Birmingham Police Department, where were they? Strutting around. Persecuting law-abiding citizens. Eating donuts. No, this one man, Officer Joe, who was probably sentenced to community relations duty for something like standing up for a citizen, is the hero. He saw the problem. He took action. He saved this child. With help from me."

She smiled big and paused to let Light ask about that.

She didn't. Instead, Light pointed her mic at me. "Officer Joe?" she said. "I like that. So, Officer Joe. What made you suspect an abduction?"

It had been a long time since I had been in front of the cameras. In front of the cameras with my boss waiting to kick my ass for any mistake.

"Well, I mean, Captain Jordan is right. It was a department effort. Detective Coltrane over there was instrumental. And the rapid response team got out here in time."

"And me," said Capulet.

I ground my teeth. "Yes, Ms. Capulet was helpful. Once she stopped battling and arguing and being a general pain-in-the-ass, she did help." The captain was grimacing. Oh well.

"Yes, yes, Detective—Officer Joe. I'm sure all the little people contributed. But there must have been a moment, a clue that you picked up on that everyone else missed."

"Well, the child missed school."

Light waited. Finally, I said, "I mean she missed school on the day I was coming."

"Are you that popular?"

"No, in fact, a lot of the older kids don't like me at all. It's just—" I looked over at the captain for help but there was none there. "It's kind of hard to explain."

"Officer Joe, I think there's a real story here. Perhaps we could give you a day or so to get your story together and do a longer interview?"

I stepped back. "No, I don't think that's such a good idea."

She turned to the captain and he gritted his teeth. "He'll be delighted."

Maria pushed forward and grabbed me around the leg, hugging hard.

"Thank you, Huggy Bear. You saved my life."

I reached down and patted her, my hand almost covering her little head. I opened my mouth to say something, but the words caught and nothing came out but a gargling sound.

"Did you get that?" Light whispered to the cameraman.

"Got it."

"Good. Stay on it for the voiceover."

She raised her voice. "This is Paula Light for Big 11 News. Tune in tomorrow night for more from Officer Joe, the Huggy Bear Hero."

When I left police headquarters and was back in my own department-issue car alone, there was no place I wanted to go and no one I wanted to see. I drove around Birmingham, drifting the black Impala in and out of city traffic without paying much attention to anything outside of my head. Horns honked, fists waved and I learned colorful new curses in half a dozen different languages.

I honked back, waved my fist and yelled my own curses. If I didn't know the language, I yelled gibberish really loud.

"Kumbaya! Kumbaya!" I screamed at a couple who had shouted something incomprehensible at me while I was stopped at a green light, thinking. They shut up and pulled around me, staring.

I drove home, parked in the driveway and sat in the car. I couldn't go inside and face the ghosts. Couldn't explain to them why, yet again today, I hadn't caught the Angel. Couldn't look at the two faces staring out of the photo, begging. "Catch him and free us. Do your job."

I got out of the car and walked up to State Street. Turned at the drug store on the corner, headed toward Johnson's and almost ran into a woman with the beginnings of crow's feet around her brown eyes.

"Joe?"

"Excuse me." I started to step around her.

"Joe? Joe Brosette? I'm Kathleen, Kathleen Clift. You probably don't remember me?"

I stepped back and my vision cleared.

"Yeah," I said. "You were married to Raekwon Clift. Young cop. At least, young when your family moved into the neighborhood, what? Ten years ago. Oh." I paused and realized how stupid I was being. "Sorry about Raekwon." I thought I should say something more. "Brave man." It sounded stupid, but she smiled.

"Thanks for remembering. Raekwon always looked up to you. We both worshipped you. You were like the funniest and smartest cop around, back when we first moved in."

"Back when."

"Yeah. Back when." She put her hand on my arm. "I saw you on the news a few minutes ago. They said you saved a child. Good for you. Good to see you doing something again."

"Yeah." I didn't want to talk about it. "Surprised to see you still in the neighborhood."

"Yeah," she laughed the same harsh laugh. "Hard to move on. You know you've got to, but it's hard to do, alone. Call me sometime and we can talk."

She gave me a flickering smile, took her hand away, and left me standing in the street wondering what any of it meant. Is this what it felt like to be hit on? Not something that happened to me often. And was that something I'd have to do someday? Move on and hit on a strange woman?

Jesus Fucking Christ.

I passed a window and saw myself. No way a woman could overlook all that. Whatever had happened with Kathleen wasn't flirting, or whatever the word was for the tentative stage just before flirting.

That was pity, and I felt my muscles tighten. Pity. What you get when you don't get your job done.

I was dog-tired turning into Johnson's. It felt like the middle of the night. I thought about going home to sleep, but my feet did what they had been doing for two years and my ass found itself on a stool.

"Early," said Wendy. "The kitchen is still open. I can get you a real meal instead of a sandwich."

"So, I can have inedible crap on a plate rather than inedible crap between two slices of bread?"

"That's our menu here. Would you like to see the more detailed version, the one that says things like, 'chicken' or 'omelet'?"

"The bunco squad lets you use words like that?"

She shrugged. "They let you guys pretend to be cops enforcing the law; we get to pretend to be citizens following it."

"Bring me something. Anything that doesn't have too many flies on it."

Wendy muttered one of those standard curse words bleached into friendly banter by constant use here and turned to walk away.

"I don't know why Joyce cooks for you heathens. I'll bring you something with a lot of vegetables." She gave me kind of a crocodile smile and said, "Because we love you here."

She left and I turned to Ron. "You always on that stool?"

"Don't know. Never sober enough when I'm other places to remember."

"Jesus. This is the future I'm staring at?"

"What future?" said Ron. "You think you're following our example? We're following you."

"Shit. So, what you got for me?"

"Same nothing I've had for years. Give it up, Joe. Get a life."

I shifted around and made a noise. "That's why I come to you, Ron, seeking a qualified life coach."

"Asshole. You come here seeking approval from other assholes."

"Yeah," I said. "Approval and love, all in the same place. Good to know I can always rely on support from the fuckups."

Wendy put a plate down in front of me.

"Shit, Wendy, there's green stuff and red stuff on this plate."

"Called veggies, Joe. They say to eat healthy these days. Make sure your plate has a lot of colors."

"Can't I just put ketchup and green Chile salsa on my fries?"

She grunted and a voice in the dark yelled, "Hey, look at the TV."

Paula Light was on, with Maria and Capulet breathlessly spinning the tale of Joe the hero and the camera turning to me.

"Crap," somebody muttered from the back.

Someone else yelled, "Turn it up," and they got quiet and listened. At the end, somebody said, "Another fairy tale from the liberal media."

I said, "Christ, Wendy, can you turn that thing off?"

She glared at me. "Fuck you, Mr. Media Star. You've had your two minutes of showing off, so now you want the TV off so we can all bask in your glory?"

"No." I said. "What? I didn't do anything. They made up that story. I never wanted to be on TV. You guys know me."

Ron said, "Damn it, Joe, I'm the closest thing you've got to a friend, and even I can see you putting on airs. Making that face for the camera and coming up with a cute nickname for yourself. Showed up here right in time for it to be on TV and rub it in our faces. Even ordered a fancy meal instead of an honest crap sandwich. Like you think you're a celebrity in a five-star restaurant or something."

"No—I didn't—five-star? Here? No. More like 'one-turd.' I didn't ask for the reporter or this food or anything. I was trying to help out a little girl."

Wendy looked bored. "So you say, Joe. So you say. But remember." She waved at the TV. "We don't like heroes in here."

What would I do without all this love and approval?

It was more effort than it was worth to move my ass off the bar stool. So, I stared into the mirror and ate and drank and stared some more. A little before midnight, Wendy pulled the almost-black Myers bottle down from the shelf and started to pour into my empty glass again.

"I didn't ask for that." I pulled my glass back and half the rum splashed onto the bar. "And I ain't paying for it."

Wendy stood there with the bottle in her hand, still canted at an angle. "You're sure as hell paying for it. You think you're too good to drink here now?' "

"No, I..." I stood up. "No, I...I didn't ask for this. Any of it."

She put the cork back in the bottle. "Hey, no skin off my ass."

A voice out of the grumbling darkness said clearly, "Too good to drink with us here, why don't you get the fuck out."

"Fuck you."

"Fuck you."

I stood up and said to the dark. "Well, if I'm not here for the rum, not here for the food. Sure not here for the scintillating conversation."

"Fuck you."

"Or for the love." I stumbled to the door.

Wendy said to my back, "We'll settle up when you come back."

I started to walk away, stopped, picked up the rum and downed it in one hot sweet gulp. No sense in wasting stuff.

Outside, it felt like I was outside of everything. Outside of the bar, outside of the police world. Outside of my own fucked-up life.

I looked around. The sidewalk was wet and slick-black with the night. What time was it? I couldn't remember when I'd last been alone on this sidewalk on this side of the witching hour.

Maybe the usually dark Birmingham streets had been bewitched, too. More colors. I was shocked at how much more you could see if you came out of Johnson's before midnight, with two drinks in you, than if you came out at two, with more drinks than you could count.

Must be the street lights.

There was a new store next to Johnson's. "Pretty Parrot," said the sign. I tried to figure it out. At first it looked like an excuse for painting the windows into a cartoon jungle of smiling, friendly animals. There was a small trike in the window, and children's clothing arranged like they were dancing. Kid's store. Hell, maybe a store for playful parrots who rode bikes. What did I know? Alabama is a state that cheers for Crimson Elephants and War Eagles. Why not Playful Parrots?

I laughed at it, laughed at the audacity of youth, at bright colors standing up to the gloom.

I tried to think what the store had been, back when Luz and I moved into what had still been a no-nonsense neighborhood in working-class Birmingham. It took effort. I looked up and down the street and worked hard not to see ghosts; just the street as it was today. Now that the Birmingham steel mills have been replaced with high-rise banks and hospitals, there's a lot of bright clean modern shops, with a few left-over derelicts like Johnson's. Typical once-decaying city battling with ambitious yuppies. We had never imagined either of those things for our home. I looked around, carefully. A lot of things I had never noticed before.

I walked along window shopping, not so much exploring the items in the windows as the windows and stores themselves. There was a wireless phone store with big letters proclaiming, "More Apps!" next to an Applebee's with a sign for half-price apps. Whatever apps were, they were clearly something on your phone that you could eat. I'd have to check up on that. Maybe the kid at the precinct—Coltrane, was that his name? —could tell me how to get food on my phone.

"Probably have to upgrade," I said out loud. I looked to see if anyone heard. Nobody around.

I turned at the CVS drugstore onto my street. There was a teen boy in a hoodie pissing on the dumpster.

"Hey! Hey!" I yelled.

The boy took one look at the bulk coming toward him and took off, not bothering to zip up, spraying as he ran.

"Jesus," I yelled. "World's going to hell."

That shook me out of the Disneyland fantasy I'd stumbled into and back to the crappy world I knew.

I looked down the street and picked out the porch light at my house. Something flickered. I stopped and stood still. Maybe it was a trick of the light.

I was starting to relax when it happened again. A flicker, nothing more. But it looked like something blocking the light, and moving.

I cut across the back of the CVS parking lot to the next street parallel to mine and walked down it. Taking the last cross street, I cut through my neighbor's back yard and came into my own yard, standing with my back to an oak tree, watching.

There were no lights on inside the house, not even small ones from a flashlight. I eased up beside my car parked in the driveway and crouched behind it and paused, listening. Something over by the porch rustled. I drew my Glock and held it by my side. Then crept around the car.

The back of the car was even with the porch. Checked the Glock, sucked in my breath and stepped out.

"Freeze!" I yelled as I brought the gun down on the figure I saw there.

Juliet Capulet looked up from the book in her lap. "You're late."

"Jesus Christ, what the hell are you doing on my porch in the middle of the night?"

"Reading. And waiting. After we solved today's abduction and saved a child, I figured we needed to talk about our future."

"*We* didn't save anyone. Birmingham PD saved that girl. And *we* don't have a future."

She shook the bag again.

"Want some?"

A light came on across the street.

I thought about what I looked like, standing under the streetlight at midnight with my gun drawn.

"Get in the house," I hissed.

Capulet closed her book and set it beside the bag, using both hands to push herself up. "Good. These old bones are getting tired of this cold concrete. Beginning to think you aren't much of a partner." She picked up the pork rinds and waved them at the locked door. "Or much of a host."

"I'd rot in hell before I picked you for a partner," I said.

My mind flashed back to Kareem Ali. Kareem was my last real partner when I was still on the homicide squad. Other cops called him "Dick Tracy," for his square-jawed insistence that everything be done right. We'd been good partners.

Now I looked at the sad, sagging heap in front of me, waving pork rinds instead of a gun. "And you sure as hell aren't what I would pick," she said. "What you are is an embarrassment."

She took her time bending down to pick up her book. "And I'm not the one standing out here waving around his substitute for manhood." She indicated the lit window across the street.

I put the Glock back in its holster. "It's called a gun. A serious piece of police equipment."

"Suit yourself. Still, I'm betting you haven't fired it for as long as you haven't fired that other phallic symbol." She smiled sweetly. "Except on the practice range, of course."

I tried to say something, but she interrupted. "Aren't you going to let me inside?"

I shoved past her, barely enough room for both of us on the small square of concrete porch. I unlocked the door, grumbling, and tried to shove her into the open door. She stayed rooted to the porch, motionless until I stopped pushing, then swept into the house on her own.

"Oh, my." She plopped her book, the pork rinds and a half-empty two-liter bottle of Pepsi next to my favorite chair, like she was a guest waiting for the hotel staff to put her things in their proper place. "This is so much homier than I would have expected."

She saw the open hallway and headed for it.

I hustled but couldn't get in front of her before she made it to the hall. The hall was too narrow to get around and politely stop her.

"No one invited you back here."

"No. They didn't."

She went straight to the first closed door and put her hand on the knob. I reached around her, no mean feat, and put my hand on hers.

"No."

"Aw, come on." I wouldn't give and she turned, no room for the two us to move around in the narrow hall without rubbing. She laughed at me at first, but paused when she saw something in my eyes.

"OK." She dropped her hand and half-turned, half-rubbed her way toward the other rooms, pointing to the other closed doors.

"No."

"OK."

She walked into the open door of my bedroom. "Like I said, not what I expected. So, what did you think of our first romantic moment here?"

"There is no romance here."

"Says the man who won't let me in any room but his bedroom."

She waited for a reaction and didn't get one.

"Well, are you going to get out of the doorway and let me go back to the front of the house, or do you think you've got a young maiden trapped in your boudoir?"

I jumped back from the door and she swept past me.

"Didn't think so. That's the effect this Juliet has on men. I'd be a lesbian if I didn't have a fascination with..." She turned around in the hall and I almost crashed into her. She looked at my belt and said, "...guns."

Then she turned into the kitchen and threw open the refrigerator.

"If we're going to work together, you're going to have to get some Pepsi."

"We're not working together. You're not staying here. In fact, you're leaving now."

"Not until." She pulled out a chair and plopped herself down at the kitchen table. "Not until we get our working relationship sorted out. Bring me my Pepsi and pork, will you? You can leave my book there. I'll get back to Hank Ryan later."

"You're not staying."

I said that as I set the Pepsi and the pork rinds down next to her.

"Of course not." She said that as she shoved her hand into the bag and pulled out a handful to wave them at me. "Let's get things worked out between us, then I'll go."

"There is nothing to work out."

I sat there and listened to her crunch pork rinds for as long as I could stand. "I'm putting on a pot of coffee. I need to be awake for this."

I got up, went to the sink and took the pot off the drying rack. Took my time loading Mr. Coffee, muttering at Joe DiMaggio for not being there to protect me.

"So, you've been sitting out there for how long?"

"A little after six. Figured you'd be home soon, but I was wrong."

"I had a stop to make."

"I'd have guessed that being a community affairs officer was more nine to five than that."

I laughed. "You mean 'clown in a cop suit'?"

Capulet reddened. It seemed somehow quaint to see blushing on a woman who was built like - and behaved like - a battleship.

"Sorry," she said. "Sometimes my mouth will say anything to piss people off." She paused. "You'd think that someone who looks like me wouldn't do things to attract attention."

I sat down and let Joe Di work on the coffee. "People look at big people like us, and sometimes think we don't have normal feelings, like we don't need anything but for people to get out of our way at the buffet line. Sometimes, even I think that's true. But it's not always the way it feels on the inside."

"No," was her answer. "After I got fired as a prosecutor, I was a librarian for a lot of years, thought I could hide behind a desk, fade away and be normal."

I raised an eyebrow.

"Until some asshole tried to check out a book proving the Holocaust was fake and I threw him out of the library."

"The library objected to that?"

"They agreed with my position, but not my—what was the word they used? —*vigor*. And they didn't like paying for his injuries in the lawsuit."

"Might be worth the cost." I paused. "OK. I'm impressed. And I appreciate your coming by. Well, sort of, I guess. But, I really can't be your partner. I'm a cop. You're not. Sorry."

She snorted. "I ain't leaving. So...to your sorry, sorry back."

I picked up the coffee pot and waved it at her.

"This time of night? My doctor would have a fit. Sure."

I poured two cups, brought them over and sat down.

"You got any sugar?"

"Sorry." I stood up. "My hosting skills are a little rusty." I rummaged around a shelf. "Actually, I'm not sure if I do...oh, wait, how about this?"

I set a yellowed box of brown sugar on the table.

"Jesus. How old is this?"

"I would guess," I said, "at least two years old."

She picked up the box. "I don't need fancy." She opened the top, unfolded the plastic bag and peeked inside. "Solid as a brick." She raised the box and slammed it on the tile floor with a bang. Picked it up and used a fingernail to dig out a couple of flakes to put into her cup.

"Now," she said, "can we get down to business?"

"There is no business. One cup of coffee, and you need to go so I can get to sleep."

She swirled her cup. "I don't think so. A man who needs sleep more than he needs help wouldn't have let me in the door."

"A man who finds an intruder on his porch—even if it is the notorious pork rind bandit—probably finds himself wide awake."

"The pork rind bandit, apprehended by the Huggy Bear. Look, I did my homework on you this afternoon. I know what happened the last time you drew your gun on that porch. And I know that Maria was the first case you've worked on since then."

"I have an active case."

"Chasing a man the real police say is dead. One phantom case for two years. How much longer?"

"Twenty, thirty years if it's needed. Till I die."

"Does the department know?"

"Yes."

"Does Birmingham PD give you any support?"

"No." I hesitated. "That's not really true. The department gives me plenty of support in community relations. Scripts to read, flyers to hand out. A paycheck. I've even got a Keystone Kops clown suit, although it's always seemed too silly to wear."

"Hey, you never know. Kids, maybe even teachers, might tell a clown things they wouldn't tell a cop. Might be worth a shot. But no, I don't mean that kind of stuff. I mean with the case."

"None. The only thing that makes the job worthwhile from my perspective is that I get to keep my gun and my badge. Got a captain who will listen. Sometimes."

"Got a partner?"

"No. Don't need or want one."

"So, you tell me: why does Birmingham PD insist that most working detectives have a partner?"

"Second set of eyes sometimes sees things. Someone to talk to. Someone to be there for you."

"You miss having a partner?"

I stood up and carried my coffee cup to the sink, dumped it and rinsed it out. Set it on the drain, just like Luz used to do.

"Yes."

"Then we're in business."

"No, we're not. I'm still a cop. I can't bring a civilian into this. You don't have the training or—"

"I told you, I'm from a family of cops."

"Not the same."

"That's the point, maybe for both of us: we're not the same. A cop in a clown suit sees things and thinks things an ordinary cop won't. And a fat old lady teacher sees things, too. Look, I've got skills we can use. I know how to research things that you can't. I know kids in ways you don't."

"You like that 'cop in a clown suit' thing, don't you? Yeah, maybe you're right. A little bit. Maybe I can call you sometime, ask you for information. But there are reasons why cops need to carry guns and teachers don't."

"But the one thing cops—at least this one—and teachers—at least this one—have in common: we want to protect kids. We can do things your department can't. And there's one other thing you need to know."

She paused and waved a pork rind at me.

"I have a legally registered shotgun, and I know how to use it."

"Heaven help us all. Still, I can't make you my partner."

She leaned across the table. "Look, I'm bored silly as a teacher. And I know that I want to help kids, but I don't think I'm helping them with what I'm doing anymore. You ever feel that way, like you want to break out and do something crazy?"

I'd been doing crazy for two years. Was getting nowhere by myself, and I knew the Angel was still out there.

She reached into the bag and pulled out a handful of rinds and shoved the bag over at me. "Share?"

I looked at the bag. Reached in and took all I could hold. "Share."

There is no place to put a gun in a clown suit.

Despite that realization, I felt like I needed to wear my Birmingham PD community-affairs-provided clown suit today. Shirley had been bugging me forever to occasionally wear the clown suit to show the soft and funny side of Birmingham PD to kids.

That was the actual phrase she used: the soft and funny side of Birmingham PD.

Jesus Fucking Christ.

But I really wanted to get on somebody's good side today. And I felt like I needed as much of a disguise as I could get on this trip.

The suit came with a gigantic plastic pistol that went "Pop" and shot out a flag with "Bang" on it in case you didn't get the point. I pulled the gun and fired it—if that was the right word—and stood looking at a sad-faced pretend cop with a suitcase-sized prop gun and a "Bang" flag drooping out of the barrel.

Jesus.

I threw the fake gun back on the bed where the rest of the clown accessories lay. There was an alternate prop: a big, plastic billy club. Oh, a much better choice for Birmingham, a city where billy clubs and police dogs had a history that was both terrible and important to be remembered for what it really was and not as a cute joke.

Once again…Jesus.

At least I didn't need any padding for the suit.

I walked over to the nightstand and picked up my own Glock, a real gun that fired real bullets. I tried it in a couple of places in the costume and couldn't make it work. Finally, I took a kitchen knife and cut a slit in the suit's chest, putting my gun in a shoulder holster underneath. Not great but it would do.

The fake cop with the real gun drove to the church and looked up at the symbol of his city.

Back in 1904, when Birmingham was an iron and steel town (Pittsburg of the South! the signs all proclaimed) the city proudly built a 56-foot-tall cast-iron statue of the Roman god Vulcan working at his forge, naked except for a leather apron, and put it on top of Red Mountain, dominating the city, and giving half the population a constant view of possibly the world's largest bare ass.

And that was why the little stone Catholic church clinging to the side of a mountain was cowering under a giant Roman god. Could be worse. It could have been on the back side.

I sat in the parking lot, trying not to look up Vulcan's apron and thinking of the last time I had been here. With Luz and our daughter Sarah, back when Luz dragged us all to church every Sunday. Our church. I stared at the door until I realized that I couldn't make the ghosts go away by staring.

I was sitting sideways in my car, wrestling to get the first oversized clown shoe on when a forty-something man in a priest's collar walked up with a big smile.

"I'm Brother Dave." He put out a hand.

I took it. "I thought the Catholic Church—at least when I went here—reserved the title of 'Brother' for monks and such."

"Yeah, I've been told. But I'm not comfortable with people calling me Father, so it's kind of a compromise."

"Didn't think priests had to compromise with their flock."

"We've kind of—uh—had a history here lately, and we're trying to build support, particularly with the parish council."

"I know the history. I used to attend. I admired Father Carson."

That caught his attention and he studied my face. Priests usually speak with the surety of their religion, but this was a man afraid of saying the wrong thing to the wrong people in whatever this church had become. He decided something and nodded. "Father Carson was a good man. Not everyone agreed with his—ah—untraditional ways, and now the church is split and I'm trying to placate both sides. I even let one of the women on the council write my homily for today. I haven't had time to look at it."

I didn't say anything and he kept looking at me.

"I hope you return, my son. This church needs people like you."

He obviously didn't know my story. I looked at the ground and waited for him to go away. He didn't. I wanted to change the topic. I pointed to a gleaming crystal spire springing skyward from the earth next to the small church, new to me and still under construction but already dominating the church itself. I tried to guess its finished height, and wondered if the Wizard of Oz was going to live there full-time or only when Dorothy and the Tin Man came by.

For once, though, I didn't say what I thought. I said, "That looks like an impressive achievement."

Another shrug. "The council thinks so. They want it to show the power of God challenging the heathen Vulcan statue above it."

"Well, it's..." I thought. "Ambitious."

"You want to know what I call it, only to myself?"

"Sure."

"God's Middle Finger." He shrugged. "But it's important to the council."

I popped the other shoe on, stood up and saluted. "Officer Joe, reporting for duty."

He laughed. "Praise Jesus. That is a perfect look for us today. We're opening Camp Jesus for our kids, there in the Children's Park next to the church. Council says we need something to compete with purple dinosaurs and gay Teletubbies for the hearts and souls of children."

I'd never contemplated the sexuality of cartoon characters before and I thought of a couple of jokes, but didn't make them. I was here to score goodwill points.

"Glad I can help."

We went over to a field of tents and games, and a happy band playing bland, upbeat praise music with a lot of hand clapping and a lot more "Praise Jesus's" than in the Catholic churches I'd grown up in. I posed for pictures and patted heads. One snarky teen-ager wanted a picture of me eating a donut and I was glad to oblige.

Brother Dave tapped me on the shoulder. "Time to get started."

He led me up onto a stage and they hooked me to a wireless mic. I said a few bland words in favor of goodness as politely as I could.

Brother Dave took over, shuffled his papers, and started spreading fire and brimstone and salvation without looking up from the page or showing any expression. Somehow the bright and happy kids shuffling in the field in front of us, so full of life that they could barely stand still for the talk, made me think of the children whose lives had been robbed by the Angel of Mercy. The ones I couldn't save.

I looked at the crowd, scanning. Praying for a magic power to see which kids were in the Angel's sights now. Wanted to tell them to fight. To live.

I could feel myself starting to cry and mutter nasty things under my breath, and tried to focus on Brother Dave's words as a distraction. He was reading a list of things the kids would go to hell for. He took a deep breath and launched into his windup.

"Remember that your life here is only a path to God and a better life in heaven. Your life here has no meaning on its own. Don't hold on too tightly to this temporary life."

I muttered, "Jesus Fucking Christ, no. Tell them to fight and scream and kick the robbers of life in the balls and..." I realized my mic was on. I looked at the shocked crowd.

"Praise Jesus?" I said into the hush.

I walked down the hill to my car, avoiding people's accusing eyes and shocked looks, feeling like God's Middle Finger was pointing right at me. Got into the car, shut the door behind me, and realized I had nowhere to go. I didn't want to go home after St. Stephens. So, I went to an out-of-the-way breakfast place that attracted construction workers and hard drinkers trying to recover from the night before.

Nobody even noticed one more clown in here.

I ate and stared out the window, ate and stared until the waitress put a paper check at my elbow and refilled my coffee cup. She patted me on the shoulder. "Time to go home, Bozo. The other forty-six clowns want their tiny car back so all of you can get in it and go to the movies."

I gave her a smile and looked at my watch. Way too early for Johnson's, and I wasn't sure the Lost Boys would let me back into their clubhouse. Only thing I could do other than stay here was to go home and bury myself in the Angel case again, and look Luz in the eye.

Saturdays are the worst.

I pushed the check back at her. "Let me have another of the Farmer's Specials."

She gave me a look with more sadness than I wanted. "You've had two already, honey. You sure?"

"Yeah. The boys at the big top can use the elephant for transportation until I get back with the car."

She picked up the check.

"And, honey," I said. "No more coffee. I've had enough coffee for one day."

She stood there a minute. "Too much coffee? Yeah, that's it."

Whether I needed the caffeine or not, I sipped the coffee I had left to have something to do to stop my thoughts.

Didn't work.

Maybe they were right.

Maybe all of them were right.

It had been two years since the Angel of Mercy had killed a child, after killing one every other month.

Two years since he had killed Luz and Sarah.

Two years since I had stood in my own front yard with my gun still smoking from killing a man who came out of the doorway of my own house waving a gun at me. Realizing that the man I had killed was my own priest. Stepping over his body to find Luz and Sarah bleeding on the floor.

Birmingham PD wrapped it up as a righteous shooting by a heroic cop who brought down a serial killer and ended a reign of terror.

It added up for them, but not for me. I had killed a man who had the blood of my wife and daughter on him. But, in my mind, too many things were wrong for him to have been the Angel. BPD disagreed with me and closed the case.

Maybe they were right. Maybe it was all my feelings of guilt from getting there too late. Maybe it was time to move on, whatever that meant.

The moment I had that thought, I could see my girls' picture looking at me, telling me I was still missing something.

Round and around I went. Drop it; no, fight like hell. Same circle I'd been stuck in for two years. Plus a hundred pounds and an ocean of rum.

I looked down and saw my plate was empty and the waitress was once again standing over me.

"Where's my third plate?" I said.

Her kindly sadness was gone. "That was your third plate, honey. I brought it and you ate it." She slapped my check down. "Pay up and get out. Bar's closed for you."

Saturdays are the worst.

The rattlesnake clattered as I was standing at the counter paying for breakfast.

"Shirley," I said. "I know what you're going to say, and you're right. This once. I screwed up big-time at St. Stephens. I'm tired of screwing up and making your life and everybody else's life miserable. I'm going to get out of the way and let you have your Brad Pitt fantasy."

There was a long silence. I looked at the caller ID. It was a number I didn't recognize.

A voice said, "You think you can let that reporter brag about what a hero you are? You think I'm gone? The Angel of Mercy is never gone. As long as there are children who need to be freed from the pain of this world and sent to the only father who truly loves them, there will be angels like me to help. Waiting, and planning. Watch carefully, and you'll see my greatest salvation is yet to come. And you'll be there to see it."

I recognized the voice. The phone went dead as I was screaming back at it.

The captain's admin was blocking me from his office and talking over his shoulder to the captain. "You told me not to let him in again."

The captain looked up at the commotion and said, "I know what I said. Let him in."

The admin gave me a dirty look and stepped aside. "You take advantage of him too much. All of you. He stays on the Commissioner's shit list for spending all his time playing Dear Abby to his men and not getting reports in."

I pushed by him. "I'll try not to interrupt him too much with police business. You know, killers and such."

He made a face and the captain sighed. "Joe, this has got to stop."

"I know, sir. Report to the Lieutenant."

"Try it for a change."

I got up to his desk.

"Yes, sir. But the Lieutenant wasn't involved with the Angel like you and I were."

"You mean the dead Angel?"

"The dead Angel who called me yesterday."

He leaned back and I saw him resign himself. "So, they have phones in hell?"

"This one was a pay phone over by Whole Foods. I had it traced."

"Good to know he's gone organic. I told my wife the only way I'd eat that shit was if I was dead. So, our dead organic Angel, conveniently calling from a phone you can't trace, told you what? Time and temperature in hell?"

I relayed the conversation.

He wasn't impressed.

"You got a call from a pay phone. Only thing remarkable was that he found one that still works. Nothing there that couldn't have come from a crank. Joe, the cop in you knows this."

"The cop in me knows you've got to trust your instincts. This was him. Something's coming."

He sighed and looked out the window. "It's not the cop in you that worries me, Joe. It's the man. And he's coming apart. It's understandable after what's happened to you the last couple of years. Maybe you imagined the call." He paused. "Hell, even if it's real, it doesn't mean anything. Once people see somebody falling apart and fucking up, they pile on. Hate to say it, but it's true. After that stunt you pulled in a church Saturday, it could even be one of them yanking your chain. Nobody more vicious than outraged church people." He looked at me. I thought he wanted to smile but wouldn't let himself. "'Jesus Fucking Christ'?"

"I thought the mic was off."

He raised an eyebrow. "Get this straight, Joe, the mic is never off. You think you can get through life riding on throwaway jokes and warped humor, but the world is always listening and you will always pay a price."

"Yes, sir. I wasn't thinking. But that doesn't change the fact that the Angel is back."

"Joe." He leaned across the desk. "Nothing changes the real facts of the Angel case. I would gladly give my stripes if I could erase it. But nothing changes all that, or ever will."

He pushed a pencil around a little and talked looking down at it.

"Maybe it's time for you to go out on your own, away from the department. The church story didn't hit the press." Pause. "Although it sure as hell hit Shirley. And the Commissioner. And they hit me."

He looked at me. If I'd ever seen the captain plead, this was it.

"Maybe it's time, Joe. Get out before you hurt somebody. Leave on a high note. Give a big interview on TV with the news babe. Go to Florida, sit on the beach and drink margaritas all day. I know a place. My wife's brother's got a house in Panama City Beach. I can get him to let you stay there, free, for a month to get you started. You can walk to a diner that has the best baked oysters on the beach. Get a tan. Get fat and happy." He paused. "Well, get happy. Maybe see a counselor."

I didn't know what to say. I stood up and looked away from him.

At my back I heard him say, "Joe, please think about it. This could be your last chance. You don't deserve all this shit."

I turned around. "Neither do these kids."

The captain was right about one thing: I had to do better.

And I had to be better.

I stood in front of my bedroom mirror in my underwear and looked at the miserable sad sack who might be some kid's only hope of staying alive.

If I were the kid, I wouldn't bet on this race horse.

I pulled on my BPD training sweats. Even that was more of a workout than I'd had in two years. Looking like the world's largest link sausage in gray, I waddled out to the front door and stood on the porch. Tried to stretch and found I could only move a little in my full-body straight jacket. I stepped down from the porch and took a couple of steps.

My old running path was four times around the half-mile block that led me up past the shops and back home. Now, I figured I'd start with one lap. Build myself up.

I made the first step strong, pushing muscles and fabric to their limits. For a moment, I remembered what it felt like to be strong and sure again, caught up in the groove of giving it all I had.

Which wasn't much. In a few steps, my lungs said, "Go on without us." Few more steps and my legs joined the chorus. I ground to a halt, hands on my knees, huffing and puffing. A neighbor passed me with a cheery, "Getting the mail, Joe?" and I realized I had stopped at my own mailbox.

Hell, no.

I pushed one leg out. Fast walk. Maybe a very, very slow jog. I shoved my body as hard as it could go without dropping.

Red-faced, groaning, cursing, I made it to the drugstore and turned down the crowded business street at mid-day. People cleared a path, and I kept going through them. Tried to thank them, but I'm not sure it sounded any different from the groans and curses. I wiped my mouth and realized that I was drooling and my tongue was hanging out.

But I kept going as hard as I could.

A small knot of people outside a coffee shop parted, and I went through them and almost crashed into a little girl in a red plaid school uniform, part of a long line of girls dressed alike and standing in a very proper straight line outside of the ice cream store.

She turned and screamed and I tried to say something calming, but it sounded like I was screaming, too.

Screaming girl took off running past the next girl, who looked back and joined her in running into the crowd, followed by the next and then the next, until the little flames of panic spread into a full forest fire of red-skirted girls screaming down the street, followed by a crazy drooling old man chasing them and making inhuman noises.

The young cop who stopped us put his gun back in his holster after I halted and put my hands up. I pointed at the

"BPD" stretched across my chest. He said something into his radio, and suggested that I join a health club. An indoor one. Maybe with no windows.

After he left, I cut over to the parallel residential street, and pushed on as hard as I could, avoiding people wherever possible.

But I made it around the block. Maybe a little bit stronger. The captain was right about one thing: this was the last chance. For a lot of us.

twenty-one

I stepped out of the shower and heard the rattlesnake. Left a dripping trail between my bathroom and bedroom, and picked up my phone.

"Partner, get your ass down here."

Capulet.

I started to tell her this was the first time I'd talked to a naked woman in years, but decided I'd horrified enough females for one day. I grunted a "Hell, no,"

"You want to catch the Angel of Mercy, you've got to deal with the Devil. Me. So, are you coming down to the Homewood library, or do I have to get my shotgun and do this on my own?"

"I'll come down," I said. "Just to stop that."

"Good. Don't stop for donuts."

I walked into the Homewood library and found Capulet at a table with a computer and a stack of books. I set the box of donuts down in front of her.

She reached in for the gooiest one and shot me a little smile. Her smile wasn't much better than mine, and didn't seem to be used much more often.

"Look," she said. "Cops do what they do, and they're blind to what they don't do. Like anybody else. If there's something you missed a month or a year ago, you're going to miss it again now. Unless I find it."

She waved her donut at me. "So, cops don't solve this crime. Librarians do."

"Be my guest." I sat down and took my own donut.

"So," she said. "If our Angel is still out there, what's he been doing for two years? Out on a universe-wide harp-playing tour?"

"No," I said. "These guys, they never stop. There's something in them that makes them come back, over and over again. Guys like him, driven by something inside, they keep pressing harder, getting sloppier and more desperate until they fuck up enough. Maybe we all do."

I looked around the library. Several people were giving us the stink-eye for talking and eating. Somehow no one came over to confront us.

She pointed her doughnut at me. "But we don't kill people." She pulled her computer over. "Yet kids are dying all the time. Kids in hospitals, kids in accidents. If he decided to be more subtle, cover his tracks better, he could have gotten away with a lot."

"Yeah. But I don't know if it would have given him the same kick."

She looked back at me. "Yeah. I mean, that's the thing, the name he took, 'Angel of Mercy.' Got a lot of meanings, but one of them is a slang term for medical workers or family members who put dying patients or family members down."

"None of these kids were dying. Look, I don't really know if I've got a beef with those kinds of people. I don't know what I'd do in their shoes. But the kids our Angel— hate that fucking name, have always hated that name for a robber of life—none of them were even sick."

"Unless you think life itself is a sickness."

"You're talking like him now. So what? Maybe life is only an earthly carbon-based disease. But you don't get to decide for someone else. Particularly kids."

She held up her hands. "Peace. I'm trying to get inside his head."

We sat there for a few minutes, her typing and clicking, me staring at the walls.

"Here's what I've got," she finally said. "Not much. Maybe nothing. Kids die all the time, for no good reason. Get anesthesia for a toothache, and don't wake up. Go into the hospital to get their tonsils out, and never leave. I'm printing out a list of cases that hospitals tagged as unusual enough to review, for anybody under twenty, in the Birmingham area. Looks like thirty or so in the last two years. Probably twenty-nine and a half of them are legitimate, but maybe there's something somewhere." She pointed at the printer across the room. "Go pick it up."

I stood up, glad to be doing something useful, and brought the pages back. Dropping them next to her I sat back down.

"Now let me pull out my basic statistics and see if there's a pattern to any of this."

"Good luck. You're on old ground. We chased that theory and looked at every nurse and medical worker in the city and found nothing."

"But you didn't look at deaths since then."

I reached for another donut, then stopped myself. Amazing the self-restraint I have. "No, being mere cops, we did not look at future deaths."

I looked at the patterns around me. A library full of kids opening books about unicorns and moms getting new recipes for apple pie. I thought about all the volumes in my own little library in my head. A hundred or more murder books going back years. Pictures of mangled body parts. Bland autopsy reports talking about blood draining away the life of someone with no more emotion than discussing an oil change. At best, if I was lucky, the murder book would end with a photograph of our catching some poor fucker so unspeakably dirty that even chasing him made you feel so dirty yourself that you couldn't be around decent people and had to live out your life in dark places with other people who had seen more than they should have.

Hell of a life I picked.

A mother walked by with a little girl and I prayed she wouldn't get close enough to hear the shit we were talking about.

Enough, I decided. "Let's get out of here."

She gathered her stuff and followed me out. "Where're we going?"

"Walking. I'm not talking in there. Besides, can't you tell I'm a fitness buff?"

"Yeah, it shows."

We cleared the door and I felt like the whole building gave a sigh of relief.

I said, "So, let's talk about this. Maybe you're right, maybe there's something we missed—are missing. But we're not going to talk around kids. All I can do around kids is watch the doors and look for threats. You do the library work and call me." I paused. "Call me in the highly unlikely event you find anything useful."

"I assume you want to hear as soon as I've got something?"

"*If* you get something. But yes. Hate to admit I'm that desperate, but I'll take any help I can get. We have to stop this guy, this time."

I sat down on a bench outside the library. Homewood was a quiet Birmingham neighborhood with a mix of well-kept houses from every decade in the last century. Pretty. Peaceful. There was a school across the street. I felt like I could see through the walls into rooms full of giggling girls and strutting boys. Kids trying different attitudes and clothes to figure out what kind of person they wanted to be. I wanted to tell them there were only a few things that were really important in this world. A tiny handful of people they would really touch and be touched by. Hold on, kids.

Of course, they would never hear me.

All I could do—maybe all any of us could do—was hold them in a safe bubble while they shed one skin after another until they were strong enough to push through and begin protecting kids of their own.

I slapped my hands on my knees. "So, you go back to the library and I go back to, you know, real police work."

She snorted. "Without your clown suit. Fine. But I need to know what you know."

I sat back down.

"Ask away."

"OK. First big thing. Everybody else thinks you've killed the Angel."

"They're wrong."

"Why?"

"Because the man I killed was an innocent man. A priest. My own priest."

"Wow. Still doesn't mean he couldn't also—"

"First crime scene, victim's name was Amanda Butler. Before we suspected much. There's always a crowd of gawkers, and you always give them a hard once over. This one guy flinched. More than that, I caught him smiling before he flinched.

"I locked eyes with him. He was distinctive, in that he was trying hard to be indistinct. Dark shirt. Brown wool cap pulled down.

"So, he smiled and flinched. I went over to talk to him and he melted away. I pushed through the crowd, saw him walking away. Yelled for him to stop. He took off running. I thought I could catch him—I could do that kind of thing back then. He was a soft-looking guy with an awkward, almost effeminate run. Thought it would be easy to catch him, but he moved fast and got away."

I looked down. "Father Carson—the guy I killed—didn't move like that. By the time I decided he wasn't the Angel and brought it up, nobody wanted to listen."

She had taken out a notebook and was making notes. "But Father Carson looked like he was the one? At least to BPD?"

"He did. Fit a lot of ways. Wasn't much of a preacher, more of a comedian. Poor sermons, bad administrator. Spent all his time with kids and the homeless. " I took a breath. "Don't ever tell a cop I said this, but here's why I didn't believe it was him. Everything Father Carson did seemed to be driven by love. Not a need to preach the gospel, not a need to straighten things out. Just love. As much as the Angel talked about sending kids to heaven out of love, I think he really hated life. I couldn't see all this pain coming out of love."

Capulet said, "But BPD believed it was him, and that it was a righteous killing."

"Yeah. He came out of the house and pointed a pistol at me. I put three slugs in him and he fell smiling, with his arms out like the Angel's victims. And we had the house surrounded. No one else came out."

She gave me a quick, small nod. "I can see why BPD didn't believe you. My family would laugh at you. Lots of bad guys look good on the surface. Never heard a murderer on trial succeed with a defense of 'he touched people with love so he couldn't have done it.' Or a cop who put that in a report. Not sure why you believe it."

I looked across the street. A line of kids was filing out to the playground like a vibrating string of ants.

"Maybe." I paused. "Maybe because, once, I was touched by love."

I laughed, uncomfortable, and stood up. "And so ends our inspirational message for today from the world's largest church lady."

She stood up with me. "No, I need more. I need to walk through the cases with you."

I looked at the sky and saw the sun starting to go down. "Tomorrow. I need to go get us some real help tonight. And I got a community affairs thing I've got to do in the morning, first thing, if I want to keep my job and my badge. Supposed to give the same inspirational message I gave your kids for a teacher named Fouch. I'll call you after that and see if you can get away. "

"I know him. You can't do any more damage in that classroom than Don Fouch has already done. He's a burnout. Probably was burned out before he started teaching." She made one of those not-funny laughs. "You know what he does? Likes to make fun of his classes by how many WoLs they have. His own little abbreviation. Waste of Life. Like in the old Rocky movie where the trainer growls, 'You're a waste of life'. How can you teach a kid if you start with that?"

"I'll tell him you said 'hi.'"

twenty-three

There was still sunlight on the street when I opened the door to Johnson's.

A couple of voices said in unison. "Close that fucking door."

I shut out the light and said to the darkness. "Sounds like the choir from hell in here."

I heard Wendy's voice from the dull glow at the bar. "Ha."

I moved toward her, feeling like a really big bull in a really dark china shop. Saw the outline of Ron's dark-blue back and found the stool next to his. He grunted.

"We good?" I said.

"Think this is fucking Oprah?" he bellowed "It's a bar. Come, go, nobody gives a fuck."

Quieter, he said, "Stay off the goddamned TV, all right."

I stared at the bottles behind Wendy and said, "Yeah."

She looked back across the bar. "You want something to get in the way of the rum? Eat now and call it lunch, have a second meal an hour later and call it dinner?"

"Jesus, Wendy, you think there's anybody so desperate they can stand that much of your crap?"

She raised an eyebrow at me and I said, "Yeah. Bring me something."

She turned, pulled the Myers's out, poured a shot and put it in front of me. I pushed it back at her and got another raised eyebrow.

"New rule," I said. "Don't pour me a drink until I actually ask for it."

She took the rum and drank it as a shooter. "Done. What is this, a health kick?"

"Yeah. What do they have in the toxic waste dump you call a kitchen that won't kill me?"

She studied me. Lots of people seemed to be studying me these days. "I think Joyce used up her supply of vegetables on you the other day. Came in today in a bad mood and wrote that on the chalkboard."

She stepped aside so I could read the words by the clip-on light on top.

"Meatloaf. Mashed Potatoes with Gravy. Onion Rings."

Below that.

"Don't ask for nothing else."

I nodded and waved a hand at it.

"Give me the heart-healthy special, then."

Wendy nodded. "Three servings?"

I hesitated. "Make it two."

She spent a little more time studying the fascinating enigma that Joe Brosette seemed to be these days, then turned and yelled something at the kitchen door. I couldn't hear all she said, but it started with, "Jesus, don't sleep in here."

I turned back to Ron. "I got to say something."

"So, talk."

"No, not like that. To everybody here."

He sat up straight and swiveled toward me. I'd never seen him move that much and I watched to be sure he didn't hurt himself.

"You mean like a public service announcement? Jesus, Joe, don't do this. Particularly after last night."

"Yeah," I said. "Something like that."

Now he was the one studying me and I wondered if I had broccoli in my teeth. Realized that nobody here would recognize broccoli.

Wendy dropped two plates in front of me and took in our faces without saying a word.

I ate and drank and thought about what I needed to say. When the plates were clean, I stood up.

"Hey, could I have everyone's attention?"

"Sit down. You're blocking *Wheel of Fortune*."

I didn't recognize the voice, but I knew the tone. Realized that I didn't really know who anybody in here was. I'd talked to most of the people in here at one time or the other, but the conversations were usually muttered exchanges of curses with faces I couldn't see.

"I only need a minute," I said.

"Well, I need to know the fucking answer to the fucking puzzle."

I turned and looked at the TV. The category was person. The letters said, "PRESI_ENT OF THE UNITE_ STATES."

I said, "President of the United States."

The voice said, "Now you ruined it."

"Look," I said. "Give me one minute. I need your help."

There was a lot of grumbling, but no real words.

"Some kids somewhere need your help."

There was enough quiet that I could talk.

"Remember the Angel of Mercy? Killed kids? He's back. And I can't convince my captain to take it seriously. So, I need you guys help. Maybe to run down leads. Help me stop this guy."

There was silence. I took it as support.

"Let me get Wendy to turn up the lights a little, see what we've got here and get organized."

There was grumbling. One voice came through clear.

"We going to wind up on TV like you?"

"I don't know. That's not important."

The grumbling clarified itself into a chorus of "Fuck you" and a consensus of "Leave us alone."

I turned to Wendy. She put a hand on my arm.

"Joe, they're good guys. Really, they are. They just don't like the light."

"Like cockroaches," said Ron.

twenty-four

Turned out that I didn't need to tell Fouch 'hi' from Capulet.

I checked in at the polished wood counter at the school office and a perky young teacher's aide led me back to the classroom. Fouch met me at the door and gave me a big handshake and an even bigger smile.

Smile. That's a funny word. I say it, and you imagine the standard smile of the salesman on TV. Or the bright sunshine of your daughter on her birthday. Or a million other things.

Fouch's smile was greasy. Made me want to wash my hands and blink my eyes to get the feeling of it out.

Hey, people have made comments about my smile, too. I try not to judge a man by the way nature happened to make him. Still could be a good guy.

"So glad to finally meet you," he said in a hoarse whisper.

Jesus. Whoever put this guy together couldn't have done anything more to make him seem like a creep.

I liked him right away.

I liked him, but somebody didn't. That somebody bumped me from behind and shoved her way between the two of us.

His smile fell. "Ms. Capulet."

"Yeah." She pushed past him into the classroom.

I said, "What are you doing here?"

He croaked. "You can't be here."

She said to me, "Helping you." Turned to him. "Sure, I can. Teachers in this district can sit in on other teachers' classes." She smiled. If he was greasy, today she was fake-sweet. "To learn from them."

Capulet took a seat in the back and I had a glimpse of what I must look like sitting in these chairs. The kids turned, looked at her, and quickly turned back.

Fouch stood there for a long minute, then seemed to give up. He motioned me to the center of the room and walked off to a corner. I stood there waiting for an introduction and realized that I was wasting my time. I held up my presentation.

"My name's Officer Joe," I said. I looked at Fouch to see if I was going to get the same objection I had gotten from Capulet. He had his arms crossed, fuming at Capulet. No interest in me.

The kids had no interest in me, either. No Jessi in this crowd, and no questioning eyes, either. Silent kids beaten into submission.

I hated adding my propaganda to it, but I flipped the page and read them the exciting story of Henry and his heroic encounter with the evil drug seller and stealer of souls.

Capulet was motioning me to speed things up. That made me slow down. Which made her gesture, *Faster*.

A little hand went up in front of Capulet.

"Yes, ma'am," I said. "Do you have a question?"

"I..." the girl said.

Capulet said at her back. "I don't think we have time for questions. Officer Joe has important work he has to get to."

"No," I said. "Questions are important."

"You have to get going," said Capulet.

I shook my head and nodded at the girl.

She said, "I have to go to the bathroom."

Fouch nodded approval. The girl said, "I need a hall pass, Mr. Fouch."

He pulled himself out of the corner and skipped to his desk, moving in kind of an awkward, almost girly little run.

I recognized that run.

I looked at Capulet and she knew that I recognized it.

twenty-five

Capulet followed me home, trying to stay invisible, but I'm pretty good at spotting a tail. I saw her park down the street and was waiting at the door as she walked up the sidewalk.

"Don't start," I said.

She hopped up onto the porch—odd-looking little move for her—and brushed past me. "You saw the way he moved. I know you did. And he's kind of a big, soft-looking guy. And—"

"And suspects don't drop into your lap like that. So, he's big and weird-looking. You can't think of any other suspects in that pool?"

"What about the 'laryngitis'? Or whatever made him disguise his voice?" She added air quotes as I closed the door behind us.

"It happens."

"I thought cops were supposed to be suspicious of coincidences?"

"Yeah," I said. "Like a suspect falling into our laps—my lap—after two years."

She started to say something, but I cut her off. "You want to face facts, or you want to stay in fantasyland?"

She nodded. "Let's see what you've got."

I led her to the war room and opened the door.

She walked in, made one slow pass and settled at the beginning, the picture of the first dead girl. I studied Capulet's face and watched for a sign of morbid fascination or horror. I got neither. Only a sense of a sadness so heavy it seemed to push her shoulders even farther to the floor. Waited for the usual polite platitudes.

"Fuck," she said.

I thought about it. "Good a word as I know," I said. "You sure you want to look at all this?"

She didn't take her eyes off the picture. "Told you, I need to see it all." She studied the picture a little longer. "You sure you're ready to show me all this?"

"Yes. I'm a cop. I've walked people through murder books before."

She gave a harsh little laugh. "Book? This is a fucking murder shrine." She paused. "How many other people have seen this room?"

"None."

I began. "Her name was Amanda Sandra Butler. She was named after her two grandmothers, the only people who ever seemed to care for her in her short life. When I interviewed them, one of them—the one named Amanda— made me promise to find who did this. It was the only time I ever actually made that promise. I tried to give her the usual, 'We'll do our best, ma'am' speech.' She told me stories of her little Amanda until I promised."

I pointed at the picture.

"She's pale because she was drained of blood. We never found the blood."

I saw Capulet close her eyes.

"July 26, 2015. A Sunday morning. We got a call and rolled on it. A worker at a big Catholic cemetery found a body posed under a statue of Christ. Wearing a white dress that could have been a confirmation dress. The child was lying on her back with her eyes open to the sky and her arms out in a tee. Posed as if she could fly, after the bastard drained her of life."

I took a breath.

"She was the first," I said, "that we knew of. Hand-sewn dress. Nothing identifiable.

"It took us a while to identify her. None of the missing children on record at the time matched—and you wouldn't believe how many children are reported missing at any given time in a city the size of Birmingham.

"Nobody had reported her missing. A little girl like that. We were checking with child protective services, putting a cleaned-up picture of her on the TV news. Looking for parents.

"You get a lot of attention and cooperation when you're looking for a child or a child killer.

"Then the prints came back with a match. Surprised us all. You get yourself in fingerprint databases by being arrested for screwing up, or for applying for a job or something else grown up. Not for being twelve years old.

"She'd been arrested a month earlier for hooking. Arrested, booked, turned loose. Ignored, like all the others.

Gave her age as twenty-one. Every hooker says they're twenty-one. Unless they're over forty. Then they say they're eighteen.

"Interest vanished when the girl turned out to be another dead hooker. They tried to pull me off, but I had a big enough rep at the time that I made them let me keep it as kind of a side job.

"Twelve-year-old hooker. Get your head around that for a minute.

"Her family in Indiana had never reported her missing. I went to tell them in person. Daddy stared at the floor when I said the words. Mama said, 'We figured she had run off. She always was a hard one to control.' Local cops up there brought in Child Services and had the other two kids removed.

"So, I came back home. The autopsy showed a couple of broken teeth. Recent. We assumed the killer did it. Wrong. Turned out her pimp did it. He said she had one appointment—not his word—at midnight before we found her. Hadn't seen her after he got paid.

"We checked him out. And we checked out the midnight john. He looked clean. Of murder at least. It looked pretty clear: sometime after midnight, Amanda Butler met the Angel."

She was still staring at the picture. "But no one knew it was the Angel then?"

"We did when we got the note a week later. Never figured why it took a week. Maybe the first note got lost.

Maybe he got mad when everybody lost interest." I pointed to the note, to the right of the photo:

This soul has been saved by the Angel of Mercy. Saved from the unspeakable living hell of the home that you, the citizens of this world, left her in, and the one you gave her on the street. And saved from the literal hell her soul would have spent eternity in. If she hadn't been saved now, while she still had some innocence, the hell you condemned her to here would have warped her sweet child soul into a monstrosity of an adult repeating the sins she saw visited on herself, and condemning her soul to an everlasting hell.

Because of you, she would have burned in hell. Because of an angel, she is in everlasting glory tonight.

She is neither the first, nor will she be the last.

"Jesus," Capulet said. She paused. "Any of your cops ever say they thought Amanda was better off?"

"Not around me. Not then, and sure as hell not later."

The lines on the page were becoming blurry. I laughed. "If you haven't noticed, I'm not very good at keeping my thoughts to myself. Don't know why. Words seem to pour out of me these days with no control."

"Like tears." She patted my cheek.

I turned away from Capulet and looked out the window. "I don't think we ought to go on to the other cases right now."

My face was wet and she pretended not to notice. "I've got to go to a staff meeting anyway."

I laughed. "So, they don't mind your missing time with your kids to play amateur cop, but you can't miss a staff meeting?"

She laughed back, which made it a little bit of a shared relief, which we both needed. "Yeah. Union guarantees that I can take time off, and I've accumulated a bunch. But, mandatory meetings are mandatory. Even in schools, kids get the short end."

"How about we get together about six? There's a diner around the corner, Blue Collar Diner. Luz and I used to eat there, basic meat-and-three place. I can meet you there, we can get something to eat and come back here."

She struck a pose. "I suppose a salad wouldn't ruin my girlish figure."

"Actually, that sounds like a good idea. Maybe we'll both get salads."

She snatched up the oversized book bag that she carried. "Oh, fuck you and your salad. I'll eat what I want."

And then she was gone and I wondered, again, what I had done wrong.

That made me turn back to the wall, looking for what I had fucked up there. Fucked it up, destroyed everything in the world worth living for. And still didn't know what I had done wrong.

I moved down the wall. Michael Williams. October 30. On the day before Halloween, the owner of a costume store, on what was supposed to be the biggest sales day of the year for him, came whistling up the walk and found a pale dead boy dressed in white, hanging Christ-like on his door. The note—pinned to the body this time—said, "On the wings of the Angel shall they be saved. No pagan holidays."

The Angel sure as hell got his wish on that part. The newsmen who had ignored the death of a child whore, and probably would have ignored the death of a homeless kid, couldn't ignore a threat to a city-wide party. October 30 was a Friday. After a day of screaming headlines and "helpful" TV personalities giving tips on how to protect your kids (consensus seemed to be to dip them in plastic and lock them in a safe), the streets of Birmingham were empty Saturday night. I do believe that any kid in a costume who knocked on a door that night would have been met with a shotgun blast.

Fortunately, no one was. Unfortunately, we—I—made no progress on the case. After a frantic week, the story faded. The kid and his dad were homeless, after all. Probably the dad's fault, somehow.

I wish I'd met the father even a day before the murder. My take was that he was an OK guy who had lost his job and was doing the best he could. If someone could have gotten him and his son off the street even a day earlier...

Of course, it doesn't work that way. No one, including me, reached out to the family the day before. And so, in the day and days after, they were just the dead boy and the deadbeat drunk dad.

People still said it couldn't happen to them. Not in their warm cozy homes.

Until Christmas day.

The city awakened Christmas morning to two fresh angels posed under the big city Christmas tree downtown. Monica and Lee Richards. Upper-middle-class, white, ten-year-old twin daughters of a corporate lawyer.

We had more to work with this time. The girls had been kidnapped out of their home, transported, killed and posed. So, we had some video, a good time frame, and a lot of opportunities for fingerprints and DNA.

A little more evidence, and a lot more pressure. I thought we were making good progress, but the papers and the mayor didn't agree. After two days, I was called into his office, chewed out in front of the news crews, and told to do something.

I did.

I was pulled out of the past by the rattlesnake clattering in my pocket. I looked at the number. Nothing I recognized.

But I recognized the voice.

"John the Baptist is coming."

I decided to play dumb and try to string this out.

"Are you trying to sell timeshares at the beach, fella? Cause nobody wants me lying on the sand in a Speedo."

"Nice try. Didn't you learn last time what happens when you piss off an angel?"

"Oh, Jesus. Is this you again? Look, buddy, the so-called Angel of Mercy retired or moved or died a long time ago. You're some sick fuck getting his rocks off trying to torture me. Won't work. I've moved on."

"Yeah - to booze and lard. What are you up to, three seventy?"

I hate to admit it, but I almost corrected him. Even with a killer, vanity wins out.

Instead, I put as much contempt as I could in my voice. "You know, your laryngitis sure got better since this morning."

There was a pause.

"Listen, you fat fuck. John the Baptist is coming soon. Then you got three days before the Second Coming. And it's going to be bigger than anything you or the city of Birmingham ever imagined."

The line was dead. I stared at the phone.

Then I thought of something. I went to the wall for the Richards twins. What I wanted wasn't there.

There was a row of file cabinets in the garage. I pulled drawers out wildly until I found what I remembered.

The Richards twins' teacher was a woman named Johnson. But, to be careful, we'd interviewed all their former teachers. And there it was.

The Richard's twins' teacher the year before their death? Don Fouch.

I called Coltrane. "I need the address and anything you've got on Don Fouch."

"Oh, hey, Star."

"Cut that shit. You going to help or not? I think I need it fast."

"Pulling it up now. Sorry about the dig, but it's for real. You've got juice down here now, man."

"Yeah, yeah. Get me the address."

There was silence while he searched.

I said, "I'm glad I did something to make the captain look good. He's put up with a lot of shit for my sake."

"He's a good one. Went to bat for a detective here last week. Guy got into a political jam and the mayor wanted him fired. Captain said they'd have to fire him first, and publicly. Good guy to work for. OK, here's your dope: Don Fouch, 105 Heritage Lane, Birmingham proper. You want his vehicle?"

"Why not?"

He gave me the dope, then said, "No record. No tickets, even." He laughed. "You sure this guy is real? Everybody's got something, man."

"Maybe a guy who's a little weird. Probably nothing."

"Like Maria Trap was nothing, man? Your hunches are good."

"Don't even know if this is a hunch, yet. But if it's a something, it may happen fast. Can you make some time if I need you?"

"Just drop the dime."

"Thanks."

I looked at my watch. Four o'clock. Fouch could be at school, home, in-between.

I drove to the school and cruised the parking lot. I was in luck. His car was still there. I parked in the convenience store across the street. Thought about running in for a snack, but was afraid I might miss him. I used the time to put his home address in my phone's NAV app and hit 'Start.' That would let me see if that was where we were headed, and it would give me a track later of where we'd been.

Good thing. He came out a minute later, by himself, and got in his car. I cranked up my engine and let him ease out alone, watching until he got to the end of the quiet street. He put on his right turn signal, and I pulled out slowly. Got to the stop sign in time to catch a glimpse of him a block away.

I sped to catch up to him. I didn't mind if he caught sight of a nondescript black car on a crowded street now, but I hadn't wanted him to notice me at the school. Most people are suspicious of cars and people they see at the start of their journey; less so of someone who comes in randomly.

We played cat-and-mouse for maybe ten minutes, following the route to his house, until he made a turn and my NAV lady gave me a cheery "Recalculating" when I turned behind him. I dropped back.

I could see why he never got a ticket. When the speed limit was 35, he did 34. No posted speed limit? 24. Probably drove people crazy.

That wouldn't bother him, I guessed. If he cared what other people thought, he'd go with the flow, like most of us do, whether the flow was ten over or five under.

He was a man who wanted to follow whatever the rules were in his head. And stay under the police radar.

And he was a man who knew where he was going. Sure motions, no hesitation.

I stayed with him until he pulled over to the curb and stopped without warning. I had to go on by. I watched him in the mirror, took the next right and parked.

I got out and sprint-waddled back to the corner. He still hadn't gotten left his car. I stayed at the corner and surveyed the neighborhood. It was mixed residential and commercial, with a gentle whoosh coming from the wind in the trees. Strip mall a block back of where he had stopped, and a chain link fence next to his car. I needed to see what he was stopped in front of, so I crossed the street and found a big tree that looked semi-natural for me to stand behind.

He was parked in front of something commercial, bright colors and a block shape. I needed to get closer, decided that a car was less noticeable than a three-hundred-pound man out for a stroll.

I got back in the car and went right-turn, right-turn, right-turn around the block as fast as I could. Following his cue, I dropped down to 24 miles-an-hour as I came up behind him, face pointed dead ahead while my eyes were cut to his side.

He was still in his car. Eating a sandwich and drinking a can of something.

Eating his dinner as he studied the children in the day-care center playground.

The Blue Collar Diner wasn't anymore. I mean, the building had a big expensive sign with the name in an elegant script. But it wasn't a blue-collar diner anymore.

At least it wasn't my idea of blue-collar. Or a diner.

The maître d' looked at my outfit and sniffed. "Do you need a tie, sir?"

"No, I'm good."

His look told me I wasn't. He reached into his stand and pulled out a tie that cost more than my sport coat.

I held it up. "Can I just hold it?"

His look said no.

It had been a while since I had tied a tie, or had a shirt whose top button buttoned. Make that top two. Six months ago, I found that I could either special-order my shirts or leave two buttons undone.

Wendy had suggested that I was going to have to order a chest toupee if I was going with that look. Ha. Ha.

I got the tie done and hoped that it covered at least some of the bare chest. The maître d' looked away, surveying the almost-empty restaurant.

"How many in your party, sir?" I think he was wondering how large a party he could seat in the kitchen. Preferably by the dumpster.

"Two."

"Ah, romantic dinner. Very good."

I didn't know a maître d' was allowed to smile at his own jokes.

"Yeah," I said. "Romantic dinner. I want candles, the works." Show that fucker.

"Very good, sir."

He led me to a table without chairs or a tablecloth beside the swinging double doors to the kitchen. Snapped his fingers and a busboy in a tux appeared from thin air with a tablecloth and a candle. The table was pulled out and two chairs made of kind of a wooden lace magically walked under the table.

The maître d' looked at one of the chairs, shook his head at the busboy and jerked his chin toward the front. The busboy took the chair away and brought one of the more substantial easy chairs from the lobby.

"Better make that two," I said.

They arranged the chairs and table so there was room for the doors. Barely.

I sat down and a waiter appeared at my elbow.

"Would you like something from the bar or shall we wait for young Madame?"

"Young Madame" chose that moment to make her entrance.

She had changed into a tie-dyed mu-mu. Apparently, that was the only style of dress she had. He opened his mouth, but she blew right by him like a magenta-yellow-cyan storm.

"Wow," she said as she took her seat. "Some diner."

"It's changed. I didn't know."

The waiter said, "Upgraded."

I said, "Changed."

He ignored me and handed Capulet a menu with a flourish. "Would Madame care for anything to drink?"

She threw her hair back with a flourish. "Yes. Madame will have champagne."

He brightened. "We have a very fine—"

"Cheapest you've got," I said. "A glass, not a bottle."

"Very well." He turned to me.

"Beer."

He nodded. "We have a very fine IPA from—"

I usually like a coffee stout from the Rocket Republic Brewery up in Madison. Not today. "You got Pabst?"

He looked at the ceiling. "No, sir."

"Bud?"

"I think so."

"Bring me one of those. I don't need a glass."

"Very good, sir."

When he was out of earshot, I said to Capulet, "Hey, I kind of hate to tell you this, but there may be something to your guy."

She was studying the menu.

"Wow," she said. "Are you going to spring for this?"

I had planned on Dutch.

"Sure."

"Have you read these prices?"

I looked at the menu. Wow. What the hell, as long as I got a receipt I could take it back to Johnson's later and have fun with Wendy and the Lost Boys.

"Fine," I said. "But no dessert."

She looked at me and I looked at her. We both laughed.

"OK," I said. "Let me tell you what I found out. We've got work to do."

She looked at me over the menu.

"I've never been in a place like this," she said. "You picked this for us?"

"No. Well, yes. It wasn't like this when we used to come here. It was—"

"Never," she said. "I've never been in a place like this. Particularly with a man. Thanks."

The waiter came with our drinks and took our orders. Capulet made a big deal of asking how everything was prepared, which country which ingredient came from. I swear she put together a meal by taking one ingredient from every item on the menu.

I got a steak.

"Never," she said again.

"I agree. I've never seen anyone make a show like that. You do know that the menu is not just a suggestion?"

She ignored me.

"I've never been fussed over like this." She reached over and took my hand. "Ever. I mean, not only the restaurant. The whole thing. I've never even had a real date. Couple of times, people tried to set me up on blind dates and the guy wouldn't show. One time, I saw the guy walk into the restaurant, take one look at me and turn around and walk out. I chased him down the street, but I couldn't catch him."

"Could have been the wrong guy. Poor slob happened to change his mind about dinner, got chased by a screaming banshee."

"He deserved it. Even tried the lesbian route once, thinking that might be my problem. Didn't work. You ever been lectured to about sexual politics from someone between your legs?"

"No." I pulled my hand away and wrapped it around my beer to protect it. My hand, not the beer. "Can't say I have."

"None of that worked for me. Nothing ever has." She was starting to get misty-eyed. "Thanks. This may be as close as I get to romance."

She laughed, embarrassed. "How about you and Luz? Was this like your favorite place?"

"Yeah. Well, not the way it is now. Our place—this place— was a little hole-in-the-wall. Woman who ran the place would talk your ear off about food. But no interest in keeping the place up or making a buck. If you complained about a rip in your stool, she'd hand you a roll of duct tape and tell you to fix it yourself. But she would spend weeks experimenting with a dish before she'd put it on the menu."

I could feel the place shifting before my eyes, returning to what I loved.

"There." I pointed to where two stools had sat years ago. "Before Sarah was born, that was our corner. If we came in and somebody else was sitting there, the old lady would move them.

"Luz and I would sit there for hours. Sometimes I felt like we did nothing but stare at each other. Other times, we did nothing but laugh. No jokes, no stories, just laughed. The world was a very funny place with Luz in it. That's where I told her I'd made detective. Where she told me we were pregnant."

I laughed and looked at the table.

"Don't know why I've got such verbal diarrhea these days."

I laughed again.

"I mean, this was a simple diner, back then. I doubt if anybody else remembered it. But you know what was the funniest thing about it? For us?"

She was staring so I went on.

"It was like the strongest aphrodisiac on earth. Not champagne and roses, candlelight and forty-dollar entrees. Just that simple breathing of the same air in the very beautiful ordinariness of our lives together."

I looked back into the past and saw Luz and me sitting there. Friendly faces, warm glow I had never noticed when it was there. "Sometimes we'd look down and find that our plates had been wrapped to-go, untouched, without our even noticing it. Old lady would say, 'I saw that look. Didn't figure you were going to finish that here.'

"We would barely make it home with our clothes on. I could always feel it, every time. The last second before I would touch her skin, I'd feel like I wasn't even real. Then, touching her skin made me feel insanely real."

I laughed again to cover the awkwardness. Tried to say, "What bullshit," but I couldn't talk.

Capulet stood up, almost pulling the tablecloth off in her hurry. She turned and bumped into the waiter bringing our food.

"Where you going?" I said.

Her face was wet and she looked mad at me. She said, "Going home. Frig myself to sleep. Or cry. What do you care?"

Then she was gone.

I never had this trouble with police partners before.

twenty-nine

Coltrane was waiting for me at the Coffee Tree next to the station when I got there. Bright, cheery, modern place with small round tables and hipster kids bending over their Macs. I placed an order at the counter and walked over to him.

"Thought about asking you to come into the station," he said. "Let a couple of guys slap you on the back, watch Vinzini turn green."

I sat down. "I don't give a shit about that kind of thing. I respect Vinzini's point of view about me, to tell you the plain truth. And I wanted to talk away from real cops."

"Yeah, didn't think you were wired for payback like that. I'm a little more self-centered, unfortunately." He smiled and pointed at the speaker in the ceiling.

I noticed a smoky saxophone playing.

"Sonny Rollins?" I said. "'Pent-Up House'?"

He laughed. "I wish. It's 'Pent-Up House' all right. But that's a cover I did a couple of years ago with a small group over in Atlanta. Owner here likes to play local music and sell CDs of local guys."

I listened for a minute. "Yeah. Rollins had kind of a restrained anger, kind of like a resignation, in everything he played. That's missing. This is more...satisfied. Still good, though."

Coltrane laughed. "Yeah. That's what they told me, 'blow with your rage, man.' I honestly don't have that much rage." He shrugged. "Got notes, but no real rage. Too happy to play jazz."

"Maybe I should play," I said. "Got so much rage I can't sleep more than an hour or two. Feel like I'm losing all the notes, though."

"You had a pretty good riff on the Maria Trap thing." He waited for me to agree. I didn't say anything. The kid from the counter put a cup on the table in front of me.

"Fair-trade organic Costa Rican pour-through," he said.

"I just asked for a cup of coffee," I said.

"It is."

He walked away.

Coltrane said. "Hey, none of my business. But you've made your chops. Why not hang it up?"

"Want to. I really do. As much as people like Vinzini tell me I'm a fuck-up and should get out, I tell it to myself more. Don't even know why I do the things I do half the time."

He leaned forward. "Don't get me wrong. I think you've still got good chops as a cop. I'll follow your lead anytime. Just seems that anybody as...tired as you deserves some rest."

"I'll rest. It's ...I've got a..." My voice trailed off and he watched me, waiting. "...I've got a promise to an old photograph." I shrugged and took a sip. "Pretty good purebred no-trees-harmed coffee. The peasant who picked this bean in between his night gig as a Thompson gunner in the revolution must be proud."

Coltrane said, "I'm guessing you didn't call me because you wanted to talk coffee."

"No. Although the coffee may be the only thing that's real here. Remember Don Fouch, guy I called you about?"

"Yeah."

I told him what I knew about Fouch.

"Sounds crazy, I know," I said when I finished. "But I still need your help on it. It's the only lead I've got, and I really need somebody who's more than a cop in a clown suit."

"Sure, man, count me in. I don't know that it sounds so crazy," he said. "Could be him, even if it seems too pat. Or some weirdo that deserves watching. Wilder things happen. We've both seen guys walk in and give themselves up and confess when we were nowhere close to nailing them. Sick as it sounds, maybe the guy got tired of playing his masterpieces to an empty house and wanted to see you face-to-face. Maybe that will let us bring down the curtain on his act."

"So, you're in on this?" I leaned forward. "Think we can go to the captain, get him to let me partner with you on this for a few days? I hate to admit it, but somebody made the point to me the other day that I really need a partner." I looked at the ceiling. "Not the one that was suggested to me, but I do need one."

He looked at the ceiling, too. "Man, I don't know. I can give you all my spare time—glad to. Little things like this—glad to. But officially? The problem isn't the captain, it's the lieutenant. Real bean counter, man. Got us filling out time cards and charging hours to specific cases, that kind of shit. I don't think this will fly with him. And he'll have my balls if I go over his head."

I nodded.

He said, "You got to blow the notes they let you play."

"Yeah."

I bought a CD on the way out.

Capulet called as I was leaving the coffee shop.

"Oh my God," she said. "We've got such a break. A woman I used to teach with called me up and wanted to have coffee sometime and we got to talking and she used to teach with Fouch and she agreed to meet with us and tell us all about him."

"Oh my God," I said. "And she's got proof that Fouch is the Angel and that he killed Kennedy?"

"No, asshat. But she might be able to help. We're meeting her at her school at ten o'clock."

So now we were sitting in a grade-school cafeteria, Capulet and I, perched on small chairs on one side of the table while the teacher sat on the other side, shoveling food in as fast as she could.

"You really have to eat lunch at ten o'clock?" I said.

"With my students." The teacher that Capulet had introduced as Debbie Holt nodded at a boiling mob of kids across the lunchroom from us. Her mouth was stuffed with food, her hand covering her mouth while she talked and it came out something like, "wish du." She tried to say something, choked and waved at Capulet to talk for her.

Capulet said, "Budget cuts. Overcrowding. Kids get fifteen minutes for lunch, staggered between ten and two.

No student aides here, so teachers have to eat with their students." She turned back to Holt. "I'm glad you could get together with us anywhere this soon."

Holt swallowed, but her voice was still muffled. "Anything to help our boys in blue."

"It's a good thing we got a seat in the corner," said Capulet. "Don't want to discuss a murderer around a bunch of kids. This detective—"

I put my hand on her arm and nodded, no. "This detective is not here to discuss a murder. Just background—"

"Jesus," Holt said. She stood up and yelled at the kids in a very clear voice. "Can you be quiet? For one blessed minute?"

The kids ignored her. She sat down, turning to Capulet with her eyes bright.

She stabbed a forkful of meatloaf from the Tupperware leftover dish, shoved it in and covered her mouth again. Her eyes looked bigger than the wilted slices of tomato on her plate. She turned them on me and mumbled, "Juliet says Fouch is a killer."

This was not going well.

"No," I said. "Mr. Fouch is not a suspect in any investigation. I'm not even an active-duty detective anymore. Please don't assume anything from this. Please don't tell anyone about this."

She waved a finger at me. "I've done my homework on you. You're the Huggy Bear, savior of small children."

"He is. He is," said Capulet.

Holt chucked me on the arm and I thought I would need a trip to the hospital. She was big, almost as tall as me. "You tried to hide that from me, Juliet. You're dating the most famous detective in Birmingham."

Capulet and I said in unison, "No."

She stage-whispered to Capulet loud enough for me to hear. "So, he's available?"

Capulet shrugged. "I guess."

I said, "No."

Ms. Holt crammed another bite of meatloaf in her mouth.

I said, "What can you tell us—"

She held up one finger past me to kids starting to line up outside the door.

Capulet said, "Talk fast. Tell us anything weird Fouch ever did."

She laughed while she shoved in an overloaded spoonful of mashed potatoes and covered her mouth to talk. "Everything. You know what's the weirdest thing about him? He teaches fourth graders, same as me. Perfect age. After they go off to middle school, kids grow up and turn to monsters. My momma used to say, 'Kids are like peaches, sweetest just before they turn rotten.' Well, Fouch these perfect little angels Wastes of Life. Can you believe that?"

Capulet nodded, excited. "Yeah, we know about that. What else? He ever do anything that made you think he was hiding something?"

Another hurried swallow. "You know why he's not at this school, right? Principal declared mandatory staff meetings for the teachers, by grades. After school. Wanted teachers to rotate having them in their homes. Fouch refused to let anyone in his house. We realized that none of us had ever been in his house, ever. Principal insisted, Fouch transferred."

A whistle blew and she jumped up.

"Gotta go. Juliet, I'll call you and we can talk about what you want me to do to help." She stuck her fork back into the last bite of meatloaf and smiled at me.

She stood up. "Hey," she yelled. "I told you to behave."

Holt shoved the last bite in her mouth, popped the top on the plate and said through her hand, "Gotta run. One of my peaches is ripening."

She took a step towards the kids before she turned back with a thankfully-food-free smile from ten feet away. Coughed a couple of times and then spoke through the hoarseness. "I'll be in touch, Detective. We've got a noble mission here, and you need my help."

Capulet crossed her arms.

"No," I said.

thirty-one

Capulet and I were sitting in my car down the street from Fouch's school later, waiting for him to come out at the end of the day.

She said, "Debbie Holt's not going away."

"Well, she has to. I've already got more help than I need."

She winced. I hadn't meant it that way, but it had hurt.

"No, I mean…We—you and me—we're…fine. And I understand Holt. She's lonely. Probably needs a hobby or some kind of purpose. But I'm not it."

"Maybe we could find something for her to do. Make her feel better."

I was tired of making people feel worse every time I turned around. "Maybe. Till then, keep her out of my hair."

"Good luck." She dug into her purse and brought out a couple of pages and shoved them at me. "I found this waiting in my email from Debbie. She asked me give this to you without reading it. And she wants your home email."

"Good luck yourself. Only Luz knew what my email is. Was. I haven't turned on the home computer since… in years. And I sure wouldn't turn it on for this."

I sighed and braced Holt's pages on the wheel so I could read and watch the parking lot.

Before I could get started, Capulet said, "I'm sorry." She took a deep breath. "Sorry for the way I am these days."

I kept my eyes on Fouch's car, but set the paper on the console and waited.

She said. "I'm sorry I ran out of the restaurant the way I did the other night. I seem to be that way these days."

"No big deal. Lot of craziness going around." I laughed. "Hey, I got to eat your meal."

She laughed, kind of a let's-join-in thing. "Yeah. Should be apologizing to myself."

If I was itching for Fouch to come out before, I was really itching for the distraction now.

"It's just..." she said.

"You don't have to explain."

Fouch blessedly appeared next to his car. I pointed. "Look. I need you to help me keep an eye on him. I brought you along because two people can shadow someone much better than one. Helps if occasionally the driver keeps his eye on the road."

"Get started, then. He's getting away."

"I want him to get away. A little."

Fouch's car got to the same corner as yesterday and I cranked up.

She turned to me. "What I was trying to say—"

"Don't look at me. Look at him, always. If he goes out of sight, then kind of scan back and forth until you find him."

I kept my eyes ahead, watching Fouch and traffic. Capulet turned forward. I hoped she was watching him as well.

"I wanted to say that I understand you," she said.

A sound came out of my mouth that was supposed to be a laugh but sounded more like "Fuck You" without the words. "You haven't drunk enough to understand me, sister."

"No, really. You don't have a monopoly on loneliness. I can see the pain of living without love."

"You can't see anything. How about concentrating on 'seeing' Fouch? If he's going home, he should make a left up here."

"There. I saw it. I'll see the next turn, too. And I do see you. I bet if I had seen you two years ago, I would have seen a much different man."

"Yeah," I said, turning the wheel and slowing down to keep from getting too close. "I was two years younger then."

"No. Hell, no. Two years ago, you probably had more like twenty more years of life in you, looking forward to every one of them, instead of wishing you were dead every day. Looking at your daughter and dreaming of her wedding, probably even more than she was. Looking at your wife's face, wondering how beautiful she'd be in old age, just two happy old farts sitting on a porch swing."

"Will you shut the fuck up?" I was screaming and couldn't stop. "Shut the fuck up and do what you have to do and get through this."

She pointed ahead and smiled. "Watch out."

I jerked the wheel and barely avoided hitting a parked car.

She said, "Now who's not paying attention?"

I was so mad I was having trouble watching Fouch.

"Concentrate," I said.

She locked her eyes forward but kept talking.

"Who you talking to, me or you? I can do two things at once. You can't. You can't even be in the present because you can't turn loose of the past."

I squeezed the steering wheel hard to force the pain to keep me here.

"It's not the years that age you, Detective. It's the years without love."

"So, what are you," I said. "About a hundred?" Regretted it, but said it.

"Thirty."

She laughed when she saw my reaction.

"All right. Fifty. Turned fifty last year. Last birthday that counts until they give you your Medicare card. Happy?"

"Swimmingly," I said. "If we're on the homeward path, the next turn up here is right. Watch for it."

Fouch turned left.

thirty-two

"You were wrong, big boy," Capulet said. "He didn't do what you told him to."

I turned and followed Fouch. The street widened from two lanes to four, the neighborhood from residential to strip malls.

"Not wrong. Something different's happening. Maybe nothing."

He pulled into a lot and parked out on the edge, away from everybody else. I kept going to the next cluster and parked at a Starbucks across the street. There were about a hundred feet between us and Fouch.

He got out and gave a casual look around. I thought he glanced at us, but who knew? He walked into the Publix, which anchored his block.

"Good," said Capulet. "I've got to pee, and I want a latte. You want anything?"

I didn't want to point out to her that the quart milk bottle in the back was there for peeing on stakeout. Didn't point that out for several good reasons.

"Yeah. Get me a large coffee. Extra shot of espresso." I started to dig out money and she waved it away.

As she opened her door I caught her arm.

"You're probably OK, but if he leaves before you come out, I've got to stay with him."

I sat there and kept scanning between Fouch's car and the Publix entrance. Pulled a notebook out of the center console, and noted as many times and locations as I could while keeping my eyes open.

I thought about walking over and peeking in his car, but decided I would be as inconspicuous as Capulet had been, so I kicked that idea to the curb. Instead, I checked the Publix door and glanced into the Starbucks window.

Capulet was fighting with the manager. Jesus.

When I looked back, Fouch was out and halfway from the store to his car. Looked back into the Starbucks. Capulet didn't seem anywhere close to finished with the poor clerk.

I cranked up.

"Come on, come on." I wanted to tap the horn, but Fouch was already showing signs of having his radar up. Revved the engine. Stole a glance back at her. Nothing.

Watched Fouch. If he turned my way, I had a few more seconds to wait. But if he went the other way...

He went the other way. I backed out in a quick quarter circle, dropped the car into Drive, headed for the road and got there just as an eighteen-wheeler came by. I hit the brakes and heard slapping on my passenger window.

Capulet was yanking at the door handle with one hand while she balanced two cups in the other. She paused when the door opened and shifted the cups.

"Hurry," I hissed and started to pull forward as the truck cleared us and the road opened. She threw herself in backwards and protected the coffee as well as she could.

Which wasn't very well. One cup sailed into my lap, the other to the floorboard.

"Go!" she yelled.

I slapped at the hot coffee in my lap, caught the cup and what was left, and slammed the accelerator. Her legs were still hanging out as we turned onto the street. She pulled them in and slammed the door.

"What'd he do?"

"What do you mean? He left. Told you, he leaves, I leave."

"You don't have to get mad."

I started to try to explain the joys of using your dick as a coffee dipstick, but decided she wouldn't understand. I accelerated around the truck. "We're following a man. Remember?"

"We'd have caught up." She put on her seat belt and pointed ahead. "Besides, we know he's going home."

"You got eyes on him?"

"No. But that's the direction of his house, right? Makes sense."

"Making sense doesn't prove anything. Stay professional."

She pointed two cars ahead. "Says the man who wet his pants. Look, there he is. Headed home, two blocks, straight ahead. Satisfied?"

I pointed ahead. Through the windshield of the car ahead we could see Fouch's car. With the right turn signal on.

thirty-three

Capulet was quiet, for once.

The light turned green, Fouch turned right onto a quiet street and I eased up as slowly as I could without being obvious. I went straight to give him space but glanced to my right as I drove by. Fouch was slow, too, had almost stopped after barely clearing the intersection. If I had turned right behind him we would have been jammed between him and the street we'd just left. Either he had spotted us, or he was that rare schoolteacher who tried to make life tough on anyone following him. I kept going to the next cross street.

I made a right and another right, fast.

"There!" Capulet pointed ahead at a cross street.

"Got it." I accelerated until I closed us to a manageable gap. Fouch was easing along, slow enough to stack up a couple of cars behind him. As soon as I met his pace — I thought, far behind him—he made a sudden left without a signal.

"Either he's paranoid, or this guy is a pro."

I made a risky pass around two cars, and turned in time to see Fouch take a right, far ahead.

I took a chance and made the next right, one street before his. Went down to the end of the block and pulled behind a parked car where we could watch for him one street over without being seen. At least not seen well.

"Lost him?" Capulet said.

"Maybe. He's being cagey. The only safe way to follow someone—particularly someone who's suspicious—is to use multiple cars. We've got to take some chances."

"Maybe next time we'll use my car, too."

"If there is a next time. I don't know what these phone calls mean. And I don't know what he's heard from your friend Holt."

I tried to calm down.

"Hey, hey," she said. "Look."

Fouch's car turned onto the side street and was coming toward us from the left. Went by without slowing down.

"Think he saw us?" she said.

I cranked the wheel left. "Maybe. Maybe not. We were hidden behind trees and the car ahead of us. And black cars are hard to see." I pulled out and made a quick three-point turn while he disappeared.

I floored it, looking down cross streets as I went.

"Shit." I turned left and stopped behind a truck parked close to the light.

"It's a chance," I said. "We're watching the same street that his house and Publix are on. If he's not coming back here, we're screwed. But people tend to run in ruts and use the same roads over and over. And, of course, if he's going home, we'll be in position."

We sat and watched.

Capulet said, "What'd he have?"

"What do you mean?"

"When he came out of Publix."

I thought.

"Two bags. Both full. Both with toilet paper sticking out. Like those big multi-roll packages."

"Why would a guy who lives alone ever buy more than one of those big packs at a time?"

"Taco Bell?"

"Ha. Ha. You keep trying to make excuses for this guy, but it's one weird thing after another with him."

"True that. Look."

"Bingo," she said," as he rolled by.

There was a pickup a hundred yards behind him. I pulled in behind it.

"The good news is, the truck will block us from him. The bad is that it hides him from us. Keep an eye out."

She wiggled left, right, trying to get a bead. Finally, she popped her seatbelt loose, rolled down her window and half-stood with her torso out the window.

"Got him. Looks like we're going home. Next light is his block."

Fouch slowed way down, the truck stacked up between us and him. The light went yellow and I thought he was going to go through and try to strand us. Instead, he slowed to a stop. The truck and I stopped behind him as the light went red.

Then Fouch blasted through a gap in traffic, horns blaring all around him.

"Shit." I yelled. "Get back in."

Capulet, still halfway out the window, dropped back in as I pulled around the truck with even more horns screaming.

I floored it, but it was too late. By the time I cleared the intersection, Fouch was pulling away at a hundred miles an hour. I kept driving blind until we came to one of Birmingham's five points intersections. I pulled over and stopped.

"What now?" she said. "APB?"

"No. If I still had juice, maybe. Even then, I'd have to justify it, and as of right now he's guilty of nothing but weirdness."

"And speeding."

"Yeah. I'll call Coltrane, find out if he see's anything about it. Speeding tickets are now on-line as soon as they're written."

"So, what now? We go back to your place and you show me the end of the old Angel story?"

"No." I cranked up the engine. "Let's go sit on his house, see if he goes back there. Maybe we can get lucky."

She snickered.

thirty-four

We stopped at a Mediterranean restaurant to pick up food before I parked up the street from the small duplex that Fouch called home.

Capulet opened the bag. "Jesus, what is this stuff?"

I looked at her. She had taken over most of the dash and spread her food on it like a buffet. Only fair, I guess, since she had to kick the wrappers and bags and cans on the floor aside to make room for her feet.

"What? Humus?"

"Looks like mayonnaise and sand."

"No. Good stuff. You don't want it, I'll eat it."

I reached over and she slapped my hand. Picked up the little cup and sniffed it.

"Here." I picked up a chunk of pita bread, loaded it up and handed it to her.

She took a bite.

"That's good. Tastes kind of like bean dip."

"Reason for that. Basically ground-up chickpeas. Kind of Greek bean dip. Luz used to make it."

"From the name, I would have guessed she was Mexican."

"Colombian. But she cooked everything. With our backgrounds—I'm Creole, a couple of generations back—

we both loved food. She got this idea from a book called *Happiness of Pursuit* a couple of years ago. She was going to fix a meal from every country on earth, one a week, so her children—she always called both Sarah and me her children—could learn from it. Each week, she'd dig in, find something from somewhere. If she knew anyone from that country, she'd invite them in and we'd eat and talk and sing music from wherever."

I fished a chicken kabob from my Styrofoam box. "Man, did we live well."

"I can see why you have your shape. Our shape. Always got to be an enabler in their somewhere."

I didn't answer for a minute.

"Two-twenty," I finally said.

She snorted. "Yeah. And I weigh one-ten."

"Not now, then. Never varied more than a couple of pounds from that. Same weight when I played football at LSU."

She was quiet.

I pulled the chicken and onions and tomatoes off the skewer. "You're kind of right, though. Whether you call it 'enabling' or 'supporting,' we really had grown together. Hard to separate where one of us ended and the other one began. At least she did that for me. Hope I gave her the same thing. At least a little."

We were quiet for a second, awkward and embarrassed.

"I'm sorry I said that," she said. "I know I've got nobody to blame for me but me. Sometimes I don't like that. I want to blame everybody else and I want someone to join me. Sorry I'm so bitter. No offense meant."

"None taken." I took a bite of chicken. Good, but not as good as Luz's.

I held up a tomato.

"Maybe this is why I eat so much crap," I said. "Hard to eat McFood and compare it to Luz's. It takes at least ten pounds of that to match the taste in one pound of hers."

Capulet said, "I can't imagine feeling torn in half like you do. Maybe it's better I never had what you had."

I swallowed the tomato.

"No," I said. "It's not."

More awkwardness. I laughed to cover it up.

"Enough about me on our Oprah show. You seem to have built a good life around children."

She hesitated before she spoke.

"I think the past tense is correct. My bitterness is turning me from a good teacher to bad. Maybe that's why this seems so important to me. Why I'm so mad at Fouch."

"If," I said, "there's anything there to be mad about."

"You still have doubts?"

"I'm a cop. You can do your job better if you don't have doubts or beliefs. Just collecting facts. If you let yourself believe things too early, you turn from an investigator to a hunter. And you make mistakes."

"Still, there are a lot of facts here."

"Yes, there are."

"So, what do you want to do? Knock on doors, ask neighbors if Fouch keeps a passel of kids tied up in the back yard?"

"I think we've given him enough warning for one day. Let's sit here quietly and see if he comes home. If you like, I can take you home and come back."

The day was ending and the sky was starting to get dark. That time of day that's either peaceful or threatening, depending on your point of view.

"And what?" she said. "Watch reality TV? Revamp lesson plans for things I've taught a hundred times? No, if you don't think this is important, you go home, and I'll stay here. I got nothing but this."

"I'd better stay here and protect Fouch from you."

We ate in silence for a few minutes. I studied the houses. It was a pretty beaten-down neighborhood, the kind where people draw the shades tight and turn the TV up loud so they can pretend they are somewhere else.

Fouch could afford better.

Capulet finished her meal and shoved the trash back into her bag. She looked at me and I gestured at the floor.

Rolling her eyes she threw the bag down. "I need to know more about the Angel of Mercy. You told me about the first murder. Skip ahead. Talk about the most recent, and we'll fill in the rest later."

"No, not here," I grunted. We needed something to distract us. The something I found was Debbie Holt's email. I had to look at the first line a couple of times before the words focused.

Joe (may I call you that?)

I can't tell you how excited I am about our mission. Most people lack the courage of their convictions and do what they're told, afraid of offending the chary wary people. Not us. I followed your work on your last case very closely and admired your determination to do what was right, at least what you understood to be right.

I feel like we've already been working together on this, and we're destined for great things.

I'm going to start by using my connections to get Fouch's personnel file. I'll contact you when I have it. This is going to be so much fun! Be bold.

I looked up and focused on the house. Bold. Yeah, I'm the boldest clown in Birmingham, hiding under a hundred pounds of flesh and an ocean of rum.

Capulet fluttered one hand in the air and said in her best Marilyn Monroe voice, "I have always wanted to go on a grand mission with you."

"I thought you didn't read this."

"Glanced. But from what I gleaned in my glancing, this doesn't sound like the Debbie Holt I know. She's got a crush on you."

"I'm uncrushable. She's your friend."

"Not really. Just someone I used to teach with. But she is trying to impress you."

I thought about it.

"Everybody's lonely," I said. "Wants an ally and a mission from God, like most people. She's got a wrong number with me."

Capulet said, "And, so you know, I can get Fouch's file myself, if we decide we want to do that."

"And if someone calls Fouch, he'll know something's up. Call her and stop that. That's the kind of boldness that will get us in trouble."

"You don't stop Holt with anything less than a cannon. Maybe I can get her to be discreet, though. Or wait a day or two."

"Do that. And tell her no more boldness. Wait for us. Her boldness can fuck things up."

I grunted. "So, you want to hear about the last—about the end. All right, let's do that. I was feeling a lot of pressure. The mayor was feeling a lot of pressure, too, and when he feels pressure he makes it clear that he wants things done, now."

I took a deep breath. "Pressure from the inside, too. I wasn't just a cop doing his job, I was angry. I did something that seemed good at the time but turned out to be a mistake.

"I called him out. Went on TV and talked about his psychological profile. How he was a coward, acting out because he was afraid of real men. Talked about how I had met with local ministers, and they all agreed he was no Christian."

I wadded up my paper bag and shoved it into the back.

"I meant that part, too. I was raised on the whole 'God-is-love' thing, and his perversion, twisting that into 'life is a hell you've got to escape from' made me as mad as the fact that he was killing kids.

"So, I laid it on thick, calling him out, trying to push him into making a mistake."

I sat and watched Fouch's house for a long time. Thought about how things might be if I had sat here two years ago, instead of reading reports in an office.

"It worked better than anybody dreamed it would. His next note was an out-of-control rant telling me, personally, about all the things I didn't know about hell. Ended with, 'Officer Joe'—he was the first guy to call me Officer Joe—'Sometimes hell is very, very personal.'

"I didn't know what that meant. Found out. At 1915 hours I got a call in my car as I was going home to catch a dinner break. Shots fired. My address. Patrol was on the way. I was a block away. I knew what it had to mean."

I was still staring at Fouch's house as I talked.

"I re-read the report on that for the millionth time last night. Every night. 'Detective Brosette was first on the scene. The door to the residence was open. An adult male came out at the sound of Detective Brosette's car. The man raised his gun and pointed it at Detective Brosette. Detective Brosette fired his weapon three times. The man was killed. The man was later identified as Father Carson of St. Stephens church.'

"My church," I said. "My priest. Didn't recognize him. He toppled off the porch, spun around backwards, yelled something at the house, and fell to the ground with his arms out, like one of the Angel's victims. I didn't have time to stop and look at him till later."

I took a breath and tried to put some distance between me and the memory. "'So, the report said: Detective Brosette entered the residence. In the living room, he discovered the body of Luz Conception Brosette, his wife, age 43. Behind her, in the kitchen, he discovered the body of his daughter, Sarah Luz Brosette, age 10. Throat cut on the child. Stab wound to the heart of the woman.' And I had done nothing until it was too late."

I sat there staring at Fouch's house, bile rising in my mouth and pounding coming back in my head. I was right in telling Holt not to be bold. But she was right too: I needed to be bolder.

"Watch the street." I said. "Anyone—particularly Fouch—comes close, call my cell." I opened the car door. "Otherwise, stay off the fucking phone."

thirty-six

Most houses are easy to break into. Fouch's wasn't.

I started at the back, which usually has an unlocked door or unlatched window. Not here. There was a porch that spanned both sides of the back of the duplex, with rotting boards and potted marijuana plants in five-gallon buckets on his neighbor's side. Fouch's side was flawless, with one reading chair adorned by a clip-on reading light. I stood back and looked at it. The chair was directly in front of a steel door.

It was orderly, but odd. Why put the chair where you would bump into it every time you came out the door to read? I stood still in the dark, listening for neighbors. I studied the chair until I saw a thin wire running from the back leg, along a groove in the floorboard, under the door. An alarm.

This guy was serious. I circled his side of the house, watching where I stepped. Every window had a sensor on it. No reason to believe the front door was any easier. I walked to the back yard and stood there thinking.

I walked around to the neighbor's side, peeking in. The place seemed empty. There was a fuse box on the back porch. I took a shot and pulled the lever.

Both porch lights went out. Good. This box controlled the power for both sides. I went to Fouch's side window and saw a small red light flashing next to the front door. Probably the alarm system, and probably on battery power.

So, that didn't help.

I stood there thinking, then got an idea. Returning to the neighbor's porch, I tried the window, which looked like it would crumble with a touch. Then I tried the door, which turned in my hand and opened before me.

I stepped inside and found his security system: an AR-15 lying on the kitchen table. Over on the kitchen counter there was a Glock next to a beer.

I crept through the house, trying to get the feel for the layout. No people. Two rooms in front, a living room and a bedroom. Two rooms in back, a kitchen and a second bedroom with a bathroom. All connected by a small square hall.

That's where I found what I wanted. There was a square opening in the ceiling to access the attic. The plywood square covering the hole had been removed, and a step ladder set under.

Thank you, sir.

Climbing up I saw why: a small collection of pot plants and a now-dark grow light.

Sorry about stealing the sun from your crops, dude. Hope I didn't harsh your mellow.

I pulled the stepladder up behind me, took out my small flashlight and shined it on my feet, moving from one rafter to the next until I got to the plywood square that was

Fouch's. There was nothing obvious in the way of alarms or anything nailing it shut, so I worked my fingers around the edge and pulled.

The square came up and I counted to thirty listening for an alarm. Nothing. I set the square aside, turned off the light and stuck my head down into the room, praying there was no motion detector in the hall. No blinking lights, no siren. I lowered the stepladder and climbed down.

I stood as still as I could while I looked around. No obvious trap door leading to a hidden dungeon. I could see a motion detector in the living room, pointed at the front door and away from me. Another in the kitchen, also pointed away from me.

The back bedroom was set up as an office. I approached the desk and went through the pile of papers on it. It was all mail addressed to this house. Nothing suspicious. I tried to pull the file drawer but it was locked.

It was the cheap lock that came with the desk. I could take my pocketknife and twist it open in a second, but it would break the lock and let him know someone had been here. He had a jar of paper clips. Even with his paranoia, I didn't think he would miss one.

A few minutes work, the lock turned and the drawer slid open. I pulled out the files one by one and saw lesson plans and tax forms. I opened last year's taxes, laid them on the floor and took pictures with my cell.

Nothing in them looked funny.

There was a folder labelled "Art Project." I opened it without taking it out, expecting a stack of finger-paintings. It was filled with bills.

I took it out. Utility bills, bills from home improvement stores, repair bills.

All with the address blacked out with a marker.

I took the bills out, laid them on the floor and took pictures. I scanned them, hoping he'd missed an address. He hadn't. I turned them over and tried to read the addresses. No luck.

I found one that appeared to be typed on an old typewriter or an impact printer. Ran my finger over it and I could feel the impressions. I turned the paper over and took a pencil from the desk and ran it lightly back and forth. Brought my phone down to a shallow angle, and snapped a picture.

117 Harbin.

thirty-seven

Capulet was standing by the car when I got back. "What the hell is that?"

I locked the pot dealer's AR-15 and Glock in my trunk, and climbed in next to her.

"Souvenirs I picked up on the way out. Figured the owner didn't need them."

"Fouch had guns?"

"No. This came from the guy next door. The more innocent tenant. Maybe more innocent. Figure I'll give the guns to Coltrane to turn into BPD. Guy who had them doesn't need them."

I cranked up.

"We're leaving? After all that, we're going to walk away?"

"Regroup. Get some intelligence." I thought about where we were going and corrected myself, "Maybe just regroup."

#

Wendy stared at us as we walked in to Johnson's. Jerked her head at Ron and he swiveled and watched, too. The place got quiet. I thought Capulet would trip in the dark, but she sailed in like a queen on tour and took my seat as if it were her own.

She put her hand out to Wendy.

"Juliet."

"Guinevere." I heard someone snicker and then choke it off when Wendy glared in his direction. She gave Capulet a dainty little shake with a hand I had seen crush cans.

Capulet smiled an actual charming smile. "So nice to meet another woman with a name from the Age of Chivalry."

Wendy looked around. "A long, long time ago."

They both laughed, sounding like steelworkers again.

"What can I get you, honey?"

"Boilermaker."

Wendy gave her an approving smile and slipped away.

I took the empty stool next to Capulet.

"Doesn't look like you need me to introduce you around."

"Nope."

Past her, I saw Ron with his head down. Could be offended that he was left out. Or he could just be being Ron.

"Ron," I said. He grunted and I jerked a thumb. "Capulet."

She said, "I prefer Juliet."

"Juliet?" I said. "We're using touchy-feely names in here? Turn this into *Downton Abbey*?"

Wendy slammed my rum down so hard I lost half of it on the counter. Sat a boilermaker in front of Capulet as if it were champagne on a sterling silver tray.

"Now that's a real drink."

I said, "Only one. For both of us. We've got work to do."

I pulled out my cell phone and put it on the bar with the first of the papers from Fouch's.

"What do you make of this?"

I felt something pressing against my back. Turned quickly in time to see a figure fading back into the darkness. A gravelly voice in that direction said, "It's a fucking light bill. What's matter with you, Joe? You never pay a bill?"

"Of course, I know a light bill."

I told my story. As I talked, I got that sense you have in the woods sometimes, when you can't see anything but you can feel the figures of the night surrounding you.

"So, I need you guys' help," I said. "I get it that you like your privacy, but I want to know what you think."

A higher voice said, "I think I can't see a fucking thing."

"Yeah," I said. "Maybe we'll have to pass my phone around. Address is 117 Harbin."

"Oh, for crying out loud," said Wendy. "I can see why you Neanderthals died out."

She picked up my phone and looked at it. "Yep." She tapped on the laptop behind the bar and the Braves game on the bar TV turned to three well-oiled naked guys each twisting to get the others' full attention. She yanked the cord out of her laptop, the screen went blank and Wendy blushed red enough to light up the bar.

"Jesus, Wendy," said the darkness.

She mumbled, "I've got to do something for amusement before the bar opens." She played with the computer again, plugged the TV cable back in and added another cable to my phone. A satellite photo of 117 Harbin appeared on the TV.

"Big house," the gravelly voice said.

A high voice added, "Or a business. Or a fucking pot farm, Mr. Former Detective."

"Still a detective, even if BPD thinks they fired me."

I took away some of the gravelliness and thought I could place the voice. Wasn't sure, and didn't have time to pursue it now.

"I know Harbin Street," said a slurred voice I didn't recognize. "At the base of Red Mountain."

"Bring up a map, Wendy."

She played on her computer for a couple of seconds and the screen zoomed out showing street names.

"What happened to Harbin?" she said.

"Won't show up," said the slurred voice. "Look there at 16th Ave South. Now pan up toward the top of the mountain."

She did.

"Still don't see Harbin," I said.

"You won't. See that wooded area between 16th and the park on top of the mountain? No streets in it? That wooded area is too steep to build on. And that little bit of color there in the trees, halfway between 16th and the park? That's our house. Gravel road cuts from 16th to the house. Harbin Street."

The gravelly voice said, "How you know that?"

"I lived there for about a year. In the woods. If I wanted to have a look at that house I wouldn't drive up there. I'd park at that convenience store right before you get to Valley View Park, walk up the Vulcan Trail from there."

A voice laughed. 'If you can walk up there."

"I can make it," I said.

"We can both make it," Capulet declared.

"You stay put," I told her.

Wendy handed me a thermos.

"Is that to keep me awake?" I asked.

She nodded at Capulet. "Keep her awake while she keeps you awake. She's going with you."

I started to argue when Capulet's phone went off. Rather than do the polite thing and walk away to take the call, she stood in the middle of the crowd yelling, the crowd laughing at the free entertainment. Finally, we all heard, "We fucking know," and she hung up. Looking up, she found the whole crowd staring at her.

She paid them little attention. "That was Holt wanting to come meet us. Threatened to go rescue the girls herself if we didn't do something."

"It's been, what?" I said. "Ten hours since we talked to her? And she thinks she can call us at midnight?"

"She said she thought we'd be on stakeout with Fouch. Wanted to come take a shift. With you."

"Keep her away from him and from us. We'll find her something to do, but tell her we don't need her right now. Jesus, she's in a rush for us to get a guy who may not even be the guy. Tell her we're aware of how serious this is."

She shrugged, "I tried."

A voice in the back, imitating Capulet, said, "We fucking know."

Nothing looks sadder than a locked-up convenience store in the dark of night. Reminds you of your mother's advice that nothing good happens after midnight.

No argument now, Ma.

We sat in the parking lot under harsh lights a-buzz with electricity and summertime insects. I looked over at Capulet in her black mu-mu.

"Sure you're ready for this?"

She hiked her dress up past her knees. "Army boots. I wear them all the time."

"I didn't need to see that."

She pulled her dress down and got out. As did I, climbing out, popping the trunk, and fishing out the black tee shirt, watch cap, flashlight and mini-binoculars I kept in my ready box. Then I unbuttoned my shirt and pulled it off.

"I'll never be able to look at a romance book cover the same way," she said. "Or a whale."

I wanted to slam the trunk shut, but I eased it down and turned to lead the way to the trail.

She was ten yards ahead, and I hurried to catch up.

The trail was steep but citified, paved and wide. After a short uphill stretch, it turned parallel to the slope and was easy going. A couple of hundred yards and a gravel road crossed the path.

"Wait," I said.

I looked up the mountain and saw lights through the trees.

I started up the road. "Stay close."

After a quarter mile, I spotted a tiny red light in a bush and stopped. Fading into the brush, I pulled Capulet with me.

I pointed at the light. "Alarm. See how the beam crosses the road to the receptor on the other side?" I pointed above it. "Camera."

"Did they see us?"

"I don't think so. But someone's watching."

We eased into the woods and wove our way around the alarm. The woods ended a little clearing surrounding the house. I sat down on a rock and patted Capulet a seat next to me. I pulled out my binoculars and gave the house a once-over.

It was one of those sprawling country houses that probably started as a cottage a hundred years ago, grew into a series of unmatched additions. Fifty feet to the left was a metal outbuilding the size of a small barn. The lawn was cut short with no bushes for a hundred feet around and carefully spaced light poles keeping the whole place lit up.

I focused and studied the windows until I found what I was looking for.

"Alarm sensor on at least one window. Same as Fouch's house."

"Guards?"

"Not patrolling the grounds, but serial killers rarely hire security services."

"The yard looks bright, but the house looks dark. Suspicious."

"Maybe."

"Maybe my ass. When will you see enough to convince that pea-brain of yours?

"When I've seen more than I've seen now."

I opened my cell and woke Coltrane up. After he grumbled and I explained, I said, "You got your laptop at home?"

"No, but I've got my personal Mac. What you need?"

"Remember that guy Fouch I asked you about?"

"Yeah. Teacher. Couldn't find anything else about him."

"I need you to check an address. Might be a little hard, because it sits on a gravel road by itself in the woods under Vulcan." I gave him the address. "See if you can find a connection. Call me when you've got something." I set the phone to vibrate and checked to make sure the rattlesnake was off.

Capulet said, "If it's registered to Don the Fucking Angel of Mercy, will you be convinced?"

"Maybe. But I don't think he would swear like that."

She swore some more, but poured me a cup of coffee.

We sat and drank in silence while I watched. I thought of Luz and Sarah, frozen in the picture forever. I thought of the day I let the Angel get away.

A light went on in the house, downstairs, followed a minute later by another light. I looked through the glasses and saw a woman in sweats working in a kitchen. I looked at my watch. 6:30.

My phone buzzed, and I put it to my ear.

"Yeah?" I said. I realized I was being even quieter, as if the woman in the house could hear me.

Coltrane said, "Interesting house you're visiting."

"Yeah. It's starting to come to life."

"It was an old Birmingham family house. Guess what family?"

"I don't know. Richard Nixon?"

"Close. Been in Judge Horton's family for a hundred years."

That explained the security.

"Until Judge Horton sold it four years ago. To Fouch."

I was silent long enough for Coltrane to say, "You there?"

"Yeah. Don't be late to work today. Keep your phone on."

I hung up.

Lights were coming on in the upstairs windows with people drifting down to the kitchen.

The people I could see were all girls. Teen-aged girls, ten-year-olds. One of them looked like she was maybe six.

"Look at that," hissed Capulet. "Do something."

"They also serve who only sit on their asses."

But I felt the same fear and itchiness she felt.

About seven we heard car wheels on the gravel road and watched a green minivan come up to the barn. A woman got out and unlocked the barn door and pulled it open. She drove in and walked out. Didn't bother to lock the door behind her.

A man came out of the house and walked to the barn and drove out.

Fouch.

I stood up. Capulet joined me.

"Done sitting on your ass?"

I brushed myself off.

"I've seen enough."

I laid out the case to the captain, with Coltrane and the Lieutenant there and Capulet with me. For once, she was mercifully silent.

The captain nodded. "Sounds like it's worth investigating."

"Investigating?" she exploded. So much for silent. "These girls are being tortured at this very moment, while you tin soldiers sit around and talk about 'investigating'—bureaucrat-speak for sitting on your asses. We need a SWAT team out there NOW."

"I'm not even sure you've got enough for an investigation," the Lieutenant said. "All you've really got is girls at the home of a teacher. No victims reported at all. Could be a class project for all we know."

I said, "Could be a serial killer with a house full of girls. He's called me twice now, threatening something a hell of a lot bigger than a class project. Something soon. Maybe now."

The Lieutenant gave me a bored stare. "Someone called you. You say."

I turned to Coltrane and put up my hands.

Coltrane said, "I checked on the purchase of the Harbin house. He bought it for less than half of its assessed value."

The Lieutenant turned on him. "So, you're using department time and resources to conduct a private investigation? One not authorized by your chain of command?"

Capulet said, "If this were a houseful of boys being raped and tortured and fattened up for a kill, you'd be calling in air strikes."

The captain put up his hands. "Enough. Joe," he said to me, "after the Maria Trap thing, you've got enough cred for us to look into this, but that's all." He turned to the Lieutenant. "I want a real investigation—by the book. Do a preliminary, and we'll meet back here tomorrow and see where we go."

The Lieutenant opened the door and stuck his head out.

"Vinzini," he said. "Get your ass in here."

I lost it. "Vinzini? Vinzini? What the fuck is wrong with you? You've got lives on the line, and you pick the one man who's more concerned with proper department appearance than saving lives? What happened to 'protect and serve'? Give me two men and—"

The captain was ramrod-straight. "That's enough, Detective. You still work for me, and the Birmingham Police Department. Get in line."

Vinzini tapped on the door jamb and the captain waved him in.

"Vinzini in. You two out."

forty

I was so mad that Capulet had to drive us home. I was in the war room, pacing a circle and cursing, sometimes under my breath and sometimes at the top of my lungs. Capulet wasn't helping, matching my curses two-for-one and my volume three-for-one. Every time I came back to Luz and Sarah I stood in silence. I wanted to tell them I'd done everything I could, but I knew I hadn't. Maybe I had done everything people said I should do, but not everything I could.

I looked at Luz. "You know I can't do that."

After three laps, I had calmed down enough to tell Luz, "Tomorrow. We'll give them until tomorrow. After tomorrow's tag-up, if they're not moving out, I'll go nuclear."

My eyes teared up. When they cleared, I saw Capulet standing by the door, holding her phone out to me.

"It's Debbie Holt. She wants to talk to you."

"Jesus. Not now. Tell her we'll find her something. Tell her it's important for her to stay undercover for now."

She shook her head. "Holt doesn't take no."

I took the phone and all I heard was static, like someone drumming on the phone. I handed it back to Capulet.

"Nothing but static. Tell her to call back."

Capulet looked at the phone and held it up to her ear. "Sounds fine." She paused and lowered the phone to talk to me. "She says to tell you that she's meeting with Fouch's principal first thing in the morning."

"Hell, no."

Capulet repeated that into the phone and went back and forth a couple of times saying the same thing but stronger. Then she said, "Hello? Hello?" and hung up the phone.

She looked at me.

"She hung up on me. Debbie says this is a teacher problem, and teachers are going to solve it."

"And warn Fouch in the process. There's no way he won't find out. And kill those girls before lunch. We've got to do something before tomorrow morning."

Capulet was talking, but all I heard was the captain saying after the Trap rescue, "If we'd followed procedure, that girl might be dead." I'd let too many girls die to let that happen.

"Tell Holt she just helped," I said as I went out the door.

The station told me Paula Light was at an opening of a new Costco. When I came up behind the reporter, she was at the sampling table for some seaweed thing.

"Do I have anything in my teeth?" she was saying to her cameraman.

"No, girl. You're good."

There was enough green in her teeth to re-sod Legion Field.

I pointed at a mirror on the reading glasses carousel. "Trust, but verify."

She trotted over, brushed her teeth with her finger and trotted back. Her smile was white, but her happy face was gone.

"You son-of-a-bitch." She was glaring at the cameraman. "You would have let me go on the air like that."

He said, "Not like they're going to put you on air tonight. They'll show a shot of the outside of the store, the anchor will mention it, and Costco will get their 15 seconds of fame. No Sunshine and Light tonight, sweetheart."

"Yeah." She stood tapping her toe until she noticed me standing there, and squinted at me. "Aren't you?"

"Yeah. The Birmingham cop."

"No, I mean...." It came to her. "The Huggy Bear!"

"Oh, yeah," I said.

She turned her back on the cameraman and focused on me.

"Your story went so well. Best rated story I've had in months. People like you."

"Yeah. People who don't know me like me a lot."

"No, we get calls from moms and dads saying they want someone like you looking out for their kids. I think the Birmingham PD should let you do a regular feature for us, if we can figure out what to do." She frowned to herself. "Needs to be something more than 'don't do drugs' and 'don't talk to strangers.'"

"Good," I said. "Not sure I'm too good at those."

I looked at a stack of clocks shaped like suns on sale. Getting late.

"Look. I've got a story now. But it has to be run tonight. Are you interested?"

She looked at her watch. "Too late for the five o'clock. I might be able to sell it for ten o'clock it if it's very hot and we do it very, very fast."

"How about Birmingham PD is closing a major homicide case and saving multiple children in the process?"

Her eyes grew wide. "How soon?"

"Within twenty-four hours. The mayor's demanding it." I didn't add, if the mayor sees this and if he pressures BPD.

She pulled her phone out of her jacket pocket. "And Birmingham PD is OK with this story?"

I had already decided on my answer.

"It will help them do their job."

She punched her phone and talked while looking around the cavernous store.

"Dave?" she said. "Yes, I know you're busy. Listen. What's your lead for the ten? Scrap it."

I could hear yelling from her phone.

"The police are raiding a killer who's holding multiple children. Save me...two minutes."

She hung up and pointed at a display of children's toys. "Set up over there," she said to the cameraman.

We quick-walked over. On the way, she said, "Where is this?"

"Can't tell you."

"Exactly when?"

"Again, can't tell you."

She nodded.

"I can work with that. Adds suspense. Makes people tune in tomorrow. OK, this is going to be your show. I'll intro you and say you have news of a major operation by Birmingham PD. You've got it from there. Watch John with the camera. He'll signal us to start, then he'll hold up one finger when we've got a minute left on-screen. Then five when we're five seconds to finish. Come as close to ending when he counts to zero as you can. We're not going to have time to edit this."

She stood me in front of a couple of cartoon characters and fluffed my hair with her fingers.

I looked into the camera and knew—prayed, at least—that this was the end. Certainly, the end of anything like a career, even as a grade school cop. Maybe, maybe the end of the Angel. I tried to think of what life would be like after this, and could imagine nothing.

She introed the Huggy Bear Hero and put the mic in my face. I tried to lay on the story of Birmingham's heroic knights in blue as thick as I could.

I meant it. I hoped they would see that, even though I knew they would feel like I had stabbed them in the back.

The fingers counted down and I said my last words and stood there, feeling sadder and more exhilarated than I could remember. No one in blue would ever forgive or understand what I was about to do, but I hoped Luz and Capulet - and even Holt - would. All of them, and maybe a house full of girls.

forty-two

It didn't take long. Ten-thirty, the snake rattled.

"Yeah?" I said.

It was Coltrane. "Man, what the hell did you do?"

I was standing in the case room. Looking at the photograph. Waiting.

"You still there?" he said when I didn't answer for a minute.

"Yes. Keeping the faith."

"Don't know what that means. The captain's called everybody back in, every swinging dick he can get. He's in his office huddled with a bunch of the big guns. Nobody here knows what's going on, but every now and then we hear your name."

"I bet it's really complimentary."

He paused. "Depends on whether you think of motherfucker as a compliment or not."

"Might be the best compliment I hear for a while. At least from anyone in blue."

"What did you do?"

"Stabbed BPD in the back. And kicked it in the ass."

I told him the whole story.

"Man, you went to the news vultures?"

"I didn't know what else to do to make things happen fast. Was afraid—am afraid—that if we don't move tonight, bad things are going to happen."

"Well, something's happening now. The bullpen outside of the captain's office is full of people doing nothing but waiting."

"Know the feeling."

"Hang loose. I got to go help with ops planning."

"If you can get someplace where people can't see your laptop, check out that Harbin Street address."

"That one they've got up on the big map in the war room? Yeah. Don't need a laptop for that."

There was some noise in the background and I heard the captain yell, "Somebody get that cocksucker Brosette down here. And that loudmouth partner of his, too."

I stood up.

"Be down there in ten," I said to Coltrane.

"Oh, hell no. Wait for someone official to call you. Don't admit that you know me at all."

forty-three

"That's enough out of you," said the Captain.

It was a little past four in the morning. Capulet and I were sitting in the Captain's conference room while people ran in and out sticking pins in maps on the wall.

Wishing they could put pins in us. Capulet wasn't helping. She had just suggested that the city give me a medal for this. And her phone had gone off as we sat there. She looked at the ID, turned it off and smiled at the roomful of angry men focused on us.

"Holt again," she said, as if that explained anything.

The Captain gave me a look that could have killed a small rodent. ""You're only here because the mayor insisted. I warned him that we weren't ready for this. He told me to take all the time I wanted, as long as it was done today and he looked good in the morning. He's planning on coming in once things are wrapped up. With your girlfriend from the TV station." He fake-smiled at Capulet. "I mean your other girlfriend. Not meaning to hurt your feelings, ma'am."

"Not hurt," she said. "You got any coffee?"

He pointed her at a pot in the back of the room.

"Captain Jordan," I said. "I'm sorry about this, but I didn't know any other way to make it happen."

"I hope the 'it' that happens is what you want." He was trying to glare at me but he broke it off and looked at the wall behind me. "Joe, you used to be a good cop. One of the best. A real cop would never have done this. We're loyal."

"I wish I could have let things go and allowed you guys to nail this down solid. But the Angel has something coming soon. And there's a houseful of girls in there with no good explanation."

"Did you ask them?"

"Knock on the door and say, 'Is this a slumber party or are you being held by a serial killer?' No, sir, I did not."

"Or follow one of them to school. Or ask one of the nine hundred Birmingham police officers to investigate, and give them time to do it? Like we were doing."

He looked at the clock and sighed. "We've had eyes on the house since we talked to you yesterday. Reports are only of girls coming home from school. Nothing suspicious. We'll be getting in position in an hour. Going in just before dawn. Soon enough?"

"Hope so."

"Hope. All you've left us, Joe. Hope to hell this doesn't go south." He gave me the saddest look anyone had given me yet. "You know your caller could be—probably is— some sick fuck messing with you. Knowing the Angel is already cold in the ground."

I didn't say anything.

"For the sake of the cop you once were, I hope you're right. I hope we ride in there and save a bunch of girls.

Catch the Angel—or at least, some kind of bad guy. Hope you're on the news with the mayor for a live eight a.m. interview."

"You know I don't care about all that."

He stood there a long time without saying a word. Finally, he said, "Yes, I know that. For the sake of all the things you do care about, I hope this works out."

Vinzini tapped the captain on the shoulder.

"We're ready for the commit briefing, Captain." He looked at me. "You want me to clear the room of civilians? And press?"

"No, let them stay." Capulet walked up with her coffee. The captain noticed her, then said, "And listen. Either of them open their mouths, shoot them." He looked at her. "I'll testify that I pulled the trigger."

I found two chairs in the back and pulled Capulet down beside me. "You have anything you want to say, say it to me now. Whisper in my ear. Better yet, keep it to yourself."

Vinzini went to the front of the room and laid out the plans for the morning. SWAT team coming down from Vulcan. Snipers in the woods in front. Same basic entry plan as the Maria Trap case: two detectives with bulletproof vests under their suits would drive up in a Human Services car and approach the house carrying innocuous-looking clipboards.

In this case, because of the number of girls we had seen, officers would flood the house the instant the door opened.

The captain interrupted Vinzini. "Let's be very clear about this: this is a house full of young girls. Nobody shoots unless they know exactly where their bullet is going." He looked at me. "As usual, our job's not that easy. In addition to the girls, there may be a serial killer or killers there. If anyone threatens any of the girls, put him down. Fast and hard. But don't hurt any civilians. Easy enough?"

There were a couple of hard laughs.

"Never is. Serve and protect, as always. No leeway on either one."

He looked at me.

"You're sure about this?"

I nodded.

"OK," he said. "Listen for my voice. From now on, this is my rodeo."

forty-four

We sat in the captain's darkened Explorer on the last bend of the gravel road beyond the sightline to the house.

"No sign of movement from the house?" the captain asked.

There was a man in black tactical gear sitting in the passenger seat with his eyes on the computer between them and wearing a headset. "None reported, sir," he said.

"Wish we had had time," the captain said, "to get in there and plant a couple of cameras or even audio transmitters. Or look into Fouch more."

I thought he looked back at me in the dark, but I couldn't be sure.

Capulet said, "What do you want us to do, sir?"

He seemed to struggle with a couple of answers.

"Nothing. Do absolutely nothing. Don't leave the car for any reason. If you hear any shooting, get down on the floor." He paused and looked at us. "As best you can. But do not leave the car for any reason." He paused again. "Ma'am."

She nodded. "Yes, sir. But what if—"

"No what if's," I said. "The captain is tactical now. Let him concentrate on his job."

He gave me a tight nod of thanks. More than I expected.

"Coming up on five minutes, sir," said the man in the passenger seat.

"Call it, Hamilton."

He keyed his mic and said, "Five minutes. Mark."

The captain said, "Roll call. On speaker."

Hamilton whispered into the mic.

A voice from the computer said, "Front of the house. Ready. No sign of movement inside or out."

"Entry. Ready."

"Rear. No movement. Ready."

"Chopper. Holding over the south side of Red Mountain. One minute away."

Hamilton said, "ELINT ready. No one's used the TV, internet or house phone since midnight."

The captain cued his mic. "Command, ready. OK, people, we're less than five minutes out. I'm going to repeat this. We have reports of multiple young females inside. An unknown number of adults. Once you're in, get everyone on the floor as fast as you can. Treat the juveniles with kid gloves, but get them down for their own protection. Treat all adults as hostile until we have the situation under control. Get them down fast any way you have to and keep eyes on them. Do not fire unless there is a clear threat, and even then, only if you know what you are going to hit.

"When I give the word, Vinzini and Toomer will drive up in the city car. Eyes, report immediately if you see any movement as the car approaches. If there's no movement, Vinzini and Toomer walk up in a non-threatening manner. Slap a charge on the door and jump back as door blows.

"As soon as they place the charges, I want the front- and rear-entry teams moving. Front, you are to hit the door on the run as soon as it blows. Rear, blow your door and flood the house.

"I'll repeat the rules of engagement. There are multiple civilians present. Do not fire unless there is an active and immediate threat present, and you are certain of hitting your target. I want an 'ack' on that from everyone."

"Front, ack."

The others followed.

Hamilton said, "Two minutes, sir."

"Two minutes, people," the captain repeated, "Places. Be safe and protect the children."

Bright headlights flashed like lightning behind us and the dark gravel road lit up like a sideshow.

"What the fuck?" said the captain.

We all turned and saw the Channel 11 news van.

The captain gave me a dirty look and turned back to his mic.

"Vinzini, we've lost surprise. Go now. Everyone, go, go, go."

He looked back at the van.

"What the fuck happened to the guys who were supposed to be blocking the road?"

He looked around for someone to blame, but everyone was busy. Looked at me. "Brosette, get back there and shut those guys down."

Once again he spoke into his mic.

I jumped out. Capulet started to come with me and I said, "No."

I got to the van as the side door opened and the cameraman jumped out and pointed his camera and lights at me. I tried to put my hand over the light, but it broke the glow into a thousand beams all clawing toward the house.

"Shut this fucking light off, now," I said. "All of these lights."

The headlights went out. A voice inside the van said, "Keep filming."

I pushed the camera down and said, "This is a police operation."

The mayor stepped out of the van, wearing black suit pants and a black turtleneck sweater in May.

"This is my operation," he said. "I promised this young lady that we would be one step behind the SWAT team."

"I'm sorry, sir. I know who you are, but I can't let you endanger this operation or the lives of the people involved. As soon as my captain tells me it's safe, I'll let you go. This is a police operation."

The police commissioner stepped out and stood beside the mayor.

"It is, and I'm now in command. The mayor is here over my objections, but if he's going to be here, I'm going to protect him. And you are, too. I don't hear any gunfire. Let's move up the road."

There was an explosion up ahead and he looked at me.

"The mayor's life is your responsibility today, detective."

forty-five

Our entourage passed the command van, and the captain looked out at the commissioner.

"We're going in," he told the captain.

"Bad idea. I don't have anyone to go with you."

"We have him." The commissioner pointed at me.

"Don't have time to argue." The captain looked at me. "Don't fuck up any more than you already have." Then at the mayor. "All of you."

He turned back to his headset and his laptop, and we went back to the road. When we rounded the bend, we saw the last of the first wave going in the front door, accompanied by a lot of shouting and lights going on throughout the house. Paula Light and the cameraman were following ten feet behind us, the reporter narrating in-between breaths.

The mayor made it a jog and we tried to keep up. At the door, the commissioner held him back.

"Wait until it's clear, sir."

The mayor looked irritated.

We heard, "All clear," from inside.

He shook the commissioner off and turned to the camera. "There are people in there who need us."

The commissioner addressed Vinzini, who was standing in the middle of the living room. "The count, detective?"

"Three adults. At least five girls. One injury. Adult female broke an arm while she was being pushed down. Mad as hell."

"I bet. I'll see her in a minute."

The mayor put his foot on the tread of the stairs.

We all heard a gunshot from upstairs. A girl screamed. Someone yelled, "Officer down."

The commissioner threw the mayor on the floor and screamed at me, "Get on top of him." He ran up the stairs with his gun drawn.

I threw myself on the mayor and we crashed to the floor. He squirmed and made muffled sounds, but I didn't move. People ran past me: officers in black accompanying two medics.

Then there was a whole crowd of medics running with a stretcher and suitcases filled with medical equipment.

The mayor's squirming stopped and I was afraid I had smothered him. I raised myself up a little and a string of curses told me he was OK, or at least alive.

The room down here was quiet, but I could hear a lot of noises from upstairs: girls crying, medics yelling tense commands at each other. Lots of cursing. Finally, I heard a heavy, slow tread coming down the stairs. The commissioner stood over us.

"You can let him up, now," he said.

I rolled off.

Between gasps, the mayor said, "You stupid fat fuck. You broke my arm and almost killed me."

The commissioner looked at him without expression.

"I think it's dislocated, sir. We'll get the medics to examine it. When they're...done. Right now, you need to come upstairs, sir."

I followed them. At the top of the stairs we came to a hall running left and right. Most of the voices were coming from the room to the left. The mayor started to go that way, but the commissioner caught his good arm.

"That's a young cop named Jenkins, sir. They thought the room was clear. There was a seven-year-old female under a bed, scared out of her mind. Holding a gun she had brought from her home. She shot him in panic. He's not going to...it doesn't look good for him right now."

"I need to be there," the mayor said.

The commissioner shook his head. "I need you in that room." He indicated the room on the right.

We walked past a big central space with bunk beds and bright cheery unicorns and rainbows on the walls. It was filled with young girls and two officers. On one bed a girl sat sobbing her eyes out.

The commissioner stepped aside at the open door to the third room. An elegant-looking older woman in red silk pajamas was sitting on a bed while a medic adjusted a sling on her arm.

"I believe you know Judge Horton," the commissioner said. "The judge had her arm broken in the entry."

When she saw the mayor, her calm, sad face twisted into something that might have escaped from hell. "You stupid motherfucking publicity-starved moron. Do you know what you've done?"

The mayor started to say something, thought better, and kept quiet.

"Do you know what this is? It's a safe house for endangered girls. Girls with abusive parents who would hunt them down and hurt them—keep on hurting them. Thirteen-year-old hookers hiding from pimps. Can your little brain imagine how hard we've worked to keep this place a secret? How hard it will be to start over? What are these girls supposed to do in the meanwhile? Stay at your house? Or mine, where these predators will come looking for them? What the fuck do you think we should do now?"

He started to say something, but she said. "I know. Don't ask politics to help. What was the line from the song, 'I'd like to help you, son, but you're too young to vote?' No wonder people like you don't look out for children like these."

"Judge Horton," I said. "We thought you'd sold this house several years ago."

"Of course I did. You think we want a secret safe house in a judge's name? The real hero here is the volunteer from the juvenile court who agreed to buy the house—with his own money—and run the program. With no public praise or acknowledgment. No money for him. Only because he wanted to protect children from predators." She glared at the mayor. "And the police and incompetent bureaucrats we have in this city. He's the hero."

I looked at a chair in the back of the room and saw Fouch sitting there. Looked behind me and saw the Channel 11 man with his camera rolling.

The mayor, the judge, and the cameraman got into a three-way over who had the right to do what, with which, to whom. I went over to Fouch, sitting in a corner with his head down.

"I'm sorry," I said.

"I know." He looked up. His eyes had gone inside himself as if he knew he was in the middle of something that would take a long, long time to get over. "I believe you. You're a good man. I admired you for the way you stood up for kids. You're a good man. But this is still a bad thing."

"I know."

He looked up at me. "Why?"

"You looked..." I couldn't think of a good reason right now. "You seemed so bitter to your kids. That crack you made to your kids about them being a 'Waste of Life,' maybe. A couple of people said you were a burnout as a teacher." Right now it sounded pretty weak. "I don't know."

He thought about it.

"I guess I was. Am. I teach in the richest elementary school in the state. I've got fourth-graders with cellphones and parents who'll call the school board if I take them away. Moms who'll take their kid out of reading class so they can go to Belk's Bargain Days in their Beemers. Yeah, I guess I'm burned out on that."

He looked up at me like a little boy lost.

"So, you know how, when you get to that point in life where you're so sick of it that there's nothing good you want to do and you start flailing around at anything in desperation to try to make something work?"

I nodded, but couldn't say anything.

"About ten years ago, I heard about this program with the juvenile court. CASA, they call it, for Court Appointed Special Advocate. Volunteers who work with juvenile court judges. See, when kids come to court, there are lawyers for the parents, lawyers for DHR, and so on. A million people all involved. But no one whose job is simply to represent the child. So, in some cases, the judge will appoint a CASA. A volunteer with no constraints and no obligations to anyone but the child. His job is to talk to the child and everyone else, and report directly to the judge.

"It was the hardest and best thing I had ever done. These kids had nothing good—abusive parents, drug-addicted parents. Often the kids had disabilities of every kind. The deck stacked against them in every way. But they would do anything to fight for a better life."

He smiled to himself.

"Often they fought in all the wrong ways and got to the court in a lot of trouble themselves.

"So, I guess you were right about my calling my rich school kids WoLs. Maybe a little strong, but the comparison of the whiners who have everything to the fighters who have nothing burned me out on my day job. When the judge approached me a few years ago with the chance to do this, I jumped at it."

He smiled to himself again.

"I took it right around the start of the Angel killings. I'd watch you on TV and think how heroic you were. Funny."

"I don't think anyone's laughing."

"No. Do you know how the officer that was shot is doing?"

"The commissioner didn't sound encouraging. Any idea what the girl was doing with a gun?"

"No. We check pretty carefully for guns, drugs and cell phones when they come in, but it happens. Can't say I blame Diana—girl they said shot the officer. She's been through a lot, from a lot of people. If she had shot the people she was carrying the gun for, we'd all be cheering."

"Not much cheering going on today."

"No."

His eyes went back inside himself and I stood up to go. He looked back at me.

"You got it wrong," he said.

I had trouble saying it, but I said, "Yes."

He seemed embarrassed. "No, I don't mean...everything. Though, I guess that's true. No, I mean about the WoL thing. What I say about my kids, even though they're spoiled, I don't think they are wastes. I tell them, 'Don't be a waste of life.' Somebody twisted what I said."

I barely heard him. A stretcher went by in the hall. Covered, except for a young man's head spattered with blood. His eyes caught mine and he struggled to say something. One of the men escorting the stretcher reached down and turned the officer's head away and hissed, "Traitor"   at   me.

forty-seven

I woke up the next morning and couldn't remember how much I'd drunk the night before.

I remembered everything else with a terrible clarity. Didn't feel like there was anything in the house that I could drink to make it go away. I had killed an innocent man once before. Now maybe it was twice.

Twice. And everything I believed as a man and a as cop said that a person shouldn't get away with killing without paying the ultimate price himself.

I put on my dress blues and stood in front of the photo with my phone in my hand, waiting for the call. Didn't have to wait long.

The captain said, "You need to get down here, now. My conference room."

I asked him how Jenkins was, but the line was dead.

I stood there for a moment and saw the faded edges of the pages on the walls curling down, almost bowing. Without reading, I could make out every word on every page.

To no purpose. I had saved no one, avenged no one and possibly killed one more innocent.

My girls' faces seemed to glow. Forgiveness? Sorrow? Condemnation? They didn't say.

The voice in my head said plenty. I was reaching the point where I was ready to do anything to shut it up.

I drove downtown and walked up to the captain's office. Head down, ignoring the looks I thought I saw.

Clarity. Unwanted today, but there it was.

The captain was in his office, dressed in jeans and a work shirt, packing things in boxes. He was giving me the broken-hearted look cops get when they have to deal with the terrible consequences of someone fucking up for the millionth time.

"I told you, conference room," he said.

I didn't move. "Jenkins?"

Same look. "Alive. Looks like he's going to stay that way and recover." Long pause. "No thanks to you. Us."

I could feel my eyes growing wet and longed for a distraction. "You've left all the pictures on the wall with you and governors and mayors."

"They can stay here."

"Only one I can see that you took with you is the one with you fishing with your son."

The look told me that I didn't have a right to this conversation.

He said, "Conference room."

I went in and looked for a corner to stand in. He followed me.

"I assume you've seen the TV news."

"No. I couldn't... No."

"Relax. You came out of it smelling like a rose. TV girl didn't want to blame the Huggy Bear she had just put on the air and might want to put on again. The mayor, of course, wasn't even there according to the story."

He waited until I opened my mouth to talk, and then he talked over it.

"I'm taking the fall. Partly my choice, partly not. I'm resigning, effective the end of the month, although I'll be gone in another hour. I'm on leave until it's final, but I'll be at Lake Tuscaloosa fishing at the old Searcy place by sundown."

"Captain, no. I'm going to get on TV tonight and straighten this thing out."

He stared at me.

"I don't mean...that. I can't straighten that out. Can I talk to Jenkins? His family?"

"No, they don't want to see you or hear from you."

"I can't fix that. But I can make sure people know the truth."

"Don't fuck things up any more. The truth is it was my rodeo. I knew the correct way to do things as a cop, and I chose to go cowboy. And now I get to spend more time fishing."

The lieutenant walked in, with new captain's bars on his shoulders. The captain—the real captain—said, "I've got to go. And you have an official duty with your new captain."

He turned and walked away without looking back.

The lieu—captain handed me a piece of paper.

"As of this date, you are officially retired from the Birmingham Police Department. You will be retained as a civilian employee of the Birmingham City Public Affairs department. You will be on probation there, including a requirement to attend counseling sessions beginning tomorrow afternoon. Do not wear your uniform. Over the objections of this department, you will be allowed to call yourself 'Officer Joe,' but do not identify yourself by your rank—your former rank. And I need you to surrender your weapons and your badge."

I pulled my badge out of my pocket and set it on the table. Unclipped my gun and holster, removed the magazine and set them all on the table.

"One minute," I said. I unbuttoned my uniform shirt and folded it next to them and stood there in my underwear shirt.

He didn't make any move to stop me.

"Is everything clear?" he said.

"Everything."

Saturday morning was the first time in twenty years I had to decide what clothes to wear. No uniform. No detective suit, which seemed too much like a police uniform to wear.

In my underwear, I stood in front of my closet. Technically, I could have put on the clown suit.

It was the only thing that seemed appropriate, but I'd rather have gone out in my underwear.

Luz had always told me what to wear when I wasn't dressed for work. The only time I'd picked out my own clothes was the black suit I'd worn for the funeral. I took it down now, laid it on my bed, put on a white shirt, and pulled on the jacket.

Tried to pull on the jacket. I forgot how much I had changed. One arm went in, but the other arm opening seemed to run away from me as I twisted toward it. I was determined to make it work so I started circling like a dog chasing its tail until I got the other arm in. Pushed my arm through and heard a small tearing sound in the back. It wouldn't button and I felt like monkeys were yanking my arms back. But it was on.

Picked up the pants. By sitting on the bed and working one leg at a time, I was able to pull them on. Sort of.

I stood up, threaded my current uniform belt through and brought it around. The belt snapped, but the zipper wouldn't begin to close. I peeled them off—tearing them in the process—and put on a pair of gray sweatpants with the black jacket and white shirt, and called it victory.

I decided a tie was too much.

I looked at my watch. Still an hour to go before my first counseling session. I told myself I didn't know where I was going to go in that hour but I did.

I stood in front of Luz and Sarah.

"I almost killed a man," I said. "A fellow officer. I have come within an inch of joining the company of killers myself. Again."

I could feel my eyes getting moist. Stop it, you fat fuck. Jenkins' wife has a right to cry. The girls you've put back in harm's way have a right to cry. You don't.

I looked into my wife"s eyes and wanted far more help than the dead could ever give.

"Please, Luz. Make it not be real."

The receptionist at the municipal counseling center pointed at me with a pencil. "This is your first time here? You're meeting your therapist, a guy who came in on a Saturday, dragged me in, too, to give you his professional help and you want to dress like that? I mean, he's probably the guy determine when you get to go back on the force."

I started to tell her how cold hell would be before that happened but didn't. "I was trying to put on a black suit. Be respectful. Decided against the pants." Didn't say why.

She sighed and went back to her magazine. "Fashion."

I wasn't sure what that meant, so I took a seat and counted ceiling tiles. After a few minutes, a door behind the receptionist opened and a small light-skinned black man with eyebrows like question marks stepped out.

He looked at the only guy in the waiting room and said, "Detective Bro..." Hesitated like he couldn't pronounce the name.

"Bro-set," I said.

He gave me a grave, sympathetic nod like it was significant that I could pronounce my own name. Maybe it was.

I followed him in. He sat in a big easy chair with a notepad on the arm. I took a seat on the couch opposite him, and waited for him to speak.

After a minute, I gave up and said, "So this is what we do?"

"If you like. The time is yours."

"How much time do we have?"

He smiled, stood up and walked over to a shelf, reached into a box and took out a small rubber ball with a globe printed on it and handed it to me.

"You have all the time in the world," he said.

I tried to hand the ball back to him, but he shook his head.

"My gift to you. All the time in the world, here in this safe space."

"We're here all day?"

"No. Your session ends at 11:50. It's a metaphor."

He sat down and scribbled in his pad. Looked up and studied the wall behind me, then gave me an intentional smile. It seemed to trouble him that I didn't comprehend the gift. I sat there.

And he sat there.

After a few minutes, I said, "So, are we supposed to talk about something?"

"Do you want to talk about something?"

"No. Yeah. No, I'm not ready to talk about what happened yesterday. But there is something I do want to talk about. Do you remember a guy a few years ago called himself the Angel of Mercy?"

He nodded gravely. "The Angel of Mercy."

"You remember him?"

"What I remember here does not matter. What do you remember?"

"Well." I was starting to get the rhythm of talking to this guy. "He killed a number of children. I was the lead on the case and we never caught him. Maybe you can help me understand him. We had profilers and forensic psychologists out the wazoo, but I never really got him."

He leaned forward and nodded. "You didn't understand."

"No. He was killing children to free them of this world and send them on to the next before they became corrupt."

He nodded and made a note.

"I mean, I get part of it. I think sometimes that I'm the one guy on earth who understands what a burden life can be."

He leaned back and put his fingers together in a church steeple.

"Life," he said, "can be a burden."

"Yeah. Right. Thanks for the insight. But you can't just put it down. Not without some kind of—I don't know— permission. And you sure can't take it from someone else, particularly not from kids, for Christ's sake. They got their whole lives ahead of them. Maybe to fuck it up, but maybe not."

I paused. "So maybe you can use your skills to help me understand this guy. How can you take an idea that's almost right, and turn it into something so horribly wrong? See yourself as a savior when you're a killer? What's missing in this guy?"

He looked grave. "Isn't that the question we all have, what's missing? What do you think?"

"I don't know. Life, I guess. I mean, that's what I always thought Christ was talking about: life, how to live it, whether you feel like living at the moment or not. No matter how bad you fuck up. I thought that was what all the religions are talking about. What comes after life—whether it's heaven or reincarnation or whatever—it's kind of the tail of the dog, not the dog." I gave a nervous laugh. "What the fuck do I know?"

"What do any of us really know?"

"I know it seems like maybe this guy kept the religion and threw away the life, kind of like throwing away the baby with the bathwater. But that doesn't help me."

"Sometimes, it seems like nothing helps." He wrote another note.

"No, it doesn't. I don't even know if the Angel is real anymore. Maybe I've been wasting my life, like everything has telescoped down to one little photograph and I'm looking at the world through it and knowing that what it shows is the only thing I really want to be real again and knowing that picture is the one thing that truly shows me how real the loss was and how big my fuck-up was. Is. And you pray and you pray, and all you want to do is join dead people, and all this guy wants is to change living people into dead and maybe he's not even real anymore and I'm only imagining him and using him as an excuse to keep screwing up and all I can do is talk and talk and what the hell does anything even mean?"

There was a small ding. He stood up and smiled.

"Well, that's all our time for today."

I was sitting on the sidewalk, leaning against Johnson's dirty wall, asleep, when Capulet shook me awake.

"That's some sight," she said.

I looked down. Somebody had left me a dollar and some change, plus a pamphlet with directions on how to find Jesus.

"You think Wendy will pay me for the free advertising I'm giving her?" I said.

"Wendy's idea of advertising is a big sign saying, 'Stay the Fuck Away.' So, yes, I think you qualify today. C'mon." She reached down and took my hand to pull me up.

"Who do you think you're kidding with that?"

Her mouth tightened into a straight line and she braced herself and yanked me up with one quick pull.

I rubbed my shoulder. "Jesus. You almost pulled my arm out of its socket."

"Consider it a warning."

She took two steps toward home, looked back and saw I was still standing there rubbing my shoulder. "You don't have any business in Johnson's tonight. C'mon."

When I kept standing there, she said, "Want to have two sore arms?"

I followed her home, walked inside and started to head toward the war room.

"We're not going in there either." She pushed me down into my reading chair, handed me the TV remote and said, "Amuse yourself somehow. I'm cooking. You don't need to be alone tonight."

I started to tell her no, and thank her. But no words came out.

She went to her car and brought in a couple of grocery bags while I sat there staring at the blank screen.

I followed her into the kitchen.

"Eggplant, ground beef, red wine—moussaka?" I said.

"Yeah. You and Luz ever get to Greece in your culinary world travels?"

"Yeah. Early. Often. One of our favorites."

I pulled a prep knife out of the knife block, flipped it and caught it.

"Hey," she said. "Don't know if I can trust you with anything sharp tonight. I heard about what happened at police HQ."

"I'm not suicidal. Probably should be. The wife of the officer I almost killed must be wishing I'd been suicidal a couple of days ago." I flipped the knife again. "I'll take it out on an innocent eggplant."

I flipped a cutting board down beside the sink and took the eggplant out of her hand. Rinsed it, chopped a slice and showed it to her.

"Thinner? Thicker?"

"A little thicker. You're pretty good with that knife."

"I was always the prep chef; Luz the boss. Tell me what you need."

It was the first time I'd done any work in the kitchen in a long time. It felt good and bad at the same time, like scar tissue ripping free.

Vegetables chopped, beef seasoned and browned, béchamel sauce perfected. We stacked the ingredients in the oven and waited at the kitchen table.

She opened a bottle of red wine and set it on the table between two glasses. "Supposed to let this stuff breath for half-an-hour."

We both laughed. She poured two glasses and we each finished in one swallow. I noticed the array on the counter.

"Three bottles?" I said.

"Those are for me." She paused. "I don't figure either of us is the talking kind."

"No," I said. "Well, I don't know what I am anymore. I used to be the strong, silent type. Now I'm the strong, silent type who's a mountain of flab babbling uncontrollably all the time. Don't know how to talk when I want to; don't know how to shut up when I need to."

"Yeah," she said. "I used to be good with talking but...I don't know." She poured herself another glass. "Maybe I can get good with enough of this."

She downed half the glass and looked at me. "I know it probably doesn't help you, but half of that guilt over the Jenkins boy should be mine. I pushed you into that."

"No. A lot of things pushed me, but I went there on my own. I don't know what to say. Not to the Jenkins. Not to the captain. Ex-Captain. Even you."

We sat there and she finished another glass. I looked at mine and saw that it was untouched.

I stood up. "Let me show you something."

We took our glasses and went down the hall. I opened the door to Sarah's room and invited her in. "This my daughter's—"

She looked at the pink ponies. "I know what it is."

I frowned. "You don't understand."

"The fuck I don't. Little girl lost. Every woman feels it; a place in your heart that looks like this and you wonder where the hell your own life went. Sad, but a beautiful little place in your heart. Your daughter never got to have that nostalgia or all the great days in between, either. And you were the one who promised to protect her. Yeah, I bet that sucks big-time. You know what I admire about you? You've been beat down. And you blame yourself, which is like a double-beating. Now it's gotten so much worse that we'd need a new math to figure what to call it. And everything in your heart tells you to wallow in it and do nothing.

"Look at this house. It's a monument to fucking self-pity. And look at what you've done to yourself? Every pound on you cries out for people to feel sorry for you."

"No shit, Sherlock," I yelled at her. "What the fuck am I supposed to do? This is all I've got for a life, no matter how much I pray that it isn't real. I can try to drink it away. I can try to joke it away. Or—"

"Or you can do what you've been doing, and channel all that pain and self-loathing into something worth your whole life. Work to stop someone who's robbing life from the people who do still care about it."

"Tell the family of Officer Jenkins."

"Yeah. I would. You think they're sitting around hating you because a fuck-up shot their father or their husband? No. Well, maybe some. But I bet they're proud that he was trying to protect the very girl that shot him."

She took my face in her hands and I could feel how hot they were.

"Look, we fucked up. *We* fucked up. Not just you. I pushed you. Holt pushed you, pushed you and now she won't even answer my calls. The captain fucked up. He could have dug his heels in and checked things a little more. The news people, the mayor—hell, even the cop who said the room was clear—we all fucked up. Fucked up, and we're left here to deal with it."

I reached up to her hands and realized I didn't want to push them away. "So what?" I said. "I can kick myself, feel sorry for myself, or go on. You know what? Luz can't. Sarah can't. And I almost made sure Jenkins couldn't feel sorry for himself, either."

She started to pull her hands away, but I wouldn't let them go. "I'm done," I said. "Done with it all. They were right. The Angel's gone. I don't know where, but I'm not getting anyone else in the line of fire so I can exorcise a ghost. I'll sit in my chair here and my barstool at Johnson's, and eat and drink myself to death. Worse ways to go."

I could feel my tears running over her hands. She didn't back away. "Look. It's tough out here without love. But a great poet—W.H. Auden—once said, 'Thousands have lived without love, but not one without water.' Give somebody some water."

"I don't know if I have any water to give."

She reached up, brushed the tears on my cheek away and showed the tears to me. "You have more water than anyone I've ever known." She pulled my face down and kissed me.

It felt like a dam breaking. I held on to her and pushed her out into the hall—not Sarah's room, not Luz's. I kissed her a little harder than I meant to and we stood there kissing and crying.

It was different from anything I'd ever felt with my wife. Luz was tiny and athletic and sexy, and lovemaking was a burning and a quenching. This didn't feel like sex but simply touching on a scale fantastically large and deep. I'm sure the sight would have horrified anyone looking in the window, but I was grateful that there was so much of her to touch, and all of it was lush and hungry and that she made little chuckles with every new spot I touched. And every spot she touched on me felt like the desert blooming when it had finally found the rain.

fifty-one

When the sun came in the window the next morning, I lay in bed and wondered what it all meant. A new day was coming up and there was a naked woman in my bed.

It looked like a movie scene for rebirth of the hero.

It wasn't.

My life since Luz seemed like one long fuck-up, which I could neither avoid nor control, interrupted occasionally by bad jokes and worse sob sessions.

And grand what-the-fuck moments.

Like this one.

I lay there for a long minute trying to think of the best way to get out of bed without waking Capulet. Folding the covers down, I lifted one leg and swung it over the bed. Swiveled on my butt, feeling like an old Ray Harryhausen stop-action movie with the Claymation monster slowly and terribly coming to life.

I stood there feeling ridiculous and naked. I looked at Capulet to see if she was still asleep. No movement, at least for now.

I tip-toed to the closet to grab anything, pulled out a uniform from habit and then remembered why I didn't want that. Put it back. I hadn't bought any clothes in the last year. My sweats lay on the floor dirty. The only pants that still fit were the clown pants, bright blue with a long white stripe down the sides.

Why the hell not.

On a hanger was a Hawaiian shirt that had once felt like an enormous flapping tent.

I showered as fast and quietly as I could, dressed, and looked in the mirror. I looked as ridiculous as I had when I was naked, but at least I wouldn't be arrested.

I peeked in before I left and was surprised at how beautiful Capulet seemed to me lying there. Not *Vogue* or *Playboy* or even Reubens beautiful, but beautiful all the same. The curves and the softness, the slow rise and fall of undisguised flesh with each breath. Even the wrinkles and sags looked like awards for a lifetime of living.

I walked out to my car and eased out of the driveway.

The clerk at BPD headquarters never gave me a second look. She got the forms I requested without comment. When I handed them back, she wiped the Monday-morning tiredness out of her eyes and said, "They ain't going to accept that without a social security number."

"Send it in. They can figure it out."

She shrugged and put it in a basket.

I went back to the car and stopped at a diner for two breakfasts to take home. I was pulling into my driveway when the rattlesnake clattered.

"Detective Brosette?" the voice said.

"Mister. Better yet, Joe. How can I help you, Miss?"

"Mrs. Jenkins."

I sucked in air and felt my head pull back to my shoulders like a turtle trying to hide in its shell.

"I'm...I'm sorry, Mrs. Jenkins. I'm so sorry. I know you don't want to talk to me now, but—"

" Why do you think that? I've been calling around trying to get your number. Then a clerk from headquarters called me for my social security number and she gave me your cell."

"To verify the insurance thing? Please, I hope you'll take it."

"No. I mean, thank you for that. I talked with Ron about it. He'd be honored. We'd be honored. I mean, in the hopefully-unlikely-event that something happens to you someday, our girls will have money for college."

"I really don't have anyone left for my life insurance. I heard that Officer Jenkins has a couple of kids. And I figured that was the least I owe him after putting him in harm's way with my fuck-up."

"Owe him? Ron was thrilled to be there. He admires you. A lot of the young officers do. You're kind of a ghost story for them, the guy who wouldn't quit, even when the department did. He called me before the raid. He wasn't supposed to, but he did, all excited. He said you were finally going to get the real Angel, and he was going to be there. The insurance isn't why I wanted to call you. I mean, thanks but, no. Every time Ron wakes up he asks if I called you yet."

I didn't say anything. Despite her kindness, there were still a lot of things Jenkins might want to say that I didn't want to hear. Deserved to hear, but wasn't ready for.

Finally, she said, "Ron wants you to know what he was trying to say to you at the Fouch house."

Now I really didn't want to hear it.

She said, "He had one word for you, sir." She paused. "Proud."

The house was quiet and empty when I got back. I set the food down on the breakfast table. The bed was made up and there was a piece of paper on my pillow. I picked it up.

The writing was shaky. "Hey, no big deal. Thanks for the quick fuck. See you later, if you need me. No big deal. A mercy fuck for the fat chick. I get it. All good. J."

Jesus. I can't even make love with someone without making them feel like crap. There should be a warning sign taped to my forehead: Danger. Stay away.

Where do people like Capulet and me go when we're hurt?

I ignored the food I had picked up, and walked up to Waffle House.

Capulet was sitting in a booth by herself, taking big bites and crying. I slid in and smiled as warmly as I could.

"Hey. Got room for a..." I couldn't come up with the right word. I hesitated too long and she laughed.

"Yeah. Whatever."

"*Whatever* can be good enough sometimes."

We sat there in silence for a long moment.

"I mean, Capulet, I don't know what...I guess, I want to say it was good for me."

A snort. "Now you going to ask me if I came?" She paused. "Yeah. Twice. First time in my life. I mean...with somebody. Believe it or not."

I started to say something, but she stopped me.

"I don't need your fucking sympathy. Don't talk to me."

"It's not—"

The waitress interrupted me. "Didn't you hear the lady? She doesn't want to hear from you. Jesus, what's wrong with you men?"

"No, look, can I get something to eat?"

She turned to Capulet. "You want him to eat somewhere else?"

Capulet said, "No, he can stay."

I ordered a cheeseburger and pie, and she went away. We just sat for a while.

"It was the truth," she finally said. "Fifty-year-old virgin. At least orgasmically."

I'd never had to figure out what to say to an orgasmic virgin.

I said, "1968 Model. Runs good, body rough."

She didn't laugh. "I know."

"Really," I said. "I meant it as a compliment. For what it's worth, I'm a couple of years older."

The waitress slammed a plate down in front of me. I looked at a salad with low-fat dressing.

"No. I ordered...This is..." I saw the look on her face. "...perfect."

She stalked away and Capulet said, "Be glad they don't throw people out of Waffle Houses."

"Yeah." I picked up a fork and ate. Like I was going to send the wrong food back.

"It's just..." she said.

I put down my fork and looked her in the eye.

"I don't know what I was expecting. Or what to do now. Should I fade away?"

"No."

"Are we still chasing the Angel?"

"No."

She leaned across. "So, what are we doing?"

I thought about it. "I think you said it best: whatever."

She thought about it. Opened her mouth to talk, but the rattlesnake clattered.

I pulled the phone out of my pocket and Capulet said, "Really? I'm pouring my heart out here and you think it's more important to find out that you didn't win the Publisher's Sweepstakes?"

I didn't recognize the number and didn't want to miss it. Maybe it was Mrs. Jenkins or someone in BPD needing to click a box on a form to make the insurance happen.

"Sorry. I've got to take this."

She turned sideways in the booth and pouted. "Tell the Dean of Clown School you don't need any more lessons." Pulled her plate over so she could eat while looking out the window and away from me.

"Det... Brosette," I said.

"I'm hurt that you haven't found my present yet."

I thought about hanging up.

I said, "Who the fuck is this?"

"You know who this is."

"Jesus Fucking Christ."

I heard him cackle and realized he was getting off on this.

I tried the calmest voice I had. "Look, pal. I know who you're not. You're not the Angel of Mercy. He's gone. Been gone. You're a fraud. Worse, you're a fraud of a fraud. Even when he was here, he was a fraud. Even when he was around, he killed for his own sick reasons, and tried to cover up the reasons even from himself."

The voice said, "Spare me the cheap psycho-babble. Like my daddy used to say, 'I've been called worse by better.' You know who I am. Pretending won't help."

"No. You're right. I've been pretending, and you've been propping that up. I'm moving on. You should too, pal. At least find somebody better to imitate. Mother Teresa, any number of real saints from the real religion you claim to believe in."

"Yeah. And how many kids did Mother Teresa save? Really save. I don't mean the ones she kept alive for a day or a year before they wound up back in a hellhole for one lifetime, doing things that would put them in a real hell for longer, longer, longer..." He kept repeating "longer" over and over until he got tired of it. "...longer than I can ever say. You, Detective—all of you are the frauds, famous frauds like Mother Teresa, cheap, sad, frauds like you. You can't save them all. You can't." He paused. "You couldn't even save two of your own."

It was getting harder to stay calm. "Listen to me, pal." I could hear myself grinding 'pal' into an epithet and tried to lower my voice. "You want to know what your idol saved them from? The Angel of Mercy saved them from heaven."

He laugh-snorted and tried to talk, but I talked over him.

"No, not your heaven where all good dogs go when they die. Real heaven. The heaven they would have made. Every day when I came home, Luz made me a little slice of heaven. Every time I hugged Sarah or saw her kick a soccer ball, I got a little slice of heaven.

"People like you twist a couple of Bible verses and want to talk like heaven is some cheap reward for going to church and avoiding the real world, and that you can tell people how to get there. You're full of shit. Heaven's something that people like Luz and Sarah built. Every day. While they were alive.

"I don't know what happens when you die, any more than you or the real Angel do. Did. I pray every night that it's a place where I'll see my girls, but who the fuck knows? I do know this, wherever they are now, when they were here, they were here every fucking minute. The Angel didn't rob them of the chance to fuck up, he robbed them of the chance to live."

I could hear the irritation in his voice. "You need to read your Bible. Read your Bible and thank me. Thank me for all the sins I saved your precious girls from."

"You didn't do shit. You're a poor, sick fuck trading on other people's pain. I'm hanging up and hoping you get some help."

"Didn't do...anything? You think I don't know anything? Listen to this, Joe. I know your taste in women has gone way downhill lately. Something else. Your wife was wearing a blue dress. A Mediterranean-Indian thing, cotton with a batik print."

I'd bought that dress for Luz at a craft fair.

"Shut the fuck up, will you? You read that in the paper, maybe, or found it on the Internet or I don't care where the fuck you found it. You're not real. I'm hanging up."

I pulled the phone away from my ear, but not far enough for me not to hear.

"You guys held that detail back, and you know it. Want to know a detail even you don't know? The last thing she did before she died, when she was watching her daughter dying and covered in blood and twisting, but not for long?"

I should have hung up the phone. I didn't.

"She prayed for me. As I put the knife in her breast, she prayed for me."

I was standing up and screaming now.

"You're not fucking real. You're not fucking real."

Just so you know, you can get thrown out of a Waffle House.

fifty-three

We stood on the sidewalk. Capulet looked at me and said, "We need to get you some fucking pants. And a shirt, even."

Neither one of us was sure of what our walking etiquette should be. There was one point where the sidewalk widened and I caught up with her, leaving us side-by-side. I glanced down and thought her hand was searching for mine. Keeping in stride and looking straight ahead, I tried to give her my hand. But as soon as skin touched skin, she jumped away a foot and quick-stepped in front of me.

Walking like this made conversation awkward, which was probably good. Had we been able to talk, that conversation might have been even more awkward.

As it was, the few words were mostly misconnections.

She threw back a few words over her shoulder, and I caught up to her.

"What's that?" I said.

Long pause while she rewrote whatever it was she had said. "I said, 'Nice weather.'"

I looked at the sky. "Hadn't noticed."

She said, "Hmmmph," and walked away.

We were walking home to pick up my car. There was a little alley that nobody but me used. As we came up to it,

Capulet stopped. "Look, I know we're intentionally not talking about last night. Whatever."

"OK," I said, "I guess—"

"No. If you're not mature enough to discuss adult matters, let's talk about the Angel and where he's gone."

"Well, my guess would be—wait, you're saying talking about a serial killer of children is easier than talking about our..."

She waited to hear my word for what we were and I stayed silent, knowing this wouldn't go well. But she waited me out and I finally said, "Our last night."

She went "Mmmph."

I walked past her into the alley. She shoved me into a brick wall and took the lead.

"That's all it was to you?" she said. "Just a night? Like, 'Oh, what to do on this night? Maybe watch TV. Maybe go drinking. Maybe fuck a vulnerable young...'"

She stopped short and I crashed into her, we both almost fell and I scraped my head against the brick.

"What the fuck is wrong with you..."

I looked at her face and saw her eyes were wide, one hand over her mouth. The other was pointing down the alley.

I looked. The alley was as deep a gray as the Birmingham sun would allow. There was one circle of bright sun shining into the dirt and filth.

In that circle was a young girl in a clean white dress, glowing in the sun and lying on her back.

With her arms thrown wide.

fifty-four

Pushing Capulet against the wall, I reached to draw my pistol and came up with a handful of baggy satin pants.

Capulet said, "She's—"

"Shh," I said. "Stay. Step back into the street, there, and call 911."

I eased by her as well as I could, trying to shake the feeling that someone was drawing a bead on me. I forced myself to look at anything but the girl and moved down the alley, back pressed to the wall. The space was only two buildings long, with no gap on the right where the buildings shared a common wall. The left side had a gap between the coffee shop and a small house behind it.

I stayed on the right and scooted along with my back to the brick, my eyes on the gap. The body was just before the gap, diagonally in the alley, more like a diamond than a cross. I paused when I was even with her, my feet no more than a foot away, and tried to study her without taking my eyes off the opening or the other end of the alley. I squatted down, knees popping with more noise than I would have liked.

Still trying to keep my attention unfocused and open, I reached a hand out until I touched her neck.

Cold and still, with no sign of a pulse.

I let my hand linger for a moment. When I pulled back, the fingertips that had touched her felt permanently scarred, like fingers pressed on a stove until the fingerprints had burned to a vague nothing.

I took my scarred fingers and wrapped them around a brick for a weapon and stood up. Eased down one more step and studied the opening into the alley. Empty and clean.

I walked back to Capulet and took the phone out of her hand.

"This is," I hesitated. What the hell. "...Detective Brosette of the Birmingham Police Department. I need you to connect me with the Southside Investigation Department." I gave her the number, and turned to scan the street. After a moment, the lieutenant-captain answered.

"Brosette, I thought I made it clear that you are no longer a detective."

"Yes, sir, you did."

"And I think I made it clear that we are no longer interested in your tin-foil fantasies, or, for that matter, anything you might have to say."

"Yes, sir, you did."

I waited him out.

"Then why are you impersonating an officer and calling this number?"

"We have a dead child. White dress."

I stood watching the street as blue lights moved toward us. Capulet disappeared for a moment and then I felt her coming up behind me.

"Where'd you go?" I said.

"Prayed over the girl."

"Stay away. Don't contaminate the crime scene."

The black-and-white stopped in front of us, blocking the alley and a middle-aged officer got out.

"I'm Joe Brosette," I said. "We discovered the body and called it in."

He nodded. "You're Detective Brosette?"

"Not now. You have to treat us both as civilians. Even possible suspects."

He shrugged. "Have it your way." He nodded to his partner, a young kid. "Get their preliminary statements."

Another car pulled up and the middle-aged cop motioned for the two officers to help him secure the alley.

The young cop said, "Sir, I need you to sit in the back of my car while I take your statement."

I nodded at Capulet. He hesitated and then said. "I guess she can sit with us."

I raised an eyebrow at him.

He said, "Maybe she should sit in the other car while we talk."

"Maybe she should."

"I'm trying to make it easier on you, sir."

"Don't."

I was still in the back of the car, after I'd given my statement, alone, when I saw the unmarked car pull up and Vinzini get out.

He walked up to the window on my side. I tapped on it for the patrolman to let me out and he took a step toward the door before Vinzini nodded, no, and the patrolman backed away.

I twisted toward the car Capulet was in, but all I could see was the back of her head. Still talking to a patrolman, or, rather, giving him hell, arms waving at the front seat. She probably could tell, even from the back seat, that he had missed a comma in his report.

I watched the inflow of personnel: coroner, techs, more detectives. Regardless of what I thought of him before, Vinzini ran the scene right, keeping everybody possible out as long as he could, sequencing the order of people into the area like a ballet. He might be a prick, but he was a good cop.

He hit a point where he'd seen all he needed to see for now. Put another detective in charge of the scene, and walked over to me. The patrolman handed him my statement and he leaned against the wall reading it. Motioned for another patrolman who brought him another clipboard and he read that, then flipped back and forth between them. Finally straightened up, cracked his back a couple of times and sauntered around to me. The patrolman stepped up and opened my door. I thought he was going to kick me out, but Vinzini motioned me to slide over. He took the seat next to me, reached back and closed the door.

He waved my statement in the air. "This about it?"

"About. You guys got anything other than what you see?"

He looked at me, dead-eyed. "What is it you think we see?"

"I see that you've kept me locked up in here long enough. Maybe you've found someone else who saw something, video camera maybe. Anything."

He looked at me for a long time.

"So, this statement is complete and accurate to the best of your recollection?"

"Yes."

"You're not a cop anymore, so you're not entitled to a department rep for questioning."

He tapped on the window and the officer let him out. Just before he closed the door, he leaned in and said, "Mr. Brosette, we don't need to talk further until I've confirmed something."

I knew the technique. Let the interviewee sweat.

After a few minutes, he slid back in. "I called in to verify what I said, that your status as a non-police city employee doesn't qualify you to a department rep. It doesn't. You are aware, of course, you are entitled to a lawyer if you wish."

"Yeah. Or I could call the Pope."

He seemed to contemplate several answers before he settled on, "Yes, you could."

He flipped through my statement.

"So, about 10:45?"

This time, I played the silent game and forced him to explain.

"When you say the body was discovered?"

"About. You should be able to bracket it from the time we left the Waffle House until the time I called it in."

He flipped back and forth between the reports.

"You didn't call it in. Ms. Capulet did."

"This is true."

"And we have someone checking at the Waffle House to corroborate your story."

"Well," I said. "There's something you should know. The Waffle House asked us to leave because I got a little loud."

He turned his head toward me for a long moment, then flipped to a blank page at the back of my report. Made a show of reaching into his pocket for a pen and wrote something in the report.

"So, you were involved in an altercation at the Waffle House prior to walking out?"

I hesitated. "Well, I was shouting at the phone. It wasn't an altercation."

He nodded, straightened up and cracked his back again in a bored motion before writing something down on the clipboard.

"Was there a reason you were shouting at the phone?"

"Yes."

He waited for me to elaborate, and I didn't. He looked back down, a bored bureaucrat filling out a mildly boring report.

"Can you tell me who you were shouting at on the phone?"

I hesitated, sighed, and decided there was no point in sugar-coating this.

"The killer."

He looked up that time.

fifty-six

"This ought to be good," Vinzini said.

"The person who claims to be the Angel of Mercy called my cell while I was in the Waffle House."

He seemed to contemplate several comments to that before he got to: "The Angel of Mercy that you shot and killed?"

"No. The real one. Or maybe not. I thought it was a fake, but somebody killed this girl."

He stared at me some more. "OK."

"The captain—the old one—convinced me it was some sick wacko pretending to be the Angel. But it was the real one."

"Captain Jordan was in the Waffle House with you?"

"No, of course not. That was earlier."

"Yeah."

I relayed the conversation. He took notes. A time or two he asked me to slow down so he didn't miss anything.

I finished. He asked me to repeat, I did, and he wrote it all again. He put the pen down and looked at me.

"So, you're telling me the killer called you and essentially told you, 'I killed someone. Why don't you go outside and stumble over the body?'"

"No, he didn't—he gloated and then we found the body."

"Placed where he knew you would find it?"

"Apparently."

"So, the Angel knew you were in the Waffle House?"

I thought about it. "Not that I know of."

He wrote that too.

He studied what he had written to be sure he had it right before he spoke again. "Brosette, you sure you want to stick with that?"

I said, "Yeah. I get it. Either I've been in communication with the killer right before finding a body he left, or I've been in communication with a crank who knew where to find the body even though he was a fake. Either way, I can't prove what was said on the phone, and I'm tied to the body."

He looked at me for what felt like an hour. "Or." He let the word hang in the air. "You got an unrelated phone call, and you're trying to use it to cover up your involvement in the crime."

We stared at each other for a long, long time.

Finally, he picked up the two statements and seemed to weigh them.

"Your girl..." He struggled for the right word. "Ms. Capulet's statement corroborates that you yelled at someone on the phone."

"Well, that's something," I said.

"In fact, her statement matches yours closely. Very, very closely. You sure you two didn't discuss your stories before we arrived?"

"No time. First responder was here right after I got off the phone."

He made a note and said, "Efficient Birmingham PD. We need to get you to talk to your friendly reporter who ran the story claiming that it takes us thirty minutes to get to a call."

He looked at me and I said nothing. He stacked my report on top of Capulet's.

"Well, I've got work to do."

He tapped on the door and the patrolman opened it.

Vinzini got out and then leaned back in. "Oh. There was one thing to clear up. 'Bout the only difference in the two reports. You said the victim's arms were out perpendicular to her body. Ms. Capulet didn't mention it."

"She didn't need to. That was one of the Angel's trademarks, posing the body with the arms out."

He nodded.

"You're sure her arms were out?"

"Perpendicular. Ninety degrees. Like all the Angel's victims."

He nodded again. I started to scoot toward the door to get out and he pushed me back in and said,

"Except, in this case, the victim's arms were at her side."

fifty-seven

Vinzini finally motioned me out of the back of the car. I saw Capulet being let out of the other car and coming our way. Vinzini motioned us over to a bench at a bus stop across the street.

"Go sit over there," he said. He motioned at Capulet. "Both of you. Don't discuss the case."

All I wanted was one little question for Capulet, but I wanted it bad. Capulet walked up to us with her mouth open like she was ready to say something, too. I shook my head, no, and started to walk across the street with her.

At my back, I heard Vinzini say, "Officer Hemingway, you sure got saddled with the wrong name. This report is a mess. Grammatical errors everywhere. I want you to go through this thing with a fine-tooth comb and clean this mess up. Go sit over on that bench with these two while you do it. Don't move your ass off that bench until I call you."

Capulet led the way across the street with her head up. The patrolman with his homework to be corrected followed, and I pulled up the rear. We got to the bench and Capulet occupied the middle. I took one side and the poor young cop squeezed into the other end. She scooted to give him more room and I felt the two of us joined hip-to-knee in an awareness of her body I hadn't felt for, oh, several hours.

I didn't say any of the things I desperately wanted to.

"Well," said Capulet. The kid hesitated with his pen in mid-air above the clipboard and both he and I leaned in toward her. "I guess we're not going to talk about what's really on our minds here."

The kid flipped his report to a blank page at the end and wrote something down.

"No," I said. I reached up to take my notebook out of my jacket pocket to make some notes while things were fresh. Patted my chest and remembered that I had no pad, no jacket.

I tried to think of a way to talk to Capulet about the girl's arms without involving the kid and came up with a list of silly suggestions but nothing that would work.

"How 'bout them Braves?" I said to the young officer, and laughed. By myself.

Capulet made a face, but the kid brightened. "Yeah. Wasn't that a boneheaded play last night? Biggest mistake you've ever seen?"

Capulet and I sat still, refusing to say anything that might be misinterpreted. Or interpreted correctly, for that matter.

But I thought I had an opening.

"Yeah, but, you know, I'm wondering more about what the Braves are doing this morning? Like, does the team get together and do something really, really stupid? Like decide to change something that absolutely, positively should not have been touched?" I looked at Capulet. "Did they do that?

I mean change something that really shouldn't have been touched, in response to the really horrible thing that had happened?"

The kid seemed a little confused, but he said, "Yeah, I guess so. The Braves might overreact to one bad play."

He didn't write anything down so I thought maybe we were OK.

"What do you think, Capulet? Why would they do something completely stupid like change something they shouldn't touch?"

Her eyes watered. "You mean like last night? You think that was stupid?"

The kid said, "Oh, hell yeah. That was—"

"No," I said. "I'm not talking about last night. That was the players trying to do their best."

"Best?" said the kid. "Jones threw to the wrong base. Boneheaded mistake."

"No," Capulet and I said in unison. "It wasn't."

The kid sighed and looked back at his clipboard.

"I'm talking about this morning. Maybe the Braves are evaluating that play, trying to make things right. Maybe they decide to change something that shouldn't have been changed. Maybe they do something stupid this morning. What do you think, Capulet? Why would somebody do something really stupid this morning?" I looked at the cop and hoped I could stretch this. "You know, go into the bullpen. Change a couple of arms that didn't need changing."

She got it and shot me a look. "I don't think changing arms was stupid. Maybe they did something good."

"Good? How the hell do you think..."

I saw the kid looking at us rather than his clipboard, and I shut up. I made little growling noises as words kept falling from my brain to my tongue and I strangled them before they got out.

I looked across the street and saw a sergeant wave over at the kid on the bench. As soon as he hit the street, Capulet hissed at me.

"I put that sweet child's arms down because I did not want the world to see her that way. I didn't want the Angel of Mercy to get that satisfaction. Besides, we had already seen it."

"We?" I said. "What about BPD? What about tampering with evidence? What about..."

Her eyes were watering. "I'm not a cop. Just someone trying to do what she can. I didn't think. I should have."

I looked across the street. Vinzini was staring at us and sending the kid back to the bench at a trot.

He wedged back in, and Capulet and I sat there with our smiles.

"Well," said Capulet. "Detective Brosette here was just commenting on what a competent investigation BPD is running here. Everything by the book. As he's sure it should be."

I'd had enough.

"Yeah. They're doing everything by the book. Everyone's doing what they can. And young girls are lying cold in the dirt with sightless eyes pleading to heaven."

The kid took out his pen, but he looked like he wasn't sure what to write.

I saw Vinzini walking across the street toward us.

"A word, Mr. Brosette."

I separated myself from Capulet and stood up. Vinzini turned and walked away, and I followed him back to the squad car. He motioned me in, but stayed standing, leaning down at me, with one hand on the roof. I noticed it was his left hand. His right hovered by his hip, the lump from his gun visible through the coat within easy reach.

"So, is the girl..." He looked over at Capulet without taking his eyes off me. "...woman involved?"

"No. How could she be? The child's neck was cold when we found her." I didn't want to go further. "Do you have a preliminary time of death yet? We were at the Waffle House this morning."

He waited a long time before he answered, and I recognized the technique. Create silence and hope the other guy will fill it in. I didn't.

"We're looking at a couple of theories, trying to clear them, one by one. You've got to know that one theory involves you. Maybe you and your lady friend."

I knew the smart play was to let him do the talking, but I said, "She's not involved."

"Reading her statement, sounds like you're Robin and she's Batman." Pause. "Although I'd just as soon not imagine either of you in tights."

I laughed. Let him think I'd like to be his buddy.

"When you moved the girl's arms down, were they already getting stiff? Or still slack?"

"Never said I moved her arms."

"No. You said her arms were in a cross when you found her. They were at her side when we found her. You sure of your statement?"

"Sure. Capulet moved the arms. Thought she was helping. Not her fault."

He stared at me a long time. "Was this the story you two came up with?"

"No. It's not a story."

"And yet you didn't mention it earlier."

"I didn't know it earlier."

We waited each other out.

"Mr. Brosette—Joe, do you mind if I call you Joe?"

I shrugged.

"Joe, you and I have had our differences, but you go way back as a detective. What would you make of that? As a detective?"

I shrugged again.

He said, "I mean, every case has its anomalies, things that never add up. But it's usually a good place to start. About the only place we've got to start here. The facts are straightforward. Somebody killed the girl. No evidence to make me think she was killed here, so the body was probably moved. Maybe they dressed her, maybe she already had the dress. We'll know more when we talk to her parents. Could be random. Maybe not. No reason at this time to think that a man who was killed by BPD two years ago is the killer. You're tied to all of it. Anything stand out for you, as a detective?"

"You got a cause of death yet?"

He thought it over.

"I really shouldn't be telling you this, you know. But, since you're a cop, and I'm asking for your help, let me tell you what I know. Professional courtesy."

Professional courtesy, my ass. Probably be in the papers by evening.

"Preliminary COD is strangulation. Won't be official until the autopsy."

I didn't say anything.

He said, "Not a method the Angel of Mercy used. When he was alive."

I squirmed, but stopped when I realized the signal that sent. "Doesn't mean he didn't do it."

"No. Although, the fact that he's dead does tend to rule him out."

I didn't take the bait.

"Well, let's go back to the anomaly. I need Joe the Detective to take a look at Joe the Suspect. You with me?"

"Sure."

"So, if Joe the Suspect is involved, it's because he's so obsessed with his old case, he's willing to kill to keep it alive."

"Joe's pretty bad, if that's true."

"I don't know, Joe. You know this business. There aren't many real bad guys. Lots of sad sacks that fuck-up. Ordinary guys under so much stress that they crack. Kind of got to sympathize with them."

He was studying me as he spoke.

"So, if you look at Joe-the-suspect's last year or so, you'd expect to see him falling apart. Less and less in control of his actions. Finally reaches the point where he can't tell up from down." He paused. "Even when he's trying to do the right thing, he fucks up. You know, the kind of guy who needs help instead of punishment."

We were both silent a long time.

"If something like that's happening and our guy is really somebody trying to do the right thing, but under so much pressure that it all comes out wrong, he might want to come in before he hurts anybody else. Even if he thinks that he's not the guy here, but somebody with the right heart but who keeps screwing up, he might want to come in and unburden himself of anything he might know. That would be the heroic thing to do."

He straightened up and said to the patrolman, "Take Mr. Brosette home. And see that someone takes Ms. Capulet home."

He leaned in to me.

"Think about what I said, and get back to me. And, of course, don't leave town."

fifty-nine

Capulet and I were sitting at the bar in Johnson's, listening to Ron and Wendy rant about politics. They were on opposite sides of whatever pseudo-issue they were butchering, but their outrage level was the same, so they thought they were singing in perfect harmony. In the mirror, I saw the flash of the door opening and Wendy stopped in mid-rant.

"Boys," she said.

She reached under the bar, pulled out her shotgun and set it on the bar. In the darkness, I heard the clicks and double-clicks of hammers being pulled back and bullets chambered across the room.

I turned to the door and saw two neighborhood toughs in baggy dark clothes with their pants halfway down their asses and hoodies pulled up. As the door closed and plunged the room back into twilight, they saw her shotgun and raised their hands.

Wendy said, "I believe you boys have made a mistake."

One of them waved at me.

"Pull back your hoods,'" Wendy said.

The hoods came back. "Coltrane," I said. "Jesus, you scared everybody half to death."

"Oh yeah," he said. "I scared them."

I said, "They're with me."

More clicks as hammers were eased and safeties re-engaged.

"Let's sit down." I stood and Capulet joined me. There was an empty table on the edge of the pool of semi-light from the bar.

I said to the two, "Bud good?"

Coltrane started to order something else, then looked around. "Bud's good."

The other guy nodded and I turned back to the bar. "Wendy, can we get a couple of Buds over here?"

She snorted, "I'll pull 'em. You carry them from the bar yourself. No credit, no table service."

A voice in the dark said, "No service, period."

"Don't forget it." The shotgun hadn't budged from the bar.

I carried the beers and my drink over to the table, and Capulet followed with hers. Coltrane and his friend had wisely taken the darker side of the table.

I set the beers in front of them. "What's wrong with you, coming in here dressed like hoodlums? Lucky to be alive."

"You told me, come after dark, wear something casual."

"I meant wear something that wouldn't look like cop. Not something that would get you killed. Jesus."

"Well." He took a sip. "Not sure about your plan to meet here without anyone knowing I was talking to you. Think every eye in the place was on me."

"They won't talk to BPD. This is mostly fired and retired. Plus a few who haven't been fired yet."

He nodded. "Birmingham's finest."

"Damned straight. But don't let them hear you say it. Or BPD." I looked at the other man. "So, this is the guy."

"Yeah. Mandrake, meet Joe Brosette. Joe, Mandrake knows everything there is to know about phones."

"Good. Capulet, this is Detective Coltrane of BPD."

She reached across the table and shook his hand. "Joe's told me about you."

Mandrake said, "Let me see your phone, sir."

I fished it out and handed it to him.

"A generation old," he said, "but it still works. So, what do we need?"

"I got a call this morning. Any way this thing still has that conversation and we can replay it?"

He raised an eyebrow. "You know how these things work?"

"Not really. Until a couple of days ago, I thought an app was something you ate."

He was going through menus and stuff I had no idea the phone had. He pointed to a number.

"That's the call, right? That's the number Coltrane asked me to check out."

"Yeah."

"It's a pay phone at a convenience store off I-65. Hard to find one of these anymore. Could have been anybody. And no, the call wasn't recorded. You need to put an app— not the kind you eat—on here to do that. Easy. I can do that now. Put a button on the screen. Press it anytime, and it'll record whatever's on the phone."

"That's good. Next time, I want to be able to play it back."

"We can do that." He seemed to notice something, muttering, "Huh." He fiddled some more and said, "You ever update the OS on this phone?"

"No. Ain't broke, don't fix it. I ignore those messages asking if I want to change anything."

"Don't. There's a war out there. Hackers always finding new ways to get into phones, the software companies issuing updates as fast as they can to protect them." He glanced up at me. "This phone's been hacked."

"What's that mean?"

"Means there's stuff running on here that you know nothing about. What it does, I don't know yet." He was thumb-typing furiously. "Oh, wait a minute." More typing and grunting. "That's it. Every five minutes, this thing sends a text with its GPS coordinates." He looked up at me and grinned.

"You think that's good?"

"It is," he said, "if we can find the number it's been sending this to." More typing. He put the phone on the table and turned it around so I could read it. "That, Detective Brosette, is the phone number that's been tracking you."

He turned it back to himself and went back to work. "So, we know who did this?"

"Probably not. If they're smart enough to do this, they're probably smart enough to use a burner phone. But it's more than we had before. Looks like...Wow, this has been on here a couple of years."

"How did that happen? I never give my phone to anybody else."

"You ever get one of those messages that ask you to hit key 1 or 2 or something?"

"Sure. Everybody gets them."

"Maybe, but not everybody responds to them. Look, we're going to update your OS here, but, in the future, if you get a call from anybody you aren't sure of and you hit a key, you may be giving them permission to send all your money to Nigeria. Or to install an app like this. Or worse.

"You got to be careful. Everybody's got to be more careful. And it's going to get worse. Everything's controlled by chips now. You think it's bad for someone to take over your phone? What about when they take over your car? Or a B-1 bomber?"

I was suitably impressed. "OK. Take it off, clean it up and I'll be a good boy from now on. Give me that thing so I can record calls. And let me pay you."

He shrugged. "No big deal. The beer makes us square. But..."

"But what?"

"Well, they got apps. I got apps. I can take their app off. And they'll immediately know we're on to them. Or I can put my own app on. It will send the same texts as their app, but with one exception: I'll give you a button on your screen. You can hit it and it will freeze what it sends out, or send out a location you enter."

He looked at me.

"Let you be two places at one time."

Coltrane said, "This whole thing may be real."

I looked at him.

"No, I mean...Look, I've always admired you for not giving up, but you've got to admit the evidence is overwhelming that the guy you killed was the Angel."

I nodded. "You mean the fact that someone in the house killed my girls and the police helicopter was emphatic that no one came out of the house except for Father Carson waving a gun?"

"Yeah."

"Yeah. I've got no answer for that. Or any of the other stuff."

Mandrake left to go home. Coltrane and Capulet and I left to walk back to my house, so I could show Coltrane the war room and walk him through the cases. I looked over at him, skulking beside me in baggy black jeans and dark gray hoodie pulled up.

"Not sure I want to be seen with you," I said.

Capulet laughed. "Like he wants to be seen with us."

"Good point."

"Two freaking a.m.," she said. "Who's going to see us anyway?"

"All right," I said. "A test of your amateur detective skills, Capulet. Without looking around, tell me who's on the street besides us?"

She thought. "No one."

"Coltrane?"

"One guy—at least that's all I saw. Window shopping at the drugstore."

Capulet looked around. "Not there now. Empty street, like I said."

"Finished his window shopping," I said.

"Yeah," she said. "Two a.m. window shopping at a drugstore. Probably wondering when they're coming out with this year's aspirin."

"Yeah. Could be up to no good. Or insomnia."

Coltrane chimed in. "Anyway, not our problem. At least not yet. So, what have you got at your house on the old cases. Just a copy of the murder book?"

"That. And every news story, every letter to the editor. Transcripts from all the crazy calls that came into the hotline. Anything else I could find to throw on the walls."

"Any of it stick?"

"Not enough. Not enough to save the kid this morning."

"You can't blame yourself for that one, man."

"Of course not. The Angel warned me this was coming and I went off and busted a safe house, nearly killed a cop and ruined the career of a good man instead of saving that child. No blame there."

"You were the only one trying, man. If it turns out the Angel is still out there, you're the only one left to catch him."

Capulet stopped. "What the fuck do you mean, 'if'? Who do you think killed that child this morning?"

We stopped with her.

"I don't know..." Coltrane said. Took a breath. "OK. Let's be cold about this. BPD doesn't believe this was an Angel killing. I respect you, Joe, and I'm hanging with you on this, and the phone thing says something's up. But there's also a chance you're wrong and this is a copycat."

"Or me," I said.

Capulet waved her arms at him. "How can you ignore the evidence? Angel called Joe. White dress. Arms wide open."

Coltrane looked at her from out of his hoodie. "BPD said her arms were down."

"They were out. They don't know."

" How come they said they were down? You saying BPD is covering this up?"

"No," I said. "They were up when we found her. Down when they saw her."

"What the fuck?"

Capulet fairly shouted. "Sue me. I'm not a cop. I'm simply a good woman who didn't want her left like that. I fucked up."

Coltrane said, "So you touched the body?"

"No. I touched the child. May be a body to you, but to me she's a child. And she didn't deserve to be left like that. I'm sorry. I was a prosecutor. I know about evidence. But that was cold. This was a real child."

"Still, that's fucked up."

I said, "She's right. She's not a cop. I never should have turned my back on her. Drop it. She's doing the best she can. All of us are, and none of us are doing good enough."

We turned on my street. As we came around the corner, I saw something.

"You see that?" I said, quiet.

"Yeah," Coltrane whispered back without breaking stride. "Dark windbreaker, dark pants. Same as the drugstore cowboy. Disappeared as we came around the corner. Someone's following you, man."

"Maybe."

"Well," he said, "maybe my shoe's untied. Maybe I'm going to bend down at this car ahead and tie it. Might go back up the street a little, too, and see what I can find. You and your sidekick go on ahead. Talk loud. I'll be along in a little bit."

"Yeah," I said. "Young black guy in a hoodie skulking around a mostly white neighborhood. What can go wrong?"

sixty-one

I put all the house lights on as we waited for Coltrane and stood watching out the window while Capulet filled the house with the smell of coffee. When he showed up, I opened the door before he knocked and motioned him into the war room.

Looking around, he said, "No sign of him out there. This guy might be a pro."

"Or we're imaging things."

He gave one of those little unfunny laughs that people give. "Yeah. Like a lot of things here."

Capulet came in with three mugs on a tray. "You want this in here?"

"Yeah."

"I'm going to heat up some Dreamland's barbecue from the other night," she said. "Either of you guys want any?"

Coltrane grinned, "No Southern boy ever turns down barbecue."

Capulet tried to be correct. "Jewish Southern boys do. Muslim, even some fundamentalist Christians refuse to eat pork."

"Depends," he said. "I'm Muslim. My best friend from school is a rabbi. We get together sometimes at Dreamlands. He has to bless it as stringy tofu first though."

She looked at him and he shrugged. "Both of us see our religions as being about doing good and not about following thousand-year-old rules."

Coltrane took the mug and brushed his hood back. He scanned the whole room and went to the picture of Luz and Sarah. He stood there for a long time.

I wondered what he saw in the picture.

"Nice family," he finally said, and moved on to begin examining all the papers I had collected. He paused in the middle of the Luz and Sarah reports. "This guy wouldn't stop. Either you killed him, or he's going to kill more. Maybe has killed more."

"How can you have any doubt?" said Capulet. "There's a dead girl in your morgue, and the Angel is calling Joe."

Coltrane opened his mouth, but I spoke first.

"He's right. Lot of evidence says the Angel's dead. We need a little cop skepticism here to go with us true believers and amateur detectives."

"You're not an amateur," she said.

"I meant you. And I'm an amateur, now, too.

"Coltrane," I said, "I was watching you. Usually when someone picks up a case, they start at the beginning. You studied the walls, and started at the end and worked back. What you got?"

"How about the priest, man, the guy you...the guy that died? How thorough was BPD in going back and nailing down his connection to the other cases?"

I waved at the wall. "See for yourself, that's the reports there."

He followed my hand and flipped a few stapled pages.

"Really? That's it? He was a priest interested in kids? Knew what a communion dress was supposed to look like? A couple of his parishioners didn't like him. They said he was more of a comedian than a priest?"

"Wasn't much need for more proof. Press got the story that we had killed the Angel and ran with it. Nobody wanted to tell them they were wrong. And people wanted all this to go away."

We all heard a rattlesnake clattering from the living room.

"Jesus, what's that?"

"Phone."

I went in and picked it up. Didn't recognize the number.

"Hey, old friend."

"I'm not your fucking friend."

I punched the new "Record" button and walked back into the war room. Capulet and Coltrane saw the look on my face.

There was a laugh of triumph on the phone.

"Maybe not friends, but certainly partners."

"Hold on a second. You caught me in the bathroom." I ground the last word. "Partner."

I ripped a sheet off the wall, turned it over and put the sheet and the phone on the floor. I pulled a pen out of my pocket, wrote, "Get there," and pointed Coltrane at the phone.

He took the pen and wrote the number on the sheet. I was about to go back to the phone when I saw he was writing something else.

"Keep him talking."

I nodded and he went to the other side of the room.

"You know who this is?" said the voice.

"I know who you claim to be," I said. I saw Coltrane looking back at me and on the phone with somebody. We stood there, eye-to-eye, each talking softly into our phone so we wouldn't disturb the other. Capulet was in the middle straining to listen to both of us.

"Julie didn't convince you?"

"Who was Julie?"

He laughed. "Are you so burned out that you don't even care about the names of your victims?"

I snapped my fingers at Capulet and made a motion of writing. She took another sheet off the wall and handed me the pen and the page.

"Girl's name is Julie," I wrote. "Call Vinzini."

I said into the phone. "Not my victims. Probably not even yours."

"You know better. Your head tells you they were mine. And your heart tells you they were yours. We're partners."

I could feel, "Fuck you" coming out of my mouth and the sweat starting to pop around my eyes. Coltrane was hanging up his phone, waving a sheet of paper and mouthing "Got it" as he headed for the door.

Stay cool. In any conversation, each side wants something. The trick to keep someone talking is not to give them what they want. He wanted to talk and be taken seriously. "Yeah, pal. We're both pretty pathetic. My biggest joy these days is pretending to be a successful clown. And you're some sad bored SOB with time on his hands and nothing better to do than claim to be a famous killer. One who we both know is dead. So, yeah, pal, I really do know where you're coming from. We're kind of two old farts—I'm guessing you're old like me—that the world doesn't need, trying to pretend that we still have a reason to get up in the morning."

There was a pause while he collected his thoughts, the first time I'd heard him have to think about what to say next.

"You know better. And I know better. I know that Julie's death is tearing you apart and—"

"Yeah, you're right about that. Really, part of me wishes I were out there with the police. But I'm not. And it's not even an Angel killing. The people working the case have already told me that it's missing several elements. So, do I wish I could have saved that girl? You bet. Honestly, I bet if you could have gotten your jollies by saving that girl rather than by listening to the police scanner and bragging that you killed her, even you would rather that, wouldn't you, pal? Be a hero instead of a wannabe?"

His voice was getting higher, struggling to regain control. "You know better. If you didn't, you wouldn't have three of you gathered in your room with all the reports. And one just left. I've got to keep this short before he finds me. And you know I wouldn't call you unless I've got something important to tell you. You need to know—"

I choked and looked out the window, halfway expecting to find someone staring at me. I turned it into a laugh. "No, I don't, pal. I don't need to know anything from you. I guess that's the one good thing about being completely unimportant. I don't need to know a goddamn thing anymore. Because nobody cares about either of us." I looked out the window again, but saw no one.

"They better. Nobody better ignore me. And they won't ignore you either. You're going to be right in the middle of the final salvation soon. Wait, what do you mean the police say this wasn't an Angel salvation? What do they think is...Never mind. You need to hear this."

I laughed again, a good ole boy laugh between friends. "You mean you need me to hear it. Look, that's fine, pal. I'm enjoying talking to you. The real Angel, he was bat-shit crazy and didn't have your pathetic need to be heard. Did you ever read any of the stupid things he said about religion?"

"He said—*I said*—read your Bible. Keep your eyes on heaven—a..."

"Yeah, yeah. OK, pal, when I was a kid I was in a church-going family. Every Sunday, some guy would tell us what was in the Bible. I got tired of it one day, and decided to read the bible for myself. So, I did. The whole thing, beginning to end. As soon as I finished it, I went back and read the gospels—particularly Matthew—over and over.

The Jesus Christ I read about didn't talk much about heaven and how you could get there by following any crazy rules, but about how to make heaven on earth.

"That Christ—the one who was really in the gospel and not in some Bible-thumper's pulpit—was a god who commands you to always fight for others. At the end of it all, He won't ask if you were somehow innocent of sin, but he will ask if you were giving it your best. Were your stars out, even at the end? Were your stars out, trying to help?

"And that Christ said you don't get to judge. Not your life. Sure as hell not some precious child's."

He tried to talk but I cut him off.

"So, I don't believe the Christ in the Bible promised some glorious reunion with the godhead, at least not unless you fought for heaven on earth every minute you were here."

I realized that I was losing control. I took a breath, forced a laugh and kept talking.

"So, maybe I believe in reunions in heaven. Reunions, and maybe a hundred-pound weight loss. How about you, pal? What do you believe? Not what that pathetic joke of an Angel believed, what you—"

"Jesus, can you be quiet for one blessed minute? You know what I believe. The truth. And you know that the truth is I am the Angel of Mercy who killed your precious darlings and made you kill a man of God who was here to save them. And now you've tried to kill a cop, too."

I pulled back to my calm voice. "You're the one who doesn't know what Father Carson was doing here. BPD says he was the Angel who killed my angels."

"Yeah? Did Father Carson know this? Know that I slid my blade between your wife's fifth and sixth ribs so she would die fast and easy while watching her daughter die?"

There were tears coming out of me, but I kept control.

"I give you credit, pal. You've got good sources. But that's not hard."

"My sources are heaven. A perfect heaven for the perfectly pure. Purified by their own blood, the way I purified your whore of a wife at the end. While she prayed for me, not you. What've you got left to pray for?"

"I pray every day," I said. "I pray that Jesus Christ is the god for the fuck-ups."

He laughed and started to say something, muttered a quick curse and then there was only street noise. After a moment I heard Coltrane's voice, "Hello? Hello? Joe, you there?"

"Come on home," I said.

"Second thought," I said into the phone. "We need to get out of here. Meet me at Mabel's on 16th."

Capulet put her hand on my arm. Coltrane hung up and I let her hug me. A long, on-the-edge-of-tears hug.

I pulled away. "Let's go."

There were only a couple of other people rattling around Mabel's this late. Capulet slid into the booth next to Coltrane.

"Close," he said. "When I got there, the phone was off the hook. Still swinging on the cord."

"Any chance of prints?"

"None. Ma Bell—or whoever does pay phones nowadays—should thank him for wiping the receiver clean. There was a guy in the convenience store who noticed him, for what that was worth. Said he was a big, sloppy guy wearing baggy jeans, a dark sweatshirt and a hat. Probably white. I asked if he could ID him and the guy gave me a shit-eating grin and said, long as he was wearing the same clothes."

"Still," I said. "It's something. Confirms my suspicion about what he looks like."

Capulet said, "Maybe we could empty the coin box and get BPD to print all the coins. One of them has to be his."

We both looked at her.

Coltrane took out his detective's notepad. "Let me have all the numbers he's called you from."

I pulled out my phone. "Before, he was using burner cell phones. BPD chased them and got nothing. It's only recently that he's switched to pay phones."

"Pay phones are a lot harder to find than burner cell phones. Bound to mean something."

"Yeah. But what?"

"Means he's cheap," said Capulet.

"Means he's not willing to make a long-term investment," I said. "Still sounds like he's after one big score. Maybe he thinks he'll move on after that. Or he's naive enough to think he's going to quit."

"One way or the other," said Coltrane, "sure feels like a countdown."

He pulled out his smartphone and started working. The waitress came by and looked at me. "Anything?" she said.

Coltrane said, "Depth bomb."

She gave him a nasty look.

"You know," he said, "large fair-trade coffee, with an extra expresso shot."

"This ain't Starbucks and I ain't a twenty-something barista with no bra and tattoos."

He sighed. "Largest coffee you got."

Capulet shook her head.

The waitress looked at me. "Let me guess, Joe. One more slice of pie, long as I'm up."

I felt sick from eating, and maybe everything.

"No."

"Well," she said. "Restraint."

Coltrane turned his phone around where we could see.

"Look at this." There was a map with dots on it. "I thought we got lucky that the pay phone today was close enough for me to run to it. But they've all been around the Rosewood neighborhood south of Five Points."

"He knows where I live. Maybe he's intentionally coming here to make his calls."

"Or he's here anyway."

"One way or the other," I said. "He's in my house as well as my phone. I think."

Coltrane said, "Yeah. I've seen that room of yours. He's in your head big time."

"No. I mean for real. He was watching us. We need to get that geek friend of yours to come to the house. Now."

sixty-four

We stood on my front porch waiting for Mandrake.

"Don't want to go inside," I said, "until we decide if we want the Angel to know we're looking for a camera or a mic. Particularly if we find it."

Capulet said, "So, he said you were standing in the room with the reports, and that makes you think he's got the place bugged?"

"Something like that."

She sighed. "He could be watching us out here, maybe from a drone or a satellite."

I smiled. "Getting a little paranoid, aren't we?"

"Better late than never."

Coltrane was scanning the street. "I'm getting to the point of believing anything on this."

Mandrake pulled up in a tricked-out Scion. He walked up and stopped on the grass. "Locked out?"

Coltrane explained.

"Is there any way," I said, "that the bug on the phone's transmitting our conversations?"

"Not anymore. Probably not before I swept the phone. I didn't find anything like that, and I was pretty thorough after we found the GPS tracker."

I looked at Coltrane. "If we go in now, and he's got a bug, do we let him know, or leave it in place?"

"Don't know. Seems late in the game. May as well let him know we know something. Might rattle him."

I nodded.

Capulet added, "And you've still got the way of spoofing your phone that he doesn't know about."

I opened the door. Mandrake went into the war room and, circled around and looked at me.

"Hobby," I said.

"Looks more like your soul."

I started to say something in response, but Mandrake was walking around, checking things. A couple of passes, and he pointed at the overhead fan/light. We walked over.

He pointed. "See those three vent holes, size of a soda straw? That one has something behind it. You got a stepladder?"

"Out in the garage."

I brought in the ladder and a toolbox. Mandrake scampered up and pulled the fan loose from the ceiling. Three wires dangled down. Three wires, and a silvery fiber optic line. He pointed with his free hand, then screwed the fan back into place.

"Where's your attic access?"

"In the hall."

He carried the ladder around, set it below the plywood square, climbed up and studied the ceiling.

"Careful of spiders and stuff. I've never been up there."

Capulet said, "Never?"

I shrugged. "Luz did the house while I played cop. As far as I know, she never went up there, but who knows?"

Mandrake pointed. "Somebody has. Look here. Somebody cut the paint with a sharp knife around the opening so the paint wouldn't tear and give him away. You'd never see it if you're not up here."

He pushed the board up and into the ceiling. His torso disappeared into the attic and we watched his feet shift around as he did a three-sixty.

He came back down and handed me his flashlight. "You need to see this."

I put my foot on the first step and tested it. A little groaning, but it felt like it would hold. I climbed up and looked out into the attic. A sheet of plywood had been cut into 4-foot-by-2-foot sections small enough to push through the opening, brought up here and assembled into a pallet with a couple of blankets. Another piece three feet away had electronics spliced into the house power and lines running all over the attic. Behind that were piles of empty gallon water jugs and Power Bar wrappers. I climbed back down.

Mandrake nodded at me. "You've had a visitor."

"Looks like they stayed for several days."

"Lot more time than they needed to set stuff up."

Capulet said, "So, someone was in the attic the other night?"

Coltrane gave us a look , then scampered up and came back down holding the Power Bar wrappers by the corners.

"I'm betting there's no prints on these, but look at the expiration dates. Nothing newer than a couple of years ago. And there's an indentation in the insulation that could have been from a ladder." He looked at Mandrake.

Mandrake said, "Two years ago, the murderer didn't have to leave the house after killing your family. Climbed up, hid out until things were quiet. He was there all the time."

Vinzini had a look of disgust when we walked in, but he wiped it clean with a friendly bored expression.

He looked at Capulet while he talked to the admin who had brought us upstairs to the detective bullpen. "This is the citizen you said had important information and wouldn't talk to anyone but me? Surprised you let them in." He looked at me. "Surprised no one shot you on sight."

I motioned at my clown pants. "I'm incognito."

"Yeah."

I motioned at Capulet.

"We're going to try this the nice way," she said. "Although I suspect that won't work with you hard-headed males. We've got proof that the Angel killed Julie."

He looked at her. "Coltrane called me. How do you know the girl's name?"

"That's what I'm trying to tell you. The Angel told Joe."

He looked back at me. He had been irritated, but now he went to that blank cop stare.

"That's a new one, don't you think? 'An angel told me'?"

"Play it," Capulet said.

I fished my phone out and started to play what we had recorded.

"Wait," he said.

He walked us around to an interrogation room. Still had a locking bar on the steel table, but at least it was clean. Apparently, he was going to be nice, too, and not handcuff us to the table. Nonetheless, the door locked with a click behind him.

We sat down, I put the phone on the table and hit "Play." He listened without expression.

"So, what's all that supposed to mean, Joe?"

Capulet leaned over at him. "It means we've got goddamned proof. The Angel is planning something big, and you're sitting here with your dick in your hand."

He opened his hands to show her they were empty and smiled at her.

"Just proves your dick is so damned small you can't even find it."

He turned to me. "You're right. It could be the Angel." Turned back to Capulet. "Or maybe a sick crime groupie who's found a cop—ex-cop—he can torque." Leaned in. "Or it could mean the killer's sitting right here playing me."

Capulet said, "More. We've got proof the Angel hid out in Joe's house after he killed Joe's family."

He raised an eyebrow at me.

"What we've got is a lot of video equipment set up in my attic, and what looks like a bed and a lot of empty food wrappers. And it looks like it's two years old. Someone could have been there when my family was killed."

"You need to check this out," Capulet said.

"Oh, we will. So, you're saying, Joe, that you've had a roommate for years, and you've never noticed it?"

"Never."

"And we didn't find all this when we cleared the house after the shooting years ago?"

"No reason to check the attic. The story seemed clear from the main floor. And the attic looked like it was painted shut."

He stared at me and then pushed himself up from the table. "Wait here."

He came back a couple of minutes later. "Breuer confirms that they didn't look in the attic. Fuck up, if you ask me, but there it is." He sighed. "How about today? Did you touch anything?"

"No. I stuck my head up and looked."

"So, we shouldn't find any of your fingerprints or DNA up there?"

"Betting you won't find mine, or anyone else's."

He stood up.

"Let the admin make a copy of the recording on the way out. Go home. A team will meet you there."

sixty-six

Wendy leaned across the bar and gave me a skeptical look, followed by a bored, "It's your funeral."

She pulled out the baseball bat from under the bar and whacked the scarred wood with a bang.

"Listen up, fuckers. Joe says he's got something to say to you."

There was a low growl, kind of like the lions in the zoo at feeding time.

There was a louder boom as she hit the bar a second time. "Get quiet, or get out. Joe's had a tough week. Left a forensics team from the Birmingham Keystone Kops climbing all over his house to come down here. Let him talk."

The place was quiet except for one voice still grumbling. Wendy stared into the dark like she could see someone in the gloom.

"Shut up, Sal. Or pay your tab on the way out."

Silence.

I couldn't see anyone but Ron, Coltrane and Capulet at the bar with me, but I knew they were there.

"Guys," I said. "Women too. I need help."

Somebody snickered.

" I'm chasing a killer. I think he's going to kill a bunch of kids. Birmingham PD thinks it's a joke, or maybe that I'm the killer."

Somebody muttered, "Birmingham PD is a joke."

There was snickering, Wendy waved the bat for silence.

"Basically, we think this sick bastard is going to call me on my cell sometime in the next few hours or maybe days. He's probably going to call from one of a handful of pay phones."

"How do you know?" The voice from the back was surprisingly clear.

"We don't know, for sure. He's been calling about the time he thinks I'm leaving the bar. We think he's tracking me from my cell phone and he seems to think it's funny to call while I'm walking home half-drunk. The pay phones have all been around here, but he's not used the same phone twice—so far. So that leaves only four phones that he hasn't used."

"Sounds pretty thin."

"It is. It may be a waste of time."

A harsh laugh at the back said, "We're good at that." .

"OK, it's not much," I said. "But it's all we've got right now. I figure, anyone who can help me, we divide up and cover the phones. Once we're all in place, I'll walk out. Maybe he'll call. Maybe he won't. I left him pretty pissed off, so I'm guessing he will. He's a big guy, but not tough."

I sensed hesitance.

"Anyone who's in, I'll buy you a beer tomorrow night, whether it works or not. But that's all I've got. Don't blame anyone for not helping out."

Wendy flipped on the lights and, one by one, they came, blinking and hesitant, to the front.

A slurred voice from the back called out, "We're your cavalry, Joe."

I recognized a couple of disgraced detectives, plus a couple of guys in blues too threadbare to still be worn on duty. A tiny elderly woman came to the front, dressed in her meter maid uniform. I recognized her.

"Courtney?"

"I'm still a cop, Joe. Even if all I've got is a ticket book and a scooter."

"Yes," I said. "Yes, you are."

They were gathered around the table with the map.

"Guys," I said. "This may turn out to be one big fuck-up."

A different voice at the back said, "We're not afraid of fuck-ups."

sixty-seven

We were all on edge, with Coltrane going over and over the plan. We gave all the teams twenty minutes to get into position and then Capulet, Coltrane and I started walking home, hoping to get a call.

Halfway home, the phone rang. I looked at the Caller ID and saw it was a number I didn't know. I showed the number to Capulet while the snake rattled for a second time. She scribbled it and looked at her list of phone numbers.

I picked it up on the third clatter. "Yeah?"

"We didn't finish."

"Yeah, we did, pal. Look, why don't you go find a good therapist to talk to? I honestly can't help you."

"I'm the one helping you. I'm going to show you hell."

Coltrane and Capulet were excited about something in the notebook. Coltrane took off running and Capulet started dialing her phone. She held it up to her ear and hit my elbow with the hand holding the notebook.

"Yeah?" I said into the phone. "Tell hell to hold on a minute."

I looked at the page. We had made a list of the locations of what we thought were the likely phones and their distances from Johnson's. One was circled furiously. I looked at the column for its distance.

Three-quarters of a mile. Coltrane would be there in minutes. That was the good news. The bad news was that the nearest team was a half-mile away at a different phone, since we couldn't cover them all. Capulet was on her cell with that team.

My bet was that Coltrane, young and fast, would get there first. Less than a thousand long steps to ending this terror before it became a nightmare for a crowd of kids and parents.

I had to keep him talking.

"OK, pal, I'm back. Look,—"

"No, you look this time. You wouldn't shut up last time. I'm talking this time. You need to know that there's soon going to be a whole new choir singing in heaven. The Joseph Brosette Choir of Mercy. Now I'm done and I've got to go. "

"Yeah, yeah, yeah. Life's so terrible, you're doing the kids a favor sending them on. Got it, and I'll tell you another thing, pal, you don't believe it either. The real Angel did, but you don't."

"I hate sin. Life in this world is sin and..."

"And you're having the time of your life. Admit it. The real Angel, now there was a guy who hated life. He wanted to kill some kids because he didn't want to live in this world, either. You, buddy, are full of life. I can hear it in your voice. You call up full of excitement. Can't wait to tell me the next sick thing you're going to do."

"No. I...Aren't you paying attention? I hate this sinful life."

"You love life. Admit it."

"No! Wait. You're the one who loves life. You mope around telling everyone you've got nothing to live for, it's all been taken away from you. But you're eating and drinking and joking and chasing girls—"

"It's hard to call Capulet—well, no, I don't mean that—but, no, I've got a lot to cry about. You've probably sitting on a pillow eating bonbons."

"Bonbons! I am mortifying myself for Jesus to prove how much I hate this sinful world."

I had him hooked. "No, you love this life."

He said, "No, you—Shit. Attack midgets…" and there was nothing on the line but street traffic.

Seconds dragged by while Capulet demanded phone updates from people too busy to give them. I kept one ear on my phone, still connected to the pay phone, and tried to listen in on hers, but both of our phones were silent.

Finally, I heard her pause and listen for a few seconds. About the time she said, "OK." I heard Coltrane pick up the pay phone.

"You there, Detective?"

"Yeah. I don't hear any cheering."

"No. Close, but you know what they say about that. I came around the corner just as the shit hit the fan. The first I saw, the meter maid was in the lead coming hard, half-way across the street, while the others were still on the sidewalk. She was fastest, but not the biggest. Angel probably had a hundred pounds on her, but she wrapped him up. He slapped her away and she jumped up, bit him on the calf, grabbed his crotch and wouldn't let go. I thought a couple of others were going to get there and we'd have him, but he boxed her ears and turned her loose.

"He took off running—and limping—and I thought I was going to get him. But he jumped in an old beater of a pickup that was already running and he was gone. We should have had a driver here, but we didn't. Probably just as well. It's hard to tell what the blood alcohol would have been for any of our guys."

"Did you get a plate?"

"Yeah, but no good. It had one of those temporary cardboard dealer plates. May even have printed it himself.

"I called it in, though. Said the driver was involved with an altercation, but that the other party had left the scene. Which will be true in a couple of minutes. Maybe someone in BPD will spot him."

"Courtney OK?"

"Depends on who you ask. Your buddy Ron is trying to convince her to go to the hospital and get her ears checked. I don't know if she can't hear or won't listen, but the G-rated version of her side is that she's going back to Johnson's to talk to you."

"Any point in staying there?"

"Probably not. And I think our team wants to get off the street."

"All right. Get them back to Johnson's. I'll tell Capulet to call in the others."

I punched the phone off and looked at her. She was already making the calls.

She hung up from the last one and put her hand on my arm.

"We're getting closer."

"So's he."

We turned and made our way in silence. The first ragtag group was walking in when we got to Johnson's.

A detective I recognized from years ago, now gone to seed, said, "Heard we almost got him."

"Almost."

He put his head down and went off into the darkness.

I followed him in and motioned for Wendy to turn the lights up.

The group with Courtney came in last.

"She needs to go to the hospital," said a guy holding her up. "I think her ears are shot. Blood coming out of one of them."

She pulled away from him. "I need to talk to you."

I nodded. "In a minute. I want to get something straight before these guys start drinking."

She nodded, but didn't seem to hear.

I shook my head and tried to explain. Realized that it was a waste of time and took her by the arm and set her in a chair.

"Scotch," she said. "While you're buying."

I looked at Wendy and shook my head, no. I turned to the back of the room.

"OK, guys, we had a swing and a miss. We don't have many more chances left. After tonight, I don't believe the Angel's going to call back again."

"We fucked up," someone said. "Right on schedule."

"No, you didn't. But I don't think he'll call from a pay phone again. Whatever's happening is happening soon, and the only people who can stop it are in this room."

"Good luck."

"We don't need luck. We need to be prepared. Anybody who hasn't given Capulet your phone number, make sure you do, and make sure you keep that phone with you."

There was some grumbling, but no outright nos.

"One more thing, and this is important. Until we get this done, I need everybody stone cold sober and ready to go."

Now there was a lot of grumbling.

Wendy shook her head, backing me up.

"Shit, man," came a voice from the back. "Only good thing about fucking up is getting drunk after."

"Save it. We'll drink when we're celebrating."

Courtney pulled my arm.

"I bit the shit out of him. Mouthful of blood."

I patted her.

"You did good."

"Maybe we can get some DNA off my shirt. It's his blood, you know."

I looked at Coltrane and he shrugged.

"Probably too little, too late," I said.

But she was pulling a rhinestone-studded switchblade out of her pants pocket. She cut a blood-stained section off her sleeve and handed it to me.

"Thanks. You never know."

"One more thing," she said.

I looked at her.

"When I grabbed him, I grabbed his crotch."

"Good try," I said.

She ignored me.

"He didn't have a dick."

The room got quiet.

A voice in the back said, "Women always say that."

sixty-nine

Capulet and I went back to my house to get some rest, figuring tomorrow might be a busy day.

We walked in the door. "I need a minute," I said.

I took my backup Glock out of my pocket and set it on the desk. I stood in front of the picture, willing the figures to breathe and move and tell me what was going on, but they didn't. Eventually I felt like I was coming apart. I understood what the Lost Boy had meant about fucking up and drinking.

Up to now, Capulet had given me my space, but she came up behind me and put her arm as far around my waist as it would go.

That broke something in me and I was crying.

"What do you need?" she said.

I tried to laugh. "A fifth of rum."

"I can't give you that, but I can give you everything I've got."

And she did. For an hour, my usually sad head was filled with images of smooth skin, big curves, a hungry woman above me with her eyes closed tight as she tried to hold on and release at the same time. And more. Something between my body and my mind was filled with the sensations of the touch of a woman who cared, the heat of her breath and, finally, for me, a sense of longing and desperation that could be resolved.

We lay on my bed as the sweat cooled and I felt, for one moment, like a lovely creature of passion.

But not for long.

As I was on the verge of drifting into a very mellow sleep, Capulet said, "I know this is what it is, and is nothing more than a momentary fuck for you, but I thank you for it."

I was wide awake now, trying to fill in the blanks in that sentence.

"Did you hear me?"

"Yes. I'm thinking about it."

She propped herself up beside me. "I want you to know that I'm sorry for whining to you about never having been loved. I know that what you had with Luz was real love, and this is not that. But I want you to know that, if it's true that people can live without love, but not without water, then this is a very satisfying kind of water."

"OK," I said. "This is not what I had with Luz."

I thought.

"I think you're wrong, though," I said.

"Nope," she said, "I feel satisfied. Nothing you're going to say can change that."

"That's not what I mean. It's what you said about love. I think you're wrong. I mean, you're right about this not being what I had with Luz. That was something...more. When two kids say, 'You're my soulmate,' they're saying they love each other, and that they want to share lives. Much more than mere love.

"Luz and I had something even beyond that. She was my air and the reason to breathe and a million other things.

"I think the poet you quoted was half-right: millions have lived without a soul-deep love. But I'm not one of them. I had it, and I don't know that I'll ever learn to live without it.

"But – and this is what I mean when I say you're wrong – I'm not living without love, today. And you aren't. This is love, if only right-now love. And it's good, this touching and caring and enjoying and treating each other as a precious gift and feeling precious ourselves. This is a love. Whether it lasts for a moment or longer, it is now and it always will have been love. So, today, right now, I didn't live without love. And neither did you." I paused and added. "Juliet."

We lay there a long time, and then I heard her crying.

"I think," she said, "you're right."

Then she sat straight up.

"I know who the Angel is."

"Where's your phone?" She jumped out of the bed, and the springs almost bounced me out of the bed.

"I would guess in my clown pants. I don't recall making any calls the last few minutes."

She trundled out to the war room where I had left my pants. I followed.

We were both standing there naked, the room starting to flood with the newly risen sun. "You know," I said, "we really should close these curtains."

"Later. I'm busy. You're going to be busy in a moment, too."

She pulled out my phone.

"Listen, remember when the Angel called the other night?"

"Of course I do."

"Remember this." She started playing the call, running back and forth until I heard the Angel say, "Can you be quiet for one blessed minute?"

"So where," she said, "have you heard that?"

"Here. The Angel."

"Where else? Think."

"Well, it's not that uncommon. I'd don't know, maybe...
Holt. Yeah, but she's got a hoarse voice and she's not a
man. She's..." I stopped.

"Oh," I said.

"What did Freud call women? Men without dicks. What
did the woman from the bar say about the Angel?"

"No dick," I said. I looked at the wall and saw it
changing with new possibilities. "I don't know. Let's be
careful this time. Be sure."

"All right," she said. "Let's go through what she said. He.
Whatever somebody said tonight."

She zipped along to tonight's call and played it back
from the start. Halfway through, I said, "I don't hear
anything that sounds like Holt. Not the voice, not
anything."

She pressed "pause."

"The voice is easy. In the cafeteria, she was talking with
her mouth full to throw you off. Then she emailed you
through me. Then her phone acted up, and she had to talk
to me. I've heard her dozens of times. This could be her."

I said, "I don't hear any of her word choices."

"She's trying to use Angel's natural phrases, until you got
her so pissed that she slipped back into her natural voice."
She hit "play." "You're really good at pissing people off."

She replayed the voice after the Angel was pissed and
uttering the same phrase as Holt had screamed at her kids. I
paid attention to the tone of the Angel's voice. Capulet was
right. There was a rise in pitch, a quickening of rhythm

symptomatic of irritation. Like a teacher with unruly students. Like Holt.

I said, "Maybe."

Capulet and I looked at each other and there was a scream outside. I grabbed my Glock from the desk and crouched by the window. I looked out and saw a horrified jogger staring in while the sunlight poured past her and lit up our room.

I closed the drapes.

We were in the car, heading to Holt's house, hoping to go through the place after she was off to school, when the rattlesnake clattered again.

I looked at the Caller ID. "Shirley, I'm kind of busy right now."

"You're going to be busier tonight. I talked to your new bosses and got you a chance to atone for your sins, or at least one."

"Right now, Shirley," I said, "it's all I can do to keep from adding to them."

I turned onto a four-lane street and got in the slow lane to listen.

"Joe, you've got to do this one. Remember the church where you gave your famous 'Jesus Fucking Christ' sermon? They're being kind enough to invite you back tonight, at six o'clock. Every year the Catholic churches from Southside have a big outdoor party-slash-confirmation for hundreds of girls from the Birmingham area. This year, they're doing it at that church. They're demanding that you attend—though I can't imagine why. And we're demanding that you say something more inspirational than your last outing with them."

I pulled over to the curb and stopped.

Capulet said, "What are you doing? We've got to get to Holt's house."

"Later," I said to her.

"No, not later," Shirley said. "Don't you hang up on me."

"Not you. I'm not hanging up. Shirley, you've got to cancel that whole confirmation. BPD has to stop this thing."

"Jesus, Joe, don't give me your crazy shit today. Put your clown suit on, go down there, smile and say something polite for a change. Look, there are people here looking for any excuse to fire you completely. You blow this off and you're gone."

"Listen, this is bigger than that. If that event goes on—if you have a hundred young girls dressed in white—people will die. Lots of them. I know it."

There was silence for a long time. Her voice was tender. "Joe, are you sure you're all right?"

"No, I'm sure I'm not. We've got to stop this."

She sighed. "Joe, if you think a confirmation is a major threat to the safety of the city, you're going to have to convince somebody other than the Public Information Officer. And, if you can't, this is going to look like you're trying to get out of doing your job. Or trying to get your old detective job back. Either way, if you're not there, you'll lose the city job you still have."

"My clown-job is not what's important here."

"Let's be clear, you lose pay, rights to do anything with Birmingham city, retirement, medical insurance, life insurance—"

"Wait." I said. She graciously gave me space for a minute. "I don't want to lose that."

"Then be there."

I thought about it.

"I'll be there."

I turned off onto a side street, made a U and went back the other way on the four-lane.

"What the hell do you think you're doing?" said Capulet.

"We've got to do this." I filled her in.

"That's important," she said, "but first we have to catch a killer."

"We don't know that Holt is the killer. We have a suspicion that we need to check out. I'm sure children will die unless we stop this other thing. First."

"I know Holt is the killer. And so do you."

I looked out the window. "Like we knew Fouch was the killer. Like we—I—knew I was smarter than a hundred years of police procedures. The angry man in me says Holt is the Angel. The cop says that all we know is that Holt doesn't have balls and walks like a girl—"

"And threatened to go public about Fouch. What was that about?"

"I'm not sure. Only one thing makes sense to me. She was listening while we were bitching about BPD dragging their heels. Called us to force our hand and keep us focused away from her. And it worked. I let her push me to fuck up. Again. And that only makes sense if she's the Angel. So, we go check her out. After we get this church-thing stopped. But we don't assume she's Hitler. Yet."

"You think this whole business of calling me up to set up a fake lunch, sending you a love note, and threatening to go to Fouch's principal, was something to distract us for a couple of days?"

"Maybe. Maybe something to taunt me. Help me screw up."

"Maybe it was real. Wanting you to be the partner she never had."

I thought about it. "Maybe all three, if we're right about her."

She pulled out her phone. "I'm calling Coltrane. Get him to investigate Holt while you're playing savior."

I reached over and put my hand on the phone. "And if Coltrane is caught helping a traitor, even if we turn out to be right, his career will be ruined. And there's no way we can convince BPD—or maybe even Coltrane—that we've got enough evidence." She pushed my hand away but didn't dial. "Look, if we can stop this confirmation, we've got time to get to Holt—or whoever. If not, it won't matter."

She thought about it. "Oh, sweet Jesus," she said. "Doesn't Birmingham PD know what's going on?"

"No. They don't. And that's my fault."

"Your fault? You're the only one trying to protect these girls. You think we should dress you up in a white communion dress and sacrifice you to the Angel as punishment?" She giggled. "The sight of that would probably kill the Angel and you two would die together. Only way either of you would be happy."

"No. We talk to someone even less likely than the police to believe anything I would ever say."

#

Brother Dave leaned back in his chair. We were in the priest's study in a small 1950's ranch house next door to the St. Stephen's church, the emerging crystal steeple and the new Children's Park. The study itself could have come straight out of central casting for a priest's study in old Ireland: dark wood, a couple of past-their-prime, overstuffed chairs, cluttered antique desk and a faint odor of strong tea and pipe tobacco. Brother Dave had added a Woodstock poster.

He smiled at Capulet and me. "Surprised the parish council invited you back."

"That's sort of what we want to talk about, the event I'm supposed to be at tonight. And I apologize for what I said at the dedication. I didn't mean what it sounded like."

He smiled. "You didn't say, 'Jesus Fucking Christ?'"

"I did. But I didn't mean it to be heard. I was reacting to something."

"You meant it. Plenty of times I've thought of saying it myself."

He sighed. "And I didn't know until today that you were the man who killed Father Carson. Father Carson was a polarizing figure here. Many people loved him. He spoke about the love of Christ and opened the church to groups that other people in the church did not entirely welcome."

He paused and rose and went to the door. "Mrs. Malamud, do you think you could bring us some tea for our guests? We may be here a while."

Brother Dave looked back at us and we nodded.

He watched her walk away before he returned and gave us a small smile.

"The priest before Father Carson was Father Mitchell. Much more intense. A man on the warpath against sin and the sinfulness of mankind. His followers were—are—still passionate, and very active."

I said, "Including Mrs. Malamud?"

"Not really. Mrs. Malamud is a very gentle soul. Who loves to talk."

"So, you're the priest of a church that's split?" Capulet said.

He thought a minute. "I believe that would be fair. I also believe it's a fair assessment of modern Christianity, and, for that matter, most religions. A wise man—in our case, literally the son of God—comes along and tells people that the essence of Godliness is simply loving one another. But—because people love rules and love to hit other people over the head with rules—the followers of that wise man splinter his teachings into a million rigid rules. Over time, the rules get twisted, and the followers who want to wage jihad against the rule-breakers in the name of God sometimes take over and run wild."

"Like the Angel of Mercy?" I said.

He looked at the ceiling. "Like the—I'm sorry, but I won't call him by that name, particularly in this context. Yes, he was clearly in error. Horrible error. Father Carson was particularly vocal from the pulpit on the subject. Some of our parishioners heard his sermons as bashing Father Mitchell—which some were petitioning the Bishop to bring back—and even bashing Christianity itself. So, I'm surprised that the parish council invited you here. Twice, now. But maybe I'm not so surprised. Some of the hard-liners think that you were doing God's work when you killed Father Carson."

He gave me a bland, measured look.

"I don't, Father," I said. "I was a big fan of Father Carson's, and I was as shocked as anyone when I saw that he was the man I'd killed. With what I know now, I'm sure I killed an innocent man. Perhaps, if we get through the next few days, you and I can sit down and talk some more."

He said, "I'd like that."

"I think I need it. But this wasn't the urgent matter we need to talk about right now."

He raised an eyebrow.

"We have reason to believe that the Angel—the killer—is still alive. And that he—or she—is planning to strike at the confirmation ceremony tonight."

He raised an eyebrow.

I explained what we had.

"It's not much," he said.

"No."

"But the stakes are incredibly high."

"They are."

He sat there a long time. "Do you mind if I make a phone call?"

I stood to step outside and he waved me down. "You might as well listen in."

He looked out into the hall and Mrs. Malamud still wasn't back. He fumbled on his desk, found a number a dialed it. "I'm calling the police representative responsible for our security tonight."

There was some chit-chat and he explained our concern. Then he listened for a long time, watching me while saying, "uh-huh, un-huh" into the phone.

He hung up. "The police are confident that their measures will keep our children safe." And then, after a long pause, "though they're not very confident in you, Detective."

He looked at me with compassion in his eyes. "I can understand, Detective, that what you've been through might cloud your judgment. But I think we have to go with the police on this."

"I understand."

As we started to leave. Capulet said, "Father, can you tell us who particularly requested Detective Brosette for tonight?"

We could see him hesitate. "I'm sorry. I don't think it matters, but I'm not comfortable giving you their name."

She said, "Was her name 'Holt'?"

I decided to push for more. "Was Holt the one who wrote your homily for the park dedication? And requested that I be there?"

The look on his face gave us our answer.

seventy-three

Capulet turned sideways in the passenger seat. "They're still wrong."

I pulled out of the church parking lot. "No, they're not. Not with the little we've given them."

"If you risk children's lives, you're wrong."

"Every soccer game is a risk. And the police are very, very sensitive to protecting children. Even one call from a crackpot is enough to shut down an event. But you do have to draw the line at something that seems totally not credible, or nothing would ever get done. Again, the fault isn't theirs but mine."

"So, what now?"

"On to Holt's. You got the address?"

"Yeah. Wait. This isn't the way."

"Short cut." I pulled into Mabel's, pulled out my phone and fumbled with it. After a minute, I shoved it at Capulet.

"Here."

"What?"

"How do I do that—whatever it was called—thing that we do so Holt can't see that we're coming to her house?"

"You mean," she held her finger over the screen, "this big button labelled, 'Lock Location'?"

"Yeah. Make it look like we're still parked here."

She punched it and I pulled out.

We parked at a convenience store around the corner from Holt's house. I reached into the back seat and pulled up a stack of catalogs I'd pulled out of the mail.

I handed her one and she looked at it. "Pottery Barn?"

"People ignore salesman and insurance agents. We walk up to the door with a handful of catalogs in our hands and big smiles on our faces, and neighbors will never remember us."

She looked at my clown pants and Hawaiian shirt.

I said, "Or the neighbors will call out SWAT on us and we get the police involved. Either way, it's good."

Holt's was a small, white frame house, well-tended in a minimal sort of way. No extraneous flowers, bushes or decorations.

I started to ring the doorbell, hesitated, and asked Capulet to stand aside.

"In case..." I said. "Never mind. Just paranoia."

I rang the bell and nothing happened but a muted buzzing from the inside of the house.

"She should be at school," said Capulet.

"So should you." I rang again, then leaned out so I could see into the window. I couldn't see anything through the thin white drapes. I turned my back to the house and surveyed the neighborhood. No one obviously watching.

"I'm going around the back."

Capulet tried the door before I could stop her and it opened in her hand. "Or we could walk in."

"We could." But I stood in the doorway a moment, holding Capulet back while I looked inside. I stepped in first and jerked my head to indicate to her that it was safe to enter.

"Thanks for protecting me from the big, bad door," she said.

I pulled the door closed and fished out two pair of latex gloves. "Even with these on, don't touch anything you don't absolutely have to."

The small living room was obviously set up for one person. Make that one person, and a holy host. There was one recliner in front of a small TV, with an uncomfortable-looking couch bridging the gap between the two and covered with books. Sad-eyed saints stared down at us from the walls and there was a big crucifix behind the TV.

Capulet was taking pictures with her phone.

"Get as much as you can, as fast as you can." I picked up the remote control and turned on the TV. Pushed a button to display the shows recorded on the DVR.

"That's the local religious channel," said Capulet.

"Yeah. And Braves baseball."

"There's a joke here somewhere."

"We'll come up with it later." I turned the TV off and went into the kitchen.

"Looks clean," Capulet said.

I opened the refrigerator. "Almost empty. I think I'd want more to come home to."

"At school," said Capulet, "her lunch was homemade. Surprised she doesn't have a lot of leftovers."

I shrugged and went into the front bedroom. It was set up as an office with a desk piled with papers and textbooks except for a bare spot where a laptop would fit.

"Computer books," I said. "Get pictures of these. And the papers, too."

"Holt used to teach programming as a language. Gave it up a few years ago when they got a real computer guy."

"Still seems to be interested."

"Yeah." I pushed a book off the top of one pile with the back of my hand. "Huh."

"What?"

"Truck driving school."

Capulet said, "Could be nothing. Teachers have to take so many educational credits to stay current. A few years ago, Alabama relaxed the rules to let almost anything count. Some teachers go to Europe for language credit, some go to cooking school."

"Truck driving school?"

She shrugged and took a picture of the cover, opened it up with her glove and took a picture of the contacts page that showed a picture of the Daimler truck she would be training on.

We went into the back bedroom, neat and tidy like the rest of the house. We poked and prodded until Capulet noticed something in the closet.

"Not much here." She took a picture and walked over to the dresser. Pulled out the drawers one by one.

"No underwear anywhere. And an empty drawer."

"She doesn't seem like the type to go commando," I said. Capulet gave me a look and went to the one bathroom.

"Toothbrush is gone." She opened the medicine cabinet. "Lot of empty spaces here." She pulled open a drawer. "And here."

I stood back and watched Capulet work. She went back into the bedroom and opened the closet again.

She took a picture and pointed.

"Look at that. Rectangular indentations in the carpet about the size of suitcases."

She looked at me.

"She's not coming back."

seventy-four

I drove while Capulet worked her phone. When we got to Johnson's, there was already a small crowd huddled around the doorway, blinking like newborn kittens in the sun. Wendy came up behind us and unlocked the door.

"About time," came a voice from the crowd. "We might turn to dust in the sun."

A couple of people laughed.

Courtney the Meter Maid said, "Or worse. I don't want to be lugging this thing around any longer than I got to." She reached into a shopping bag and pulled out a pistol the size of a cannon

"Jesus," I said. "What the hell is that thing?"

"Desert Eagle Long Colt, 5-pound, 15-inch pistol chambered for a single .410 shotgun shell. Destroy anything it hits."

Someone said, "If you hit anything. Beyond ten feet, you're better off throwing the damned thing."

Someone else said, "If you can throw it."

"Well," I said. "Let's get Godzilla inside before you drop it and it destroys a building or two."

Wendy threw the lights on to grumbling and we gathered around a table. More people drifted in, one guy tried to order a beer and Wendy told him the bar was closed. People looked at me and I said, "Wait."

Coltrane and the computer geek walked in with a stack of printouts.

"OK," I said. "Let's get started."

Coltrane put together four sheets to make an aerial shot of the church.

"This is Saint Stephen's," I said. "We think the Angel of Mercy, same guy that killed kids two years ago, is going to try to run up a big score at Saint Stephen's tonight. Except that he's not a guy, it's a woman." Coltrane set a stack of Holt's driver's license photos next to the map. "And we don't have much idea of what exactly she's going to do."

"Bomb, AR-15?"

"Could be anything."

"How much proof do we have?"

I tried to make eye contact with the person speaking and couldn't find him.

"Very little," I said.

"What are the police doing?"

"Very little there too. They aren't convinced."

"What if you're wrong?" Courtney said.

Capulet pushed her way beside me. "What if he's right?"

There was some grumbling, but finally a voice in the back said, "At least the pretty-boy cops won't get in our way."

"Yes, they will," I said. "The police are providing security like at any other event. They don't think the threat justifies anything more. We'll have to watch out for them, and don't expect any real help."

Ron said, "That's the way it always is. We're the ones who get it done."

"So, let's figure out what the 'it' is that we've got to get done." I did a quick head count. "Thirteen. I've got to be onstage in my clown suit, which may be good. Or not. Coltrane, I want you to be in reserve somewhere so you can get to where the action is, since you're our one official cop."

He nodded. I looked at Mandrake.

"Can you set up a conference call so we can all hear each other on our cells?"

"Easy."

"One more thing. We took pictures of a lot of handwritten notes that Holt made for some computer code she was writing. Gobbledygook to me. Can I get you to transfer it to your phone while we're working, so you can look at it and see what it means?"

"Again, easy."

Capulet handed him her phone and he went off to the side.

"So, I'm onstage, Coltrane's our ready reserve, and Mandrake focuses on anything technical. That leaves..." I looked at Capulet and was lost in my thoughts for a moment, realizing that I didn't want to put her in harm's way. She didn't belong in the field.

Good luck stopping her.

"That leaves ten of us. Not many, given the size of the field and the fact that we don't even know exactly what the threat is."

I looked at the layout and saw a hundred places we needed to cover.

"I think I want a couple of people in cars cruising around. Who's got a good car and isn't too bad a driver?"

I got a couple of volunteers. "OK, get a description of her car from Coltrane. But keep your eyes open for anything. And keep an ear on your phone."

Capulet said, "What about the stuff we found from truck-driving school?"

"Good point. Could mean everything." I said. "Or nothing."

I looked at the layout. The I-65 exit opened into the street directly across from the church, lined up with the Children's Park.

Like a bowling alley lined up for a strike.

I pointed to it. "We can cover that," said one of the car guys. "We'll stage a fender bender on the bottom of the exit, blocking both lanes, ten minutes before the event starts. If they get a tow truck, we can pull the same thing up top. Keep them tied up until the crowd goes home."

I looked around and saw a room full of bright eyes. Bright eyes in wrinkled and dirty faces, but bright.

Someone said, "We got this, boss. We'll have this guy— gal—by morning. She'll never know what hit her."

Capulet squeezed my arm.

"By morning. You'll see. By morning, Holt will be in jail, the girls will all be safe, you'll be a hero and—more than that, you'll be at peace."

The only image I could come up with for peace was sitting on a cloud surrounded by lilies. "Oh yeah," I said. "Sounds like me."

seventy-five

One hour before showtime. I walked around the church, already in full police clown regalia with my personal gun in a shoulder holster I could get to from a slit in the absurd blue tent I wore. Sweating like a pig, but I couldn't sit down and rest in the shade. I counted heads, again, and scanned the crowd, again. Tried to smile at every family drifting in and resist the urge to tell them to run.

Run from a giant runaway truck.

Or a bomb.

Or bullets.

Or the imagination of a fat old man who had outlived his usefulness.

I heard myself say out loud, "Jesus Fucking Christ."

A woman looked at me and I forced a smile and said, "Welcome to Saint Stephen's. Jesus Fabulous Christ."

She gave me a weak smile back and moved on.

There was a pile of dirty laundry piled up on the side of the convenience store across the street. I walked over to check it out and found Claude of the Lost Boys making snoring noises on the pavement with a ball cap pulled low and a bottle in a paper bag propped on his stomach. I took the bag away and sniffed Mountain Dew. I set it back down and saw his right hand with the Eagle, Globe and Anchor tattoo resting on the butt of a pistol hidden under his ass.

Between snores, he whispered, "Semper Fi."

"Yes, sir," I said.

Waiting to cross the street, I saw an old three-quarter-ton truck drift by. The driver gave me a terse nod and I recognized him.

Let a tow truck try to budge that monster.

I found Coltrane in the crowd and stood alongside him, both of us surveying the growing crowd in different directions as we talked.

"Maybe we're going to pull this off," he said.

"Yeah. Or maybe the Angel is," I said.

Capulet's voice came out of the phone in my pocket. "Brother Dave says he wants you up on the altar."

I pulled it up, pocket and all. "On my way."

The outdoor altar was on a metal scaffolding, twenty feet high. I stood at the frail-looking stairway made of steel pipe and said, "You sure about this?" to nobody in particular. Put my foot on the first step. It didn't collapse so I climbed up, one unsure step at a time as the metal groaned and swayed. At the top, the stage seemed a little more stable and a lot more gaudy, with an altar and chairs made out of stainless steel. Brother Dave was standing at the back. He didn't look happy.

"Did you steal this stage from the Catholic church of Oz?" I asked him.

"I'd like to give it back," he said. "Feels more like a disco. Like the crystal steeple beside us."

He turned back to the sea of white below us. "At least the children look beautiful. Even tin-foil heaven can't outshine them."

"No." He looked at the children and beamed; I looked at the circle around them and worried.

I pointed. "What's that?"

"What? You mean the alley beside the spire?"

"Yeah. Wasn't there on Google. Only way in was off I-65."

"Added during construction. Gave us another entrance for the trucks."

I stepped away and pulled up my phone again.

"There's an alley running into the park. I need somebody to cover that."

A woman's voice said, "Got it." I looked down and saw Courtney block the alley with her Vespa. Not much, but maybe enough.

Capulet came up behind me.

I pointed at the Vespa. "That'll work for some things. But if Holt's driving a truck through there, we need more."

"I've been thinking about that. All these truck scenarios are suicidal. Holt's not suicidal. She's always proud of herself and sure she's right."

I said, "Maybe she thinks God will save her."

"Maybe. But she packed up three suitcases to take with her. Unless she thinks God will let her fly checked bags to heaven, she thinks she's walking away from this."

I nodded at the children below.

"I hope they do."

seventy-six

They herded us to the dignitary seats at the back of the stage and Brother Dave got his altar boys ready for their short processional to the front. I stared at the flimsy folding chair the usher was pointing me to and looked back at him.

"Take two," he said.

I wedged in carefully and they seemed to hold. The usher set up another chair next to me and I looked up as the assistant commissioner sat down.

He talked to me out of the side of his mouth without looking at me. "Don't screw up."

I nodded. My phone squawked. Coltrane said, "Mandrake, you got anything on that computer code yet?"

"Yeah. Give me a minute to be sure."

The assistant commissioner hissed, "Turn that fucking thing off."

I nodded and fiddled with the phone, but left it on.

I scanned the crowd from right to left. A sea of white, dotted with proud families sweating in the Alabama sun in their Sunday best. Here and there, a Lost Boy stood out like a sore thumb. But they were there, and they were ready. Behind the crowd, I saw the three-quarter-ton truck pull across the interstate exit and slam on his brakes. An old van smashed into it and the two of them blocked the exit. Both drivers got out and started cursing at each other.

At last, something we were good at.

The crowd looked toward the crash, then turned back. That doorway to the park was now slammed shut to the Angel and would stay that way until the crowd dispersed.

Maybe it was enough.

I kept turning to my left, looking past the assistant commissioner to the neighborhood beside the church, then up to the wooded side of Red Mountain behind everything. I saw Coltrane back there, checking on a retired officer covering the woods. Above them the head and arm of Vulcan loomed out from the trees, dominating the sky.

"Eyes front," said the assistant commissioner.

I looked front, but kept turning so I could survey the right side of the church. I saw Courtney and followed the new alley into the neighborhood. The street behind the alley looked clear and I squinted at the rest of the neighborhood.

I thought I saw something on a side street a block away, and I squinted harder. I wasn't sure, so I stood up just as the processional began.

The assistant commissioner hissed, "Sit your ass down."

"Excuse me." I tried to wedge by him as unobtrusively as I could, which wasn't very. He pushed back, I shoved, and he went sprawling onto the stage. The altar boys in the processional looked back, but I couldn't stop. I hit the ladder and slid down it.

Capulet was at the bottom.

I muted my phone. "Here." I pulled off my bobby helmet and jammed it on her head. "Get up on stage and cover for me."

"I can't..."

"Yes, you can. Take a seat. When the priest calls your name—my name—stand up and wave. They'll expect you to come to the mic and say something, but when you keep waving, they'll move on."

"Where are you going?"

"I've got to check on something. May be...nothing."

"Why don't you stay and ask Coltrane or one of the others?"

"Cause I'm not sure. Cause I want Coltrane to stay here. Look, I'm not crying wolf again. Cover for me. I'll check it out, make sure it's nothing and be right back."

I stopped at where Courtney was standing. "See if you can find something bigger than your scooter to block the alley. Anything big."

"Why? What's going on?"

"Probably nothing."

seventy-seven

The sweat was pouring off me when I turned onto the side street and saw the truck. I pulled up short and sucked in my breath.

New Daimler truck and trailer. Shiny, clean, no commercial markings.

All white.

I stood there for a minute, looked in all the windows and couldn't see anyone looking out. I went up to the truck's door. Unlocked.

The seats still had plastic on them and there was a smell of what? Bleach?

I climbed in and opened the glove box. Then I fished around for the registration, hoping it would have the name and address of a someone on this street. A guy who had bought a truck for his business and hadn't painted it yet. I'd tap on his door, congratulate him on his toy, and ease back to the church.

No such luck. The owner was some nebulous corporation, probably owned by another nebulous corporation. I pulled out my phone and took a picture for later and set the phone down on the seat.

Straightening up I wondered what to do next, when I heard a click.

I slid into the driver's seat and grabbed at the door handle. It was locked and somehow wouldn't open. I heard the phone I'd left on the passenger seat.

"The code the Angel was working on," said Mandrake, "is truck automation code."

There was a pause and then he said. "Looks like it could be for a European truck—Daimler, maybe. It's kind of a long shot but they're a little ahead of us in self-driving trucks. So, keep your eyes open."

He paused again.

The engine cranked and I yelled at the phone, "Long shot, my ass." I forgot that the phone was muted.

I reached for it as the truck lurched forward. The phone slid off the seat.

I stomped on the brakes, and that stopped the truck for just a second before the engine revved harder and the truck jumped forward even faster. I stood on the brakes with both feet and all that bought me was a second's hesitation before the brakes released themselves.

I looked around. Someone had to be controlling this thing and I bet that they were keeping it in sight.

The windows along the street stared back at me. Nothing, not even someone out cutting the grass or walking the dog.

The first cross street was coming up. The church was to the left. I grabbed the wheel and slammed it to the right with all my weight. For a second, the truck went right across a lawn and I thought I had it, but then the wheel spun left and threw me into the door. Tires screamed as the truck spun back, taking out a mailbox and throwing up flowers from a yard until it made it back on to the road.

Pulling myself back onto my seat, I looked up and saw Vulcan's head through the trees. There was someone on the observation platform, holding a computer tablet in their hands. I wanted to see more, but I couldn't.

Back in the seat, I saw the speedometer climbing past thirty. One more turn until we would come to the alley and the church.

seventy-eight

I prayed for a tree big enough to stand up to my runaway monster. This street had a long straightaway before a hard right that would take it—take us— on a straight shot to the alley. I kept stomping the brakes and jerking the wheel back and forth, forcing the truck to scrub off as much speed as possible. Every time I turned one way, something would seize control and jerk it back the other way.

We were at forty-five when we came to the turn. I saw a tree the size of a telephone pole and put all my weight into the wheel.

It worked. We crashed full into the tree and I was thrown into the windshield. For a moment, scrambling back into the seat, I thought we had stopped, but the engine kept roaring until the trunk snapped and we jumped past and back onto the road.

I had bled the speed down but straight ahead I could see the alley. At the end of the alley was a sea of white dresses.

I jerked the wheel violently back and forth, but I could move the truck only a foot or two off the road before it was pulled back.

Thirty miles an hour and a hundred feet to go. I started pushing the wheel to the left as hard as I could toward the open field beside the alley. Each time, I had a second before the wheel fought back and the Angel jerked the wheel back the other way.

We were at the entrance to the alley with nothing but the field to the left and the spire to the right. This time, I kept pushing to the left, forcing the Angel to push harder and harder to the right. Just before the curb, I swung back hard to the right and joined her; the truck jerked violently over the right-hand curb at the last second.

The megaton monster slammed into the church spire and all I could see was glass and steel raining around me and the truck as the spire collapsed.

Maybe I had been wrong to make fun of the spire. God's middle finger sure looked like salvation to me now.

seventy-nine

The truck was impaled on the spire's base, with its wheels spinning harmlessly in the air. My right arm was broken and bleeding, but I pulled myself out with the other arm, hoping I was in time, and stumbled through the shining shards. I met Courtney coming in.

"Give me your scooter," I said. "The Angel's on top of Vulcan. I'll go up the road. Tell everyone to go straight up the hill and cut her off that way. And tell Coltrane to call the captain. Tell him to pull every string he can to get troops down here."

She fished out her keys. I patted my holster and realized I had lost my gun in the crash.

"Your scooter," I said, "and your blunderbuss."

I grabbed her gun and swung a leg over the Vespa. I had to look twice to be sure my big rear end wasn't hanging over the side and dragging on the ground.

Close, but I was floating a few inches off the pavement with the invisible scooter buried somewhere in my ass.

I balanced the gun across the handlebars and cranked the scooter with my good hand. I felt like I could probably have pushed the scooter faster with my feet, but gradually I picked up speed and headed up the winding road to Vulcan.

The Vespa coughed, sputtered and smoked its way into the parking lot and I saw Holt running for a car. I pushed the scooter as hard as I could. She heard the noise and gave me a look of horror. She pulled out a pistol and fired one careless shot before I got to her. She twisted away before I hit and took off for the far edge of the lot on the brow of the mountain. I ran after her. She found the opening to a trail that led down the mountain and ducked down it. I followed, losing ground with every step, praying there was an oxygen tank somewhere up ahead.

"Halt," I yelled. I waved the big gun and realized that firing a shotgun shell from a pistol probably meant I couldn't hit anything. Worse, I realized that this monstrosity only fired one shell. And, from the dirty look of the gun, the shell was probably rusted in place and wouldn't fire anyway.

My legs were dying from a lack of oxygen and turning rubbery as I pushed down the steep hill. I saw Holt through a gap in the trees twenty feet below me. She looked back and laughed; we both knew I couldn't catch up to her on the path.

I saw a flat rock ledge between us. I shoved the gun into my pants and pushed hard with the last few steps I had left in my legs and leaped off the rock as far as I could. I sailed through the air for a long second, noting her look of terror as she watched the world's largest angel in blue polyester crashing down on her.

When I hit, it felt like a dream where every ache of the last two years was made manifest on my body until there was no place left to bruise. I wrapped my arms around the Angel and thought it was the end for us both. She was swept up with me, the two of us rolling together out of control, down the steep hill, past one open-mouthed Lost Boy after another coming up the hill. We hit the big rock that loomed over the church and came to a stop.

I rolled on top of Holt and pinned her under me, waiting for people to catch up. I could feel attempts at wiggling underneath me, but then they stopped. I rolled off enough for her to breathe.

"So, maybe," she whispered, "we die here together. Mission complete."

"No. The State of Alabama will kill you. And that's after every real preacher in the state gets a chance to tell you how wrong, evil and un-Christian you are." I paused. "Father Carson's relatives, too."

"Got what he deserved. I told him if he came out of your house and pointed the gun at you, I'd let your family live. Stupid bleeding-heart liberal actually believed I'd keep my word."

I pushed down on top of her harder, longing to kill her with the very monstrosity she had helped create. I pressed with all my might, and then I felt something solid against my ribs and a muffled explosion, followed by a pain sharper than any of the others in my chest. She rolled me off her and sat up, her gun still smoking.

"Got to go," she said. "You wouldn't have been much without me anyway. But I've got a lot of the Lord's work still left for me."

I said. "One last prayer."

I raised the giant silly weapon from my pants and pulled the trigger. The explosion tore a hole through her midsection and threw her off the rock. I pulled myself over to the edge and looked down at her, lying at the base of her broken church spire, unmoving.

I lay back and waited. Coltrane got there first. He put his hand on my chest and tried to stop the bleeding.

"Who are you kidding?" I said.

"Don't give up."

"This isn't giving up. It's accepting. Did you call the captain?"

"Yeah. He's got folks coming."

"Good. Maybe he'll get credit and they'll give him his job back."

"Maybe."

Capulet's face swam into view.

I didn't know what to say. "Thank you for some very fine water, Juliet."

I heard footsteps and shouting and sirens in the distance. I felt all the pain and sorrow and need draining out of me in a bright red stream. Capulet took hold of my good hand and I squeezed back as hard as I could before letting her go.

It was time to finally pay for all my fuck-ups. I closed my eyes and saw the photo with Luz and Sarah frozen forever in it. Then Luz gave a tiny shake of her shoulders and they both breathed and smiled and came to life. Sarah's leg came up in a slow-motion start of running out of the photo and into her daddy's arms, and I saw that she was holding an enormous armful of lilies for me, with a cloud for three waiting behind them. Luz spread her arms wide to receive me. I felt the joy spreading on all our faces, and I prayed this was real.

But then Luz came to me and took my battered face in her hands. I felt warmth and life flowing back into me as she kissed my cheek and whispered,

"Not yet."

Free stuff for you!

I've included the first chapter from one of my books for you to sample.

And more! First chapters from Kathleen Cosgrove and Maxine Nunes.

Turn the page for a bonus chapter

from Michael Guillebeau's book

MAD LIBRARIAN

A Southern librarian has to fight back to save her library and her community.

PUBLISHER'S WEEKLY SAYS, "Guillebeau blends humor and mystery perfectly in this comic thriller."

2017 FOREWORD REVIEWS INDIE GOLD WINNER FOR BEST HUMOR NOVEL!

o n e

....

little pricks

SERENITY TRIED.

She tried to be a model librarian: professional, polite and as gentle-spoken on the outside as she could possibly be.

Her library was America at its best. In its public spaces, the MAD—as the librarians called the Maddington Public Library, from the abbreviation stamped on its books—was the eminently normal center of an eminently normal small Southern city. No matter what else was going on in the city outside: failing schools, drugs in the street, too few good jobs, teen-aged boys wearing their pants too low and homeless men with no pants at all—the city fathers expected Head Librarian Serenity Hammer to keep the MAD a calm oasis of normalcy as proof that the city fathers themselves were actually doing their jobs. And, they expected her to do that whether they did anything themselves or even supplied the library with actual support.

Serenity tried to live up to that, too.

Which was why, on a hot August morning, she was locked alone in a children's reading room with a coffee cup of rum for fortitude, a rat named Faulkner for company, a copy of Harper Lee's *To Kill a Mockingbird* for guidance, and a highly illegal choice before her.

Serenity Hammer was a librarian. And Serenity was mad.

• • •

TWO DAYS BEFORE she wrestled with moral dilemma, Serenity threw open the library's glass doors on a hot Wednesday morning in August. She smiled as patrons flowed past on their way to her books.

She picked up a handful of books from the "to be shelved" cart and turned to the stacks. She ran her finger along the spine of one, inhaled the paper-and-ink smell, and smiled again.

Someone screamed, "Damned stupid computers." She put the books back on the cart.

Maybe later.

She then walked up to a worn-out older woman who was slapping a worn-out library computer like it had stole from her. Serenity took the woman's hands away from the computer and held them.

"I knowed this was a bad idea," the woman said. "I told my councilman I needed a job and he said they had to close the employment office and he told me to go to the library. But your damned computer just tells me what books you got here. Don't want a book; want a job."

The woman tried to pull her hands away but Serenity held on. The woman's jaw was still jutting out but her eyes were full of fear and shame.

Serenity put the woman's hands in her lap and pulled up a chair. "Then let's find you a job. What can you do?"

"Not a goddamned thing. Forty years looking after my husband and he died. Now I don't know what to do and they ain't nobody to ask that won't charge more money than I got and I just feel like everybody's letting me get torn to pieces."

"So, what have you been doing in those forty years?"

"Cooking and cleaning and raising kids and—"

"There. Know much about baking?"

"Well, of course. Who do you think made all them cupcakes the kids took to school?"

"Good." The woman slid over and Serenity brought up a web page. "There's a bakery out on Segers Road. They specialize in making treats for people who have special dietary needs. They were in here yesterday looking for a book on hiring folks."

The woman shook her finger at the screen. "They better be careful. My husband Christopher was a diabetic. There's some stuff you got to know if you're cooking for diabetics."

Serenity touched her on the shoulder. "You're just what they need. But you'll need a resume." Serenity slid back and turned the keyboard to the woman. "You type, and I'll help you."

A few minutes later, a warm sheet of paper slid out of the printer, and Serenity handed it to the woman. "Take that to Stacey out at Liberated Specialty Foods, see if you can help each other."

The woman's tears were gone, "What would we do if the library wasn't here?"

Serenity said, "My library will always—"

A blue-haired woman grabbed her elbow.

"This thing ain't got nothing in it."

She shoved a book in Serenity's hands and Serenity smiled. The woman was the wife of the Church of Christ's choir director. She had joined the Romance

Book Club so she could condemn immorality. Flipping through the pages, Serenity handed the book back and pointed to the middle of a page. "Here."

The choir director's wife bobbed her head up and down like a nervous bird, studying the page and popping up to make sure no one saw her. She raised her head one last time with her mouth open.

"Praise Jesus. This is terrible."

Anything to keep them coming in.

Serenity headed for her office door. A twenty-something woman with books clutched to her chest and a librarian's badge blocked her path.

Fine. She didn't want to face what was waiting behind that door anyway.

"Ms. Hammer, he's back."

"Who?"

Amanda Doom pulled one hand from under her books and slowly raised her index finger until it was straight up. "Do you want me to get security?"

Serenity looked over at the high school boy who had volunteered to wear the red "Security" tee shirt today.

"No."

"I can call the police."

"Take them a half-hour to get here," Serenity said. "Besides, he's cousin to the wife of the district attorney. We'll just wind up in a long discussion about his constitutional rights, again. No, we need to end this once and for all. We're a library. Our power is books."

She pulled out the biggest atlas she could carry. "Keep his attention so he won't see me coming."

Serenity weaved through the stacks until she heard two teen-aged girls giggling.

"Smaller than I thought it would be," said one. More giggles.

Serenity peeked through a gap in the books and saw the back of a 1940's style trench coat. She eased her way around behind him and stepped into his aisle.

Doom was standing in front of the man as requested, looking shocked, but now she smiled at Serenity and the surprise was gone. The trench coat spun toward her. Move fast. She opened the atlas and took one giant step forward. The opening of the trench coat rotated into view followed by the man's grinning face and his . . . pride.

Serenity slammed the heavy book shut on the man with a vengeance. He jumped and screamed and she yanked the book away with a nasty jerk.

He fell back against the stacks and put his hands over himself. "My rights."

She held the book up in both hands like Moses handing down the commandments. "Freedom of the press trumps freedom of expression." Shook it at him. "By. The. Book."

She shoved him aside.

"Come back again, Cy, and I'm going for the unabridged dictionary." The teenaged girls giggled at "dictionary." She held the book out to Doom and the girl took it like she was accepting a dead rat.

"Shelve this, please." Serenity looked back at Cy and said, "I'm tired of wasting my big books on you little pricks."

Turn the page for a bonus chapter

from Kathleen Cosgrove's book

ENGULFED

My introduction to Kathleen Cosgrove's writing came when my wife came running up from the beach with a copy of Engulfed in her hands, yelling, "You have got to read this book until page 187." She was right. Kathleen's Maggie Finn books are the funniest Florida weird mysteries out there, bar none.

CHAPTER ONE

When you're a divorced woman from an Irish Catholic home, you sort of expect God to punish you once in a while. It's his benevolent way of making you pay here, so you don't have to burn in hell later; at least that's how I look at it. Therefore, I was not really surprised when Hurricane Fanny, who was supposed to make landfall in Mexico, changed her trajectory and headed toward southwest Florida the moment my plane touched down at the Fort Myers airport. I did take exception this time since I was here to do a good deed and help my folks move into their fancy new retirement home. But, such is my relationship with The Almighty and my reason for being in a place that I consider to be only slightly more livable than the sun.

The drive to Shell Harbor Assisted living took me ten minutes and two bottled waters. By the time I got there, I was so damp from the humidity no less than two people stopped to ask if it was raining,

Before I could find a ladies room to freshen up, I heard the sound of high heels clicking down the hall and turned to see a young, attractive woman making her way to me at a near gallop speed. Her brown, shoulder length hair bounced and glistened like in a shampoo commercial; the type of woman who wouldn't sweat in a steam room, so naturally I disliked her.

"Mrs. Finn? I'm so glad you could come. I'm Brandy," she said, a bit out of breath. "I'm the director here. I met your folks, lovely couple, we're super excited they'll be living here. I know we promised you a tour this morning but since the hurricane tomorrow—well, this may not be the best time."

"I know," I said, "I think I have to go buy a flashlight or something, but I thought I'd just take a quick peek if you don't mind."

She looked at the receptionist who was giving her the wide-eyed, *please don't make me take this sweaty lady around,* look. Then she put her arm through mine like we were on a date, smiled, glanced at my hair and asked, "Is it raining?"

*****

"What's going on here?" I asked when we approached the patio. A large contingency of seniors were gathered round a group of men setting up sound equipment.

"Oh," she said, "The radio station is here today to do a live broadcast from 9:00 to 11:00. It's always so much fun when they come that we decided not to cancel. They give out prizes and the D.J. they send is so funny, Ziggy he calls himself. They all love him here, they never miss his show. I can introduce you if you'd like."

"Gee thanks, but I think I'll pass," I said. "I've still got lots of stuff to get ready at my parents' home."

I raised my voice attempting to be heard over the sound of a dozen people speaking to each other at the same level you would if you were standing in front of a jet engine.

I spotted a van parked in the circular drive that separated the building from the lake and adjacent golf course. The vehicle had a satellite dish attached to the side and a painted mural of a beach that included crabs, seagulls and a leaping dolphin, all with images of people where the animal head should be. I assumed these were the radio personalities and I recognized the *crab man* as the one seated at the long table in the center of the lobby. The call letters for the station were painted on the side of the van in large green letters—WWTF.

"The radio station is WWTF?" I asked Brandy.

"Yes, it stands for Waving Through Florida."

"But, surely they must get kid..."

Brandy interrupted me, "Oh Ziggy!" she waved to the crab man.

Ziggy stood up and made his way toward us. He was about my age, tall, thin and nice looking. He wore shorts that went mid-calf, a long sleeve *Tommy Bahama* shirt, and a leather necklace with an Indian head nickel dangling from it. I suddenly felt a little more self-conscious of my appearance and reached up to tame my hair, instantly regretting it; it looked so obvious.

"Brandy! Long time no see. How've you been darlin'?" he asked with a smile and an arm around her shoulder.

"Hi Ziggy," Brandy gushed. "It's really great you're here. Everyone's been asking when you were coming back."

He looked at me and smiled.

"Ziggy, this is Mrs. Finn." Brandy said. "Her parents are moving in the beginning of the month."

"Maggie," I said as I shook his hand, "nice to meet you."

"Nice to meet you Maggie," he said. "This joint is pretty nice huh? If I weren't so young, I'd be looking at moving in myself."

"Well, it's very nice to meet you too," I said. "Brandy says you're quite a hit here at The Shell."

"Ah, yeah, they love me here, they're my best audience. All the markets I've worked in, this is definitely my favorite."

He looked around and waved at a couple of elderly women who giggled and waved back.

"I really lucked out getting this gig," he continued, "great folks down here. Yep, I love it."

He stopped himself, probably aware that he was going too far out of his way to sound convincing, but I think Brandy, at least, was buying it. From the tattoos and long hair I was certain he was more used to playing Pearl Jam than String of Pearls.

"You gonna stick around and watch the show?" he asked. "We have a lot of fun and some company's comin' out later to demo a new mobility device."

"Gee, that does sound fun," I said, more sarcastically than I had wanted, "but I've got an appointment."

"Suit yourself," he said, and looked at his audience. "I gotta get back to work."

He sauntered back to his table in long, easy strides and began talking to one of the set up crew.

"I think I insulted him," I told Brandy, "I didn't really mean it like that."

"Oh, I'm sure he wasn't insulted, he says crazy things himself all the time."

On our walk back Brandy stopped suddenly and yelled, "Jesus!"

I don't know if I was more surprised by her sudden outburst or the fact that she was cursing.

"Jesus," she hollered again, and a man hurried over to us.

"Si Miss Brandi?"

"Jesus, there's a raccoon in the bird bath again, take him away, quickly!" she said in a tone more suited to an impending avalanche.

The animal had something it was tossing about that looked like a small bone. "It looks kind of cute," I said, "look, it's washing its food in the water."

We watched as Jesus approached the animal stealthily, looking at it, then back at us, then at the animal again. When he got within five feet of it the raccoon tossed the bone at Jesus and ran across the lawn into the brush near the lake. I stopped watching the animal when I heard Jesus let out a blood curdling scream.

By the time Brandy and I reached him he was staring at the ground mumbling in Spanish and crossing himself.

"Jesus," I said, "I could be wrong, but that sure does look like a man's..."

"Si," agreed Jesus, "a pene."

"Yep," I said, "that's a pene alright. And if there's a pene here," I pointed at the object, "then there must be..."

Brandy looked at the thing, stood motionless for a minute as though someone had hit the pause button on the remote, and then fainted.

"Someone call a doctor!" I yelled.

A cleaning lady came over with a bottle of Windex, waving it under Brandy's nose.

Someone tapped me on the shoulder. I jumped and turned to see one of the landscapers holding a leaf bag out to me. He said something in Spanish that sounded like a question.

"Does anyone here speak Spanish?" I asked the crowd.

One of the women, part of the kitchen staff, came over and said something to him in Spanish, he replied in the same language. She turned to me and said, "He wants to know what he should do with this."

The man held up the bag.

"What's in it?" I asked.

"A leg," she said, dramatically in her heavy Cuban accent.

"Si, leg," the man said.

I looked in the bag, felt woozy and yelled, "Someone bring me the Windex!"

Turn the page for a bonus chapter

from Maxine Nunes book

DAZZLED

If you want the dark underbelly of Hollywood glamor, vividly written, Maxine Nunes is the writer for you.

CHAPTER 1

What's real? Darla used to ask me. *How do you know what's real?* I never understood the question. But then I didn't have platinum hair and cheekbones that could cut glass, and no one ever offered to buy me a Rolls if I spent one night naked in his bed. Darla was a brilliant neon sign flashing pure escape. You almost didn't notice that those lovely green eyes didn't blaze like the rest of her. She was both main attraction and sad observer at the carnival. Something had damaged her at a very young age. We never talked much about it, but we recognized this in each other from the start. Isn't that what friendship is?

The week she disappeared was as extreme as she was. Triple-digit heat in late August and wavy layers of smog suffocating the city. By ten in the morning, it was brutal everywhere, and on the sidewalks in front of the homeless shelter, with the sun bouncing off the film crew trailers and the odor of unwashed bodies and general decay, it was a very special episode of hell. Beneath an archway, a tall man with a filthy blanket draped over his head rolled his eyes heavenward like a biblical prophet. Or a *Star Trek* castaway waiting to be beamed up.

In one of those trailers, where air conditioning brought the temperature down to the high nineties, I was being stuffed into a fitted leather jacket two sizes too small. Perspiration had already ruined my makeup and the dark circles under my eyes were starting to show through.

Heat keeping you up, hon? the makeup girl had asked. I'd nodded. Half the truth.

Mykel Z, the costume designer, was trying to zip me into the jacket, but his fingers were sweating and frustrating his attempts. "If you'd get yourself boobs, Nikki," he said, "we wouldn't have to squeeze you into size zero to work up a little cleavage."

"Bigger boobs for you, smaller nose for my agent. Average it out and I'm perfect."

"Almost. Legs from here to eternity, long dark hair to die for. But the nose *is* a bit roller derby, darling. Did you break it?"

"When I was a kid."

"I'll give you the name of a marvelous doctor, a genius with noses. And his lifts for my older ladies . . . I swear the seams don't even show."

"I'm not sure I want to wake up one morning and see someone else in the mirror."

"An idealist. Good luck, honey."

I was used to this. At my first Hollywood party, a guy asked me what I did. When I told him, he looked bewildered. Then he brightened. "Oh," he said, "I guess you could play a real person."

Outside, a prop guy was spraying a couple of shopping carts to dull down their newness, and a wardrobe assistant walked a few extras onto the set.

"No, no, no!" Mykel cried, running out the door, letting in a flush of hot air. "Layers! They need layers!" With a broad motion of his arm, he pointed to some people in the little park on the corner. "Use your eyes! The homeless *totally* invented layering!"

I took advantage of the break, managed to find my phone in the junk shop that is my shoulder bag, and called Darla's cell again. It flipped straight over to her voice mail. Like it had for three days, since this shoot had begun. No point leaving another message.

Mykel flew back into the trailer and stared at me for a few seconds, blinked like he was fighting back tears, then began to tackle the zipper again. It moved up an inch before it caught on the leather.

He dropped his arms, his lips trembled, then he opened the trailer door again and stuck his head out.

"*Benito!*" he hollered, with an edge of real panic in his voice. When Benito, his "shlepper," did not appear, Mykel flopped down on a chair and blotted his face with a tissue.

"Where the hell has he gone?"

"You sent him for a Frappuccino," I said.

"Ten minutes ago!"

"It's hard to find a decent barista on Skid Row, Mykel."

"Maybe that's why these people look so depressed."

"You know what," I said, "let's forget the jacket for a while. They're nowhere near ready to shoot. I'm gonna grab some water from the fridge. Want a bottle?"

"Thank you, sweetie." Mykel placed the jacket back on its hanger with all the tenderness due a garment that cost more than I was being paid for a week's work.

Beneath my tank top, a trickle of sweat from my bra reminded me I was still padded with chicken cutlets—the silicone inserts the director wanted for every female in the cast over the age of twelve. When I removed them, I felt almost human again.

Outside, an assistant was trying to wrangle the extras—a task that had turned chaotic, since real street people kept slipping past security to get to the bagel table. But even from this distance, it was easy to tell them apart. You only had to look at their faces. On some, the flesh itself was infused with misery, the eyes dazed with hopelessness. The rest, in the same soiled layers, were radiant and eager to be noticed.

I'd had a taste of both, but a year on the streets at fifteen had been enough. I got a false ID, found jobs, and managed to take care of myself. But there was something restless in me and I never stayed in one place too long. Somehow, more than a decade slipped by. And what had seemed like freedom began to close in on me.

Then I wound up in L.A. and started picking up rent money working as an extra. A crime show was shooting a Manhattan street scene in downtown Los Angeles, and I got pulled out of the crowd because of my "New York face" for a line they had added: *Ain't seen her in a long time, mistah.* That amazing stroke of luck—and the three-thousand dollar initiation fee I was still paying off—got me my union card.

Now I had pictures and an agent and classes, and that was what really hooked me. Acting may be make believe, but in class the truth beneath the face you showed the world was not only welcome but demanded.

Only that wasn't exactly what working as an actor was like.

This job was a midseason pilot called *Street*, a "fish out of water" comedy about three girls from Beverly Hills who start a gourmet soup kitchen for the homeless. "*Clueless* meets *Pursuit of Happyness*" is how my agent described it. My role—two days' work that could "go to semi-recurring"—was as a homeless person who gets a makeover.

A wave of hot air blew into the trailer, followed by the production assistant, who looked at me and let out a shriek.

"*Mykel!* Why isn't she in costume? They're *ready* for her."

And they were.

Four hours later.

* * *

By the time they released me it was past ten, and as the crew struck the lights and equipment, the homeless began crawling into makeshift tents of newspapers and old blankets and cartons, or gathering in doorways, palming small packets that would get them through the night.

Hot stale air still hung over the city as I walked to my car, an ancient MGB that looked right at home in its own version of layers—black over Haight-Ashbury psychedelic over the original British racing green. The standard joke about MGs is that you share custody with your mechanic, but someone had replaced the temperamental English parts with American ones, and it actually started up every time I turned the ignition key.

With the top down, the hot Santa Anas were better than no breeze at all as I passed the rolling lawns and swaying palms of MacArthur Park, moonlight dusting the lake and the silhouetted figures of dealers and users.

A half hour later, I turned onto La Cienega and headed north past the cool stone facades of restaurant row, past Beverly Center whose colored lights bounced off gleaming Mercedes, Lexus SUVs and the occasional virtuous Prius, past the mansard-roofed Sofitel, past the crowds milling outside a few nightspots.

My little cottage still held all the heat of the day. I stripped down to panties, then finished off a pint of Chunky Monkey— ate it straight from the carton in a current of cold air from the open fridge door—and dragged myself into the bedroom.

I used up all the cool spots on the sheet in about five minutes and picked up a mystery from the night table. But no matter how hunky the hero, an old paperback cannot fill the other side of the bed, and I started to think about the man who'd occupied that space until a couple of weeks ago. Dan Ackerman. A good, solid guy, and I left him . . . why? Maybe because he was a good, solid guy.

The only other person in my life who mattered was Darla, and she hadn't returned my calls, which really wasn't like her at all. Even when she was on location, she'd phone and talk about anything—what they had for lunch, how filthy the honey wagons got— just to keep from feeling lonely.

I wondered if she was mad at me, if maybe I shouldn't have been so blunt about her ex-boyfriend Jimmy. It was past midnight and too late to call. But I sent a quick text, then found myself listening in the silence for the phone to chime with her answer.

I turned on the TV. Fourteen dead in the Middle East and four dead in a murder in the Hollywood Hills. But no worries. Just wait for election day. Mike Ryle, TV Land western star/turned senate candidate, was saying, "Let's return to the America I grew up in." He sounded so earnest, you could almost forget that he'd grown up in the America of Vietnam and segregation and backstreet abortions.

When the infomercials started, I flicked the TV off and watched the minutes and the hours on the clock change. As the city was waking up, I fell asleep.

Made in the USA
Middletown, DE
16 November 2020